IN A CLASS
OF THEIR OWN

IN A CLASS
OF THEIR OWN

MILLIE GRAY

BLACK & WHITE PUBLISHING

First published in this edition 2009
by Black & White Publishing Ltd
29 Ocean Drive, Edinburgh EH6 6JL

1 3 5 7 9 10 8 6 4 2   09 10 11 12 13

ISBN: 978 1 84502 256 3

First published in 2008 by The Bellfield Press, Edinburgh

Printed and bound by Cox & Wyman, Reading

To my husband Bob

AUTHOR'S NOTE

This story tells of one family's life in Leith in the years before, during and after the Second World War. Although it echoes some of the writer's experiences and personal feelings, the characters portrayed in the book are wholly fictitious and bear no relation to any persons, living or dead. Many of the street names, localities and other details from that period in Leith's history have been preserved however.

CHAPTER 1
1939: MOVING UPWARDS

"We're here, Sam," Carrie called out. Her brother, who had been so busy making sure that his legs didn't buckle under him, slowed to a halt once he discovered that he had run right past the big, highly-polished door with its gleaming brass plate that said: ***Edinburgh Corporation Housing Department.***

Sam trotted back obediently to where his mother, Rachel, was busy straightening baby Paul's legs after having lifted Carrie out of the foot of the pram. He shrugged stoically at not having had his usual turn of getting a hurl in the pram. Obviously his mother had been preoccupied ever since they had left home in Leith and he'd wisely resisted the impulse to remind her that a four-year-old found it wearying to run for ninety minutes non-stop through all that teeming rain and driving wind. Sam knew full well that this was a Monday, the day when Mam *had* to be at the Housing Office before the door opened; but that didn't stop him making his customary plaintive query, "Mammy, why've we come here?"

Rachel turned abruptly to look at Sam as if she hadn't known he was there.

"Sam!" she said in exasperation, "you ask the same bleeding question every week and the answer I give you is the same bleeding answer, week in and week out. We're here because I want you and Carrie to go to a good school when you start in April next year."

Sam sniffed, lifting his hand to wipe away the water that was dripping steadily from his hair and tickling his nose. "But, Mam," he whined, pointing to the brass plate, "ye telt me it says there, '*Hoosing* Department'."

His mother glanced at the storm-tossed heavens for a second before muttering through clenched teeth, "Aye, that's right, Sam.

We're here cos I'm aiming to get us a good address. That means that the schools there will be very good as well."

"Oh," was all he could reply.

"Nae like the Ragged School you and your sister will have to go to if we can't get out of Admiralty Street."

"But Mammy," Carrie butted in, "our Hannah says Couper Street is a guid school and *she* kens aw her readin' and coontin'."

Rachel turned on her daughter, who had taken off her hat so that the rain could plaster her fair curls tight to her skull. "Carrie," she said with exasperation as she grabbed the hat and rammed it back on. "The words are 'reading' and 'counting'; and the reason Hannah does very well at Couper Street is all due to her being so clever and streets ahead of the rest."

But to herself she muttered: "Nae like you pair. Lord, gie me patience. Only just turned four an' they baith argue black's white an' syne turn it black again."

She sighed audibly, reflecting that, even although the midwife had explained how they *couldn't* be identical twins, they certainly were in *her* estimation. They had the same thrawn natures; the same fair, red-tinted curls (though Carrie's were less fiery than Sam's); the same snub nose; the same big eyes – except Sam's were blue and Carrie's were … Rachel shook her head wearily, thinking that if one of them *had* to have such bad squints why couldn't it have been Sam? Cross-eyes make even the prettiest girl look – and she gulped before mentally changing *ugly* to *different*.

But doing something about Carrie's eyes would have to wait. The most important thing was whether their long, rain-sodden trek to the Housing Office would bring the result she so dearly wished for. In spite of the depressing weather, she felt momentarily buoyed up with confidence. Then, as the wind tore at her face and the rain began to turn to sleet, she acknowledged to herself that they were such buggers in the Office here that it could well take a good few weeks more before she could really wear them down. The noise of the door being opened suddenly broke into Rachel's thoughts.

"You again?" grunted the janitor. "Every effing Monday for a hale year I've opened up this door and found you lot." He stuck his hand out to decide if it was raining or not. "Ye nae got a bed ti bide in wi' weather like this?"

"I'm no layabout," declared Rachel. "And before you go on, no, I haven't got money to throw away on buses either."

What an ass that man was, she thought, to be putting his hand out like that to feel if it was raining! Anyone could see it was simply lashing down. Then she noticed Sam and Carrie were both trying to climb into the pram at the same time. "Here! What d'you two bairns think you're at? Now, just stand there by that pram. And don't let nobody – and I mean nobody – touch it till I come back. Understand?"

Sam and Carrie both nodded so vigorously that spray from their drenched heads cascaded over their mother. Satisfied that neither would move and that baby Paul would be safe, Rachel climbed the five steps to the Housing Office, simultaneously pushing back her nut-brown hair and hastily brushing the drips from her faded coat.

"Wish I wasnae so down-at-heel," she said to herself.

In reality, Rachel had no need to worry unduly about her appearance. Thanks to Eugenie Fraser's coaching, she always walked with a stately, almost regal air that seemed to add inches to her stature. Rachel had been only thirteen when she'd first gone to work, as a teenie, at Miss Fraser's elegant New Town mansion in Moray Place. From the very start, Eugenie had taken a personal interest in the young girl and, after only six months' training, had promoted her from scullery-maid to upstairs duties where she quickly learned to welcome visitors and wait upon the guests. When mistress and servant were alone together, Eugenie would patiently instruct Rachel on how to speak the King's English correctly, how to walk with head held high and how to make the most of her personal appearance – of which her gleaming green eyes were by no means the least of her striking features.

"Rachel, my dear," Eugenie would say, "I can't possibly imagine how a little gem like you managed to pick the parents you have! But never mind, you have good looks, some brains and that *je ne sais quoi* that we all wish we had – the capacity to look genteel even when dressed in a coal sack."

The memory of those encouraging words always made Rachel smile: Eugenie's attitude had stemmed from having been a suffragette possessed with the fervent desire to improve the lot of all women. She had wanted to make others of her sex realise they all had the potential to become more than mere chattels of men.

"All very well for you, Eugenie," chuckled Rachel to herself. "Your father died leaving all his money to you. So you never had to see a coal sack, let alone wear one."

At that moment the receptionist – an officious old maid – broke abruptly into Rachel's reminiscences with an imperious click of the fingers.

"And what can we do for you today?" she demanded sourly, as Rachel planted her rent book on the counter. "I know you have a clear rent book, Mrs Campbell, but, as I have already explained more than once to you, we can only offer you re-housing to the North of the City, along with all the other Leith slum clearance families in Admiralty, East and West Cromwell Streets; and ..."

"... And as I have already explained to *you*, sixty times over," Rachel broke in, "I'm not going to the North. I wish to be re-housed in the East."

"The East of the City?" said the receptionist incredulously, lifting her mascara-laden eyes to the ceiling.

"That's right. The *East* of the City. And in particular, the estate across Leith Links and up beyond Restalrig Brae."

The woman sighed and this time scrutinised her enamelled fingernails as if only then becoming aware of them. "I don't think, Mrs Campbell, that you quite understand. We have *no* vacancies in that area. Besides, all our tenants there are most carefully vetted."

"You telling me I'm not good enough to go there?" retorted Rachel with fury. She leaned threateningly across the counter as if to grab the women's throat but halted suddenly, remembering Eugenie's warning that a lady must *never* let herself down in public. If one gave way to anger, the battle was lost.

But the receptionist had seen the danger and drew back. "No, n-n-no," she stammered. "What I'm saying is that the tenants there are all hand-picked so they will all fit in properly."

"Fit in? And what exactly do you mean by 'fit in'?" demanded Rachel fiercely.

"Er … just that they all have to be … er … you know, be in the same class." She paused before adding, "I mean, I don't think anybody from the Leith slums could imagine …"

"I beg your pardon!" Before Rachel could launch into a tirade against this pen-pushing bureaucrat, she caught sight of Councillor Smith sidling along the wall towards the Council Chambers.

"One moment, Councillor Smith," she called out.

"Ah! It's Mrs Campbell, is it not? And what may we do for you today?"

"Fine you know, Councillor Smith. It's the same old thing I see you about every week. This here's my rent book and it's never been in arrears these past two years. All I want is to be re-housed in the Restalrig district."

"Yes, I realise you do but, as I've already explained to you, we have to look at prospective tenants and the available vacancies. Unfortunately at this precise moment we have no vacancies in Restalrig."

Rachel drew a deep breath before allowing a sly smile to cross her face. "Oh, but you *have*," she gently intoned.

"We *have*?"

"Oh yes. You see, the bairns an' me took a walk up there yesterday. Just for a wander. And guess what we found!" She paused, relishing the moment. "An *empty house*! In Learig Close. You know, the close on the left of Restalrig Brae, just before the railway bridge."

"The railway bridge?"

"Aye, where your four-in-a-block houses are on one side of the street and the private- owned ones on the other."

"Oh, *that* Learig Close," the Councillor exclaimed, before collecting himself and proceeding in a conciliatory manner. "Now, correct me if I'm wrong, Mrs Campbell, but are you saying you wish to be re-housed in Learig Close?"

"Aye, and don't you be surprised at that. After all, I'm not asking to be re-housed in Holyrood Palace. No, no! All I'm asking is to be re-housed in that empty house in Learig Close."

"Well," he paused. "I don't know. We would need to look at where you are on the list and then ... er ... could you maybe ... perhaps ... make out a special case for yourself?"

"Special case?" said Rachel. "Well, I don't think there can be anyone more entitled to be re-housed than me."

Councillor Smith smiled patronisingly, which only served to infuriate Rachel. She swallowed hard and pulled herself up to her full five feet four inches before continuing.

"D'you not know that right now in Admiralty Street there's me an' my man; there's a lassie of six; there's my twins just turned four; a one-year-old bairn; an' – as you can well see for yourself – another about to drop. An' we're all livin' in a damp, bug-infested, verminous single-end wi' but the one cold water tap?"

During this harangue, the councillor had twice attempted without success to interrupt. He raised his hand and opened his mouth but Rachel wasn't finished.

"And the only convenience we have – if you can call it that – is a solitary lavvie on the downstairs half-landing. And that's used by *five* families!"

By now all Councillor Smith could utter was a prolonged "Tut-tut; tut-tut; tut-tut-tut."

"Aye, well may ye tut! The fact is that thirty of us have to use that one lavvie."

"Thirty?"

"Aye, *thirty*! So maybe you know now why I *have* to be re-housed in Learig Close."

The councillor stared long and hard at Rachel, until she could stand the silence no longer. "Well, all right, it's true. I *do* have delusions of grandeur, I suppose. Every day and every night I dream of flushing a lavatory. A lavatory, that is, for the sole use of my man, my bairns and myself. A lavatory where just maybe sometimes the seat gets cold."

Councillor Smith went on staring at her until she began nervously to gnaw at her thumb. She desperately hoped he might appreciate (as Eugenie had) that she truly was a refined woman, a person of some intelligence and someone not to be lightly dismissed. As the deafening silence continued, Rachel could see that he was weakening. She began to take short, panting breaths. Surely, dear God, she thought, he must realise I've never felt at home in the slums. Knows just how much being re-housed in Learig Close means to me. And that I'll go any lengths to get my way.

"Tell you what, Mrs Campbell," he finally said, blowing out his lips. "I'll go and see where you are on the list and whether I can do anything to help. Where'd you say that house was?"

"Number 16, Learig Close," said Rachel with emphasis.

"Right. Now, off you go home because my enquiries may take some time."

"No! That house is vacant and I mean to bide here till you give me an answer!"

The councillor nodded and turned on his heel. Rachel was pleased to see that he had a smile on his face. That seemed a good omen. She moved towards the outer door, only to have the receptionist call out: "That'll be you going now, Mrs Campbell?"

"No, no, my dear," said Rachel in her sweetest tones. "I'm only going to bring my bairns in out of the rain. Then I mean to bide here till I get the answer I want about the house at Learig Close!"

The following Saturday afternoon, Rachel was pleasantly surprised by the sun's warmth. Was it, she wondered, a sign that summer would soon be coming? Or was it just the warm glow inside herself that she'd experienced ever since she'd picked up the keys for 16 Learig Close?

"Aw, Rachel! Hoo much further?" bleated her husband plaintively. "Twenty meenits we've been walkin' an' we're only just across the Links."

"So what, Johnny?" she answered, pushing Paul's pram into Gladstone Place. Then she turned her attention to the twins. "You two bairns! Let go this pram right now! Restalrig Brae will be hard enough for me to get to the top of without havin' to haul the pair of you as well."

Then she silently contemplated the man at her side. Johnny was tall, dark-haired, grey-eyed and strongly built. She couldn't remember how old he'd been when she first thought him handsome – maybe he'd been only seven when she'd considered him quite dishy. Rachel herself had been brought up by Johnny's Auntie Anna, who always claimed that her darling nephew's wife might not always have something to eat but she sure would always have something worth looking at. She smiled whimsically, thinking it might have been a lot better to have heeded Eugenie's advice and not thrown herself away so lightly in return for a glad eyeful. Better maybe to have settled instead for a decent plateful.

Her speculations came to a sudden end as she tilted the pram to guide it over the kerb. Seized with agonising cramps in the pit of her stomach, Rachel's whole body buckled in pain.

"Johnny! Oh, Johnny!" she gasped. "I'm no feelin' great. Got a wee pain. Could you push this pram for me up the brae?"

"C'mon, Rachel! If ony pals o mine saw me pushin' a pram they'd think me a richt Jessie."

His wife looked down ruefully at her swollen belly and muttered caustically: "D'you no think you've proved you're no Jessie?"

Johnny flushed deeply and shuffled his feet in embarrassment. "Look, I'll pit yin hand on the pram and help ye push. Okay? It's nae wonder ye're wearied. It's twenty-five meenits noo we've been hikin' up here."

Rachel didn't answer. Her thoughts turned to Hannah, her first-born, who was lightly skipping up the brae in front of them. Bright wee thing, my Hannah, she mused. Just six year old she is but already you can see that some day she'll go places. Oh aye, *she'll* no need to beg for help pushing any pram up a brae. I'll see to that, so I will. No, no! She'll no make the mistakes I've made and land up grateful for someone standing by her.

"D'ye no hear me, Rachel? Twenty-six meenits noo an' we're only half-wey up this flamin' brae. Ken somethin'? If I'd kent ye wanted me tae gang mountaineerin', I'd hae took masel up Arthur Seat."

Rachel laughed in spite of the pain. "Arthur Seat, Johnny? Come off it! You cannae even climb the Plague Mound in Leith Links without gettin' dizzy."

"Look, Rachel, what I'm tryin' to get through to ye is this. Livin' in Admiralty Street means I'm nae mair nor ten minutes frae my work at the Cold Store. This Learig Close'll mean I'd be hoofin' it for thirty-five minutes or mair!"

"Don't be daft, Johnny. When you're goin' to work from the new house you'll be stopping at the Cold Store, no goin' on another ten minutes to Admiralty Street."

"Ye're splittin' hairs, Rachel! An' my sister Ella says only the King and Queen would dream o takin' on a rent o nine bob a week."

"Well that makes a change from her rantin' on about your soul bein' damned because you didnae get married in the Chapel," Rachel said, before stopping to take a long breath.

"And in case you dinnae ken it," Johnny went on, ignoring Rachel's reminder of the price he'd paid for marrying a Protestant. "At fower bob a week we just manage tae get by – wi' a few coppers left ower tae jingle in ma pooch. A man needs that when he's wi' the ither lads on the street corner. But bidin' here, whit'll I hae in ma pooch?"

"How about the loose screws from Ella's stupid head?"

Johnny bridled at this slur on his sister. "See this? Oor Ella says ye aye think ye're a cut above awbody else. She's richt at that."

"Compared to her, I am! Oh, look!" Rachel halted. "The Learig Pub. The Close is just round the corner."

Only then did Rachel notice that Carrie and Sam had run ahead and were trying to climb the wall of the railway bridge to watch a train slowly rumble past.

"For the love of heaven, come down out o that!" she cried, as they disappeared in a cloud of smoke from the engine. "That's a coal train an' if you fall in you'll be smothered in dirt for weeks – nae to say landin' in hospital."

"Mammy," Carrie spluttered and coughed as she reappeared out of the smoke. "See there. Up the road there's a Chippie!"

"Where? Where?" squealed Sam in excitement. "Oh aye! I see't. Can we no hae some chips, Mammy?"

"No, you can't."

"But I *dae* want some chips!"

"An' I've told you – you can't have any. Besides it doesn't open till five."

"A Chippie!" Johnny joined in. "Next thing, we'll be findin' there's civilisation hereaboots."

"Well, if you mean everything civilised folk need – the butcher, the grocer, the Co-op, the Post Office, the doctor and the midwife – then they're all here."

"Fair enough," her husband responded grudgingly, "but that's thirty-five meenits it's taen tae get here."

"Aye, but just you wait! Round the corner here, an' – there we are! Learig Close!"

"Oh, ma God, Rachel! You've really flipped proper if ye think we could bide here an' feel at hame. Which yin's oors?" Johnny panted as he tried to keep his panic in check.

Rachel stopped and was silent for several minutes. The broad street basking in the spring sunshine seemed even lovelier than she'd remembered: pink and grey harled Corporation four-in-a-block housing with red-tiled roofs and daffodil-strewn gardens beckoning cheerfully to her. Tears came into her eyes as she breathed the sweet scent of lilac and new-mown grass. So different by far from Admiralty Street, where vile body odours met with the smells of stale cooking in dark, dank, narrow lobbies.

"The left-hand bottom one," she whispered dreamily, as she pointed to their new home. "All it needs is the grass cutting."

"Grass cuttin'!" Where the hell d'ye think we'll get the money for a pair o shears? Let alane a bluidy lawn-mower! Look, let's awa oot o here richt noo."

"You want us to give up this house just because we've not got a lawn-mower?"

"Naw! Cos we'd nae feel at hame here. Aw snobs they'll be across the wey there. They'll no want tae ken us," moaned Johnny, jerking a finger at the elegant stone-built villas facing them.

Rachel shrugged her shoulders. "But we won't be living across the way. We'll be staying *here*!" She pushed open the gate and marched up the pathway. With a shake of his head Johnny slowly trailed behind while she fished the precious keys from her pocket and unlocked the door, which swung open to welcome them into a sun-drenched, two-windowed living-room that was half as big again as the one in Admiralty Street. She didn't linger there though, because the scullery beyond seemed to invite Rachel to enter through its open door.

Johnny gaped. That scullery was near as big as their single-end living room. To his right stood a three-ringed gas cooker and beside it a large storage cupboard – a walk-in cupboard at that, complete with shelves. He turned to speak to Rachel but she was now standing by the sink and wash-tub. Both had hot and cold water taps which she immediately turned on full and gurgled rapturously in unison with the cascading water that ran bubbling into the drain.

"Hot and cauld water on tap, eh?" said Johnny.

"Aye, four taps. And see outbye there."

Johnny crossed to look out at a manicured drying-green with its dancing lines of washing: shirts, blouses, towels and sheets, all flapping boisterously in the wind. His eyes strayed beyond the green to the spot where Sam was already playing happily with the wee lad from next door.

"Want a gemme?" Chalky had asked, lobbing a football to him.

"Aye," said Sam. "Cos yin day I'm to be playin' for the Herts."

"Herts! Nae Herts for me," his new friend retorted. "Naw. Naw, I'll be goalie tae the Hi-bees."

Without saying a word, Johnny sought Rachel's hand and guided her back though the living-room, this time noticing the brightly polished brass canopy over the fireplace with its pipe-clayed hearth. Hesitating only for a moment, he drew her gently into the small hall that led towards the two bedrooms – but it was the adjacent bathroom that compelled his attention – a room without bed, table or chairs. Just a bath, a wash-hand basin and a lavatory. A lavvie they wouldn't have to share with anyone else. His eyes strayed back to the bath: Johnny was thirty years old and had never taken a bath in a house. Until he married Rachel, he'd lived in a room and kitchen with his Mum, his Dad, his sister and his younger brother.

"I'm away oot for half an hour, Johnny," his mother would say. "So ye get yer private bits washed at the sink. There's enough hot water for ye in the kettle on the range."

But when he had married, Rachel insisted he'd queue up at the public baths in Junction Place. Sixpence it cost if you allowed them to run the water but they never put in more than would just cover your legs. For ninepence though you could run your own bath – a luxury he'd never experienced. Johnny nodded his head silently. Rachel was right after all. Times were changing and the bairns deserved better than he'd had. Maybe too she was right about them going to a better school hereabouts. Or maybe Ella knew better when she'd said that Rachel was giving them delusions of grandeur.

"Heavens alive!" he thought to himself. "What if we cannae find the nine bob a week for the rent?" Terror-stricken, he hardly heard Rachel speaking to him.

"Well, Johnny, what d'you think?"

"It's … it's just great, it is. Absolutely … dandy in fact."

Then, after a lengthy pause: "I was just wonderin'." He needed more time to think; time to find a good reason to run away from the problem. Something that Rachel would accept gracefully. Then it came to him suddenly. "What if we hae tae gang tae war?"

"And what on earth would a war wi' Hitler have to do wi' us taking on this house?"

Johnny could only shake his head and stare blankly at her.

"Surely you're not saying that if Chamberlain wakes up and finds he's been hoodwinked an' there's a war on, then we cannae take this house?"

"What I'm sayin' is …" Johnny hunted desperately for words. "… that even though I'm in an exempted job I wid still need to volunteer for some sort o Hame Guard duties or somethin'."

"So?"

"Well, ye'd be up here all alane wi the fower bairns – five bairns I mean – ye wuidna be aside my Ma or Ella when the bombs stairted."

There was silence for a moment as the words sank in. Rachel turned away to hide the triumphant expression on her face. Then Johnny put his head in his hands as enlightenment dawned.

CHAPTER 2
RATIONING

Johnny had just turned the key in the lock and opened the door when he yelled, "Carrie! Sam! For heaven's sake, pit a sock in it."

"It no me, Dad. It's him," Carrie screeched as she swung another punch at Sam.

"Me? Never. She's ayeways at it," Sam retaliated, pushing Carrie over and on to the floor.

"I am *not*," she said defiantly, kicking out at Sam.

"But ye *are*," Sam retorted before chanting, "Fower eyes. Fower eyes. Just like mince pies."

Johnny breenged forward, grabbed Sam by the arm and yanked him to his feet. "Look, my lad," he said threateningly as he shook Sam, "Dinnae ever, *ever* let me hear ye say such a thing to yer sister again."

This reaction emboldened Carrie who smirked at Sam before leaping from the floor on to his back. Curling her legs tightly round his waist, she began pummelling him with her clenched fists.

"That's enough," Johnny commanded. "Is there no enough fightin' goin' on the noo withoot you twa startin' anither war in here?"

He heaved Carrie off Sam's back and propelled her into the scullery.

"Rachel!" he called. "Could ye no hear the racket they twa were makin'? Heard their shrieks from the tap of the back lane, so I did."

Rachel didn't answer. She just sat there on her rickety wooden chair, staring vacantly into space.

Johnny hesitated before shaking his head. "Em … em," he stammered. "Ye just gang back ben the hoose, Carrie. But keep awa frae Sam."

He closed the door quietly but firmly on both children and turned to his wife. "Noo then, Rachel. What's up? You cannae be awa wi' a bairn again. Hiv ah no been getting' aff at Haymarket for months noo?"

Rachel well understood Johnny's euphemism for a practice that so often dulled her sex life. She blinked her half-misted eyes. "Och, if it was only you forgetting to get off afore the Waverley, I'd be more than happy."

Johnny pulled up another chair and slumped himself down in front of Rachel. Then he patted her hand and took a deep breath: "So ye've mebbe heard aboot whit happened to me at work the day?"

"No," said Rachel, pulling her hand away impatiently.

"Then whit on earth's wrang?"

"Mind how you wanted me to get your shoes out of the mending the day?"

"Dinnae say ye didnae hae enough to pey for them?"

"No… Aye… . What I mean is, I hadnae at the start. No till I pawned your suit."

Johnny jumped to his feet, the chair toppling over with a thud, and shrieked, "Pawned ma suit! But Rachel, you ken it's the Trade Union meetin' the nicht. The AGM. An' I'm chairin' it."

Rachel didn't speak so Johnny continued: "I cannae staun up in a boiler suit to address the brithers. I'd be the laughin'-stock." She still made no comment so he bent down and picked up the chair before starting to pace about the scullery. "Pawned ma suit? Pawned ma suit? Pawned ma only suit?"

"Now just a minute, Johnny," Rachel said sharply as she slowly got to her feet. "What you said this morning was that, whatever else, you had to have your dress shoes out of the mending."

"Aye but surely the likes of you, whae's sae hoity-toity, kens ye dinnae wear dress shoes wi' a boiler suit."

"Look! Why don't you go in your Home Guard uniform then?" Rachel said brusquely. "But right now we've a lot more to worry us."

Johnny stopped his pacing. Rachel could see he was realising that the Home Guard uniform was his solution. Smart and authoritative he looked in it. Especially now there were three stripes on his sleeve.

"Richt enough," he conceded, "I cannae dae onything aboot the suit noo. And there could be an air raid the nicht. So it's just as weel that they ken whae's in chairge."

Rachel nodded. "Now listen to me, Johnny. They shoes of yours were mended by yon Polish refugee, Roman, who's working there the now."

"Did he no mak a guid job o them like?" Johnny asked, picking up the shoes to examine them.

"Och aye. But when I got talking to him, know what he told me?"

"Naw."

"That it's true about Hitler no liking the Jews."

Johnny was still admiring the shoes, giving them a wee rub up on his boiler suit sleeve, and he casually replied. "Well wi' aw their dosh, the Jews'll no be bothering a whit aboot that."

"Look, will you just listen to me?" Rachel said in an exasperated whisper. "He says Hitler puts Jews into concentration camps and I've been thinking – what if he invades us?"

"Dinnae be daft," said Johnny with a chuckle. "There's nae wey he'd bypass Dover and Portsmouth and start his invasion doon at Leith Docks." He pushed out his chest and began strutting around the table. "And even if he was daft enough to tak' on me and ma lads first, whit's him no bein' keen on the Jews got to dae wi' us?"

"You're forgetting my Mammy was a Jew."

"Aye, but she's deid and I dinnae think he'll dig her up just tae tell her he disnae care ower muckle for her."

"But, Johnny, Roman says they're arresting *all* of the Jews."

"And I say again what the hell has that to dae wi' us?" Johnny replied emphatically, laying down his shoes and looking vaguely about the scullery.

"Well, Roman says that even half-Jews, like me, have to be sent away to be – *cleansed*."

Johnny now slowly raised his head to examine the clothes pulley. Freshly washed garments hung neatly from every bar.

"Cleanse *you*? For heaven's sake, wumman, there's naebody wid need to cleanse you wi' aw the bleachin' and carbolickin' ye're forever daeing."

Rachel went on as if he hadn't spoken. "And no only me but the bairns an aw – because they're a quarter."

"Behave yerself, Rachel! Even Hitler widnae mak war on innocent bairns."

"Oh but he does. They get taken away too and they're looking for a final solution. One that will be ..." She hesitated as she drummed her fingers on the table ... "Final!"

"Final solution? Weel, let me tell ye, I'd like a final solution richt noo – like when am I, the breid winner in this hoose, gonnae get ma tea. And is there onybody gonnae show ony interest in whit happened to me the day?"

Rachel went on talking as if Johnny had said nothing. "Look," she said as she rose mechanically and lit the gas underneath the chip pan and lifted up a handful of chips that were sitting ready in a bowl of water. "We'll need to make plans." She breathed in deeply as she laid the chips on a tea towel and began vigorously patting them dry.

Carrie, who had grown tired of being jabbed and punched by Sam, now pushed open the door and crawled into the scullery. Without being noticed by either Rachel or Johnny, she huddled up in the corner beside the children's bench.

"Aye, we have to make plans," Rachel repeated more to herself.

"Plans? What kinna plans?"

Rachel flung the first handful of chips into the chip pan and the fat sizzled and spat. "Like how we get to be like the Free French."

"Free French?" Johnny exclaimed as his eyes widened.

"Aye, a hit-and-run resistance."

"But, but … but ye could get killed daein' that."

"So?"

"Ye ken fine it's against my principles to kill onybody that hasnae put an end to me first," Johnny moralised as he picked up his dress shoes again and held them to his chest.

"Naw! Naw! Mammy," Carrie cried, bumping along the floor on her backside.

"No what?" Rachel demanded.

"I dinnae want to get killed either."

"And why for no, Carrie? A guid killin' wid dae ye the world o guid." This admonition came from Sam, who had now joined the others.

"It wud not!" asserted his sister indignantly.

"Aye, wud it. Cos ye're just a great big yelly belly," said Sam, jabbing Carrie in the shoulder.

"Careful, Rachel, ye're scarin' the bairns," warned Johnny, pulling Sam and Carrie apart.

Rachel stopped slicing the bread when she realised how terrified Carrie looked. The knife slipped from her grasp as she stretched out her hand towards the child but when she saw Carrie shy away she instinctively pulled back and turned again to Johnny.

"Richt!" he said. "Let's forget aboot aw this cleansin' nonsense. There's a mair pressin' problem that we *hae* to get to grips with the nicht."

"Aye, you were saying there was something up at work," Rachel said slowly.

"Somethin' up? It's mair than somethin' up," said Johnny, with a note of alarm in his voice.

"Oh?"

"Aye, an' it's no as simple as getting' to grips wi' Hitler the meenit he gets here. This is serious, very serious, and we've got to get it sorted oot this very nicht," said Johnny with conviction.

Without another word he turned to Carrie and Sam and with a jab of his thumb signalled for them to get out.

"But, Mammy?" Carrie protested.

"Your Dad's right. Now off you go. The pair of you."

Carrie sniffed but without further protest followed Sam out of the scullery, Johnny slamming the door after them.

"Now what is it, Johnny?" Rachel asked wearily as she shoogled the chip pan.

Johnny began to pace the floor. "I just dinnae ken what t'dae aboot it. An' if I dae nothin' I could end up daein' time in Saughton."

"The prison?"

"Of course the bluidy prison!"

"But why?"

"Well, ye ken hoo they've put in the polis at the Store?"

"Aye, cos there's been a lot more food going missing since you were put in charge?" Rachel said quietly but firmly as she began to lift the chips out of the pan.

"Well, the nicht, wi'oot ony warnin'," Johnny continued, ignoring this slight on his managerial abilities. "dae they no lock aw the doors and start to dae full body searches o awbody?"

"Everybody?"

"Aye, even me. There wis I waitin' to gang through to be searched when Fingers, whae was standin' richt aside me, threw a wobbly. Honestly, what a state he got himsel' in. And then he gasps, 'Christ, Johnny, I didnae ken there was to be a bluidy body search the nicht. Ma auld hert'll no staun it. Hae an attack, it wull.' So I says to him that I could see he was haein' bother with his hert but he then tells me that the problem's no his hert – it's his liver!"

"His liver?" Rachel said incredulously.

"Aye, and ye're never gonnae believe this, Rachel. But just as we were getting' near the tap of the queue, there was a loud swishin' kinna plop." Johnny stopped and nodded emphatically to Rachel who was staring at him as though he had gone quite mad. "An' the poor sod's liver, aw drippin' wi' bluid, careered doon his trouser leg and fell on the tae o my boot."

Rachel gaped at Johnny's boot. "Now, let me get this straight – you're tellin' me Fingers' liver dropped right out of him, on to the toe of your boot?"

"Aye, an' Fingers looked doon at it and says, 'Ah telt ye it was a liver problem, Johnny, didn't I? But noo I'm rid of the bleeding bugger, I'm ready to face onythin'!' An' he jumps richt to the heid o the queue and demands to be searched immediately. And as they couldnae find onythin' on him they let him bolt oot the door and the last that we saw of him was him goin' like the clappers alang Tower Place."

"So that was that then?"

"Naw. The sergeant turns to me and says, 'What's that there on the tap of yer boot, Johnny?' I tells him, 'Fingers' liver'. 'That richt?' says he. 'Weel, just pick it up an' you and me'll go ben an' hae a wee chat aboot it.' So I picked up the liver, and believe it or no, it wis still warm."

"Well, seein' it had just fell out of Fingers' belly, it would be," said Rachel as she went to wind down the clothes pulley. She had just began to take the sheets off for folding when she discovered Johnny had followed so closely that he was now entangled in the washing.

"Where was I?" he went on relentlessly. "Oh aye. Well, I lays the bleedin' thing on his desk and ye should hae seen the cairry-on yon liver was haein'. Shakin' and wobblin'. Ye'd hae thocht it was still alive. But ken something, Rachel? That sergeant wasnae lookin' at it. Naw, he was starin' at me. Wantin' an answer, so he wis."

"And what did you tell him?" said Rachel before calling to Hannah to come and take the washing away.

"Just that the liver wasnae mine. That it was Fingers'. Then he asks me if I could explain hoo my alibi was now daein' a Powderhall sprint alang Constitution Street?"

"And did ye?" Rachel asked trying hard to keep her laughter in check.

"Naw. Cos I couldnae. And I kent, cos I couldnae, I'd be nicked and chairged."

"Oh, my God! You've no lost your job, Johnny? Please say you havnae lost your job." Rachel was almost hysterical by now.

"Naw, naw. I didnae lose my job but I wish to hell I hud," Johnny replied as he choked back the tears. "In fact, droonin' mysel' or volunteerin' seems like a guid idea."

"You joking?"

"Naw, I'm no jokin'. Ye see, whit happened next wis he tells me to sit doon. And I'm aw shakin' and shiverin' aside yon bleedin' liver. Then he says that, starting the morn, he's gonnae get real tough with them that's nickin' grub oot the Cold Store. An' he needs ma help."

Johnny followed Rachel over to the sink where she measured out a tablespoon of water that she added to the sauce bottle.

"Stopped him richt there and then, I did," Johnny explained. "Telt him straight oot that I was nae shopper. Against ma religion that'd be. But afore I could go on, he says, 'Aw, I think the twa o us could come to some kinna arrangement'."

Rachel pushed past Johnny and shook the sauce bottle vigorously before setting it on the table, "Arrangement? What kind of arrangement?" she asked, sucking the sauce that was sticking to her fingers.

"I thocht he meant spyin' on ma mates. So I says, 'Look! I've already telt ye, I cannae help ye. I …'. "

"For heaven's sake, Johnny! Hurry up and get to the end of your tale. The chips are burning," said Rachel before calling Hannah for a second time to take the clean clothes away.

"Weel to cut a long story short … An' here, Rachel, is there onythin' to gae wi' they chips?"

"Aye, that tomato sauce I've just doctored."

"Are we that hard up?"

"Wednesday, is it no?"

Johnny shrugged. "Aye, richt enough."

"But you're damned lucky you're getting your chips. Cos I've had mine – in more ways than one."

Before Johnny could answer the scullery door creaked open and Hannah tiptoed in. "Just finishing the chapter of my book, Mammy, I was."

"Good grief, Hannah. Every time I want you, your nose is buried in a book."

"Sorry."

"You always are. Here, take this washing and put it on top of the boiler to air off."

"I was sayin'," said Johnny, ignoring Hannah. "Then the sergeant says his wife's findin' it awfae hard to make ends meet. And then he brings his face that close to mine I could smell his mingin' breath an' he whispers in my ear that there'd be only yin person smugglin' food frae the Cold Store frae noo on. An' that it wid be," Johnny hesitated and took a deep breath – "me!"

"You?" Rachel said incredulously, as she took out the second batch of chips and put in another.

"Aye, me! An' afore I could reply he just cairried on, sayin', 'An' ye'll tak it hame wi' ye an' I'll ca' by later to your hoose for my hauf and ye can dae what the hell you like wi' the ither hauf'." Johnny paused, waiting for Rachel to react, but she didn't; so he went on, "Struck dumb, I was. And when I managed to speak I says to him, "I'm nae thief. It's against my religion to get caught thievin'.""

Rachel began dividing the chips on to the plates before scraping some margarine on to the bread: one slice for each child and two for Johnny.

"Well, Rachel, I cannae get caught breakin' the Commandments. I just cannae."

Still making no comment, Rachel emptied the last basket of chips on to a plate for Johnny. Opening the scullery door, she called the children through for their tea.

All four dashed in from the living room to take their places at the table. Johnny ignored Rachel's instructions to sit down and went on with his harangue. "Then he says, 'It's like this, Johnny. Either we cement oor arrangement, or I'm gonnae hae to chairge ye wi' the theft of this bleeding liver and it will be in aw the papers that ye're a greedy black-marketeer and then ye'll either be hung …'." Here Johnny stopped and sobbed but the children were too busy gorging themselves to notice his distress, " '… or ye'll end up in Saughton afore bein' shipped oot to join Montgomery in North Africa.' So. Rachel, whit else could I dae ither than say, 'Look, sergeant. Haud aff till I gang hame and speak tae ma Missus'."

The following evening, Sam and Carrie were playing Cowboys and Indians in the Empty Room. It was really the second bedroom of the house but had no furniture in it, nor any linoleum on the floor. However, Sanderson chintz curtains tied back with red silk cords adorned the windows.

Sam, who had found a better use for the silk cords, now had Carrie securely tied to a chair and was doing a war dance around her. She in turn was quite happy to be captive and played the role well, widening her violet eyes and sniffing loudly. Happy enough, that is, until Sam, brandishing a large pair of scissors, advanced closer to her, chanting, "I'm Big Chief Sweeney Todd."

"Mammy, Mammy!" she cried loudly. "Come quick! He's gonnae scalp me. Really scalp me."

Rachel was busily bathing Alice in the washing tub in the scullery but stopped abruptly when Carrie's screams penetrated the kitchen. Carefully, however, she lifted the baby out of the tub and placed her safely on the floor before rushing to Carrie's aid.

"Sam, Sam! What in the name of heaven is going on in here?" she yelled, bounding into the bedroom. "And why d'you always have to have this lassie bawling her head off?" She paused. "Here – that's surely no my Jenner's Sale tie-backs you've got there?" she shouted.

Sam nodded. Rachel snorted and shook her head in exasperation before grabbing him fiercely. "Don't you realise they curtains and tiebacks are to fool the neighbours? Stood for four hours in a blinking freezing queue to get them," she continued as she dunted him mercilessly on the shoulder. "And here's you using them for bloody ropes."

Without hesitation, Sam began to untie Carrie but in doing so only succeeded in tightening the cord around her neck.

"Mammy, Mammy! He's chokin' me now," Carrie cried out, as she started to turn blue.

The next thing Sam knew was his head rocking, as Rachel's open hand whacked his ear. Still sobbing loudly, Carrie was led by her mother into the scullery where she wiped her nose piteously with the back of her hand, looking about her at the same time in the hope of seeing signs of the tea being prepared. But there was no pot of porridge bubbling on the cooker. No bread was waiting to be spread with the twopence-worth of roast dripping that Carrie had been sent for to the butcher's when she had come in from school. The thought of roast dripping sprinkled with salt and spread on fresh bread made Carrie lick her lips, reminding her that she was hungry – very hungry. "Mammy," she whined. "I'm starvin'."

"Aye," Rachel replied absently as she picked Alice up to rub her dry.

"Mammy, did you no hear me say I'm hungry?"

"I heard you. And you'll get your tea in a wee while. Now then, Alice, you're all clean and beautiful again. Off you go and play ben the house," Rachel thrust a yellow wool-tufted rag doll with shirt-button eyes into Alice's hands.

"But I'm starvin' hungry, Mammy," Carrie wheedled.

"Aye, Carrie, I know you are. You'll get your tea in a wee while."

"Bit could I no just hae a wee piece on white jam the noo?"

"How often have I to tell you to speak proper and that white jam is condensed milk?" Rachel retorted, testing the temperature of the water she had just washed Alice in. She smiled, thinking it was just warm enough and, lifting up a pile of dirty washing from the floor, began putting it into the tub to steep.

"Okay then, so could I have a piece on that condensed …?"

Sheer exasperation made Rachel interrupt. "See, Carrie! You were fed last night and you'll be fed tonight in due course but right now I'm too busy for making blooming pieces."

"But, Mammy," Carrie began once more.

Before she could go on, Sam bounced through the scullery door, having speedily recovered from his punishment. "Mammy, I'm stervin'! Can I no hae a piece?" he pleaded, running his finger round the top of the condensed milk tin and making sure it dipped into the milk before sticking it in his mouth.

Rachel turned just in time to see Sam suck his finger. Without a word of warning she smacked his hand away from the tin before grabbing it and putting it on the top shelf above the window. "See this, you two wee pests," she yelled, "you've got appetites like bloody vultures. And as I told you last night," she went on through clenched teeth "you've no any God-given right to expect to be fed every day. Some of us … "

Sam, who wasn't paying any attention, interrupted. "Mammy," he said, "Why are ye walkin' up and doon and then lookin' oot o the windae?"

"Aye, what are you lookin' for, Mammy?" added Carrie.

"For some bloody peace, would you believe!"

"Peace, Mammy? But why?"

"I'm just lookin' for your Dad comin'." Rachel craned her neck to get a better view out of the window.

"You dinnae usually look oot for him."

"Too right, Sam. But I'm looking for your useless Dad coming the night. So will you just be bloody quiet?"

Carrie scrambled on to the bunker so that she too could look up the back lane. "Mammy," she cried. "Here's our Daddy comin' noo. There's somethin' awfae wrang wi' him. He cannae walk right."

"Neither he can. Fair buckling he is," Rachel said gleefully before she clasped her hands and looked to the ceiling, "Oh, thank you so much, God, for answering my prayers!"

"You prayed for Daddy to be ill?" Carrie asked tearfully as she jumped down. "I'm awa to help him."

"You stay right where you are, my lady. And Sam, don't you dare go out neither," She grabbed hold of both children. "You two's the bane of my life. Aye on about being bloody hungry. So I'm trying …" Rachel halted mid-sentence and loosened her grip on the children because the outside door had opened and

Johnny, pale and gaunt, staggered in.

"Oh, Daddy, are you awfae no weel?" Carrie whimpered.

"Dinnae tell us ye've a sair back again," said Sam shaking his head dolefully.

"Carrie! Sam!" Rachel shouted , "Bide here and don't take another breath until I tell you."

Turning to Johnny. "C'mon now, son. You're going to be all right. Here, let me help you ben the scullery."

Johnny's mouth opened and shut like a fish. Gasping, he tried to form words but Rachel gestured to him to keep quiet. Then the two of them staggered into the scullery and the door was slammed shut.

"Sam, did you see that there's nae porridge pot on the gas?"

"Is there no?"

"Naw. And it's Thursday – so we should be getting porridge and a drippin' piece."

Sam shrugged. "Maybe Mammy meant it and we're no gonnae get fed every day."

Carrie was about to answer when there came a loud knock at the outside door.

"Will I answer the door, Mammy?" shouted Sam, as he went over and flung the outside door wide open.

"Yer Daddy in, son?" asked the big police sergeant who framed the doorway.

"Naw," Sam replied, 'He's awa to North Africa to get shot."

Rachel rushed out of the scullery and, grabbing Sam by the scruff of the neck, thrust him backwards across the room.

"Yer man hame?" the sergeant asked.

"Aye, he's ben the scullery," Rachel replied, pointing towards the door.

The scullery door slammed again on the twins and Sam commented bitterly: "Oor Mammy's a stinkin' shopper. Handed oor Daddy ower to the polis, she has."

"I ken. But what can we dae"

"Rescue him! Whit else?"

The children were still hatching their rescue plan, part of which would mean Sam attacking the policeman by jumping on his back while Carrie grabbed him round the legs, when the sergeant emerged from the scullery with a bulging kit bag that he swung on to his shoulder.

"Weel done, Johnny lad," he said with a chuckle, as he opened the outside door. "On Monday I'll gie ye the order for next week."

Carrie and Sam, who had now been joined by Hannah, looked questioningly from one to the other as the sergeant peered warily into the dark passageway to ascertain there was no one hanging about. Then, quickly and quietly, he made off into the night.

No sooner had the door closed than all three children scampered into the scullery. Simultaneously they all pulled up sharply. Carrie's mouth gaped.

"Wid ye look at that!" said Sam in amazement.

There, displayed on the table, sat the rear quarters of a large pig chopped into roasting joints. Beside them lay a row of pork chops – enough to feed an army – and in front of those half of a roughly-hacked lamb's liver that spewed blood everywhere. And to complete this astonishing gastronomic exhibition there was an enormous five-pound tin of New Zealand butter.

"Where did aw this come from, Mammy?"

"None of your business, my lady," Rachel snapped at Carrie.

"Here, does this mean that I can gang intae school the morn and tell aw the boys that my Daddy's no a coward? That he's noo the heid o the Leith Black Mairket!" Sam asked hoarsely, adding – as he grabbed the front of his trousers – "Oh ma God! Ah think I'm gonnae pee masel'.."

"You'll no tell nobody nothing!" Rachel shouted, lifting Sam by his jumper again and shaking him so vigorously that a thin dribble trickled down his leg. "There's no one to be told a word about what's going on in this house."

Johnny, who was bent over on a chair wringing his hands, just shook his head. "Yer Mammy's richt, son. You cannae tell onybody that yer faither's a common thief – an' no prepared to be rationed like ither folk."

Carrie was upset at this and sidled over to him, whispering, "It'll be all right, Dad. You're a Catholic and my pal Bernie says that Catholics, nae like us Proddies, can dae awfae things. Then aw they need tae dae is confess. An' then God forgives them and lets them intae heaven."

"That reminds me, Rachel. I met Father O'Hara in the street the day so I telt him aw aboot this." Johnny nodded his head towards the spread of food on the table.

"Have you lost your marbles, Johnny?" said Rachel in utter disbelief.

"Nae problem. Father O'Hara's very discreet."

"Oh aye. And what did he tell you to do?"

"Just to let ma conscience be ma guide."

Rachel's response was to dump the frying pan on to the stove and fling the twopence worth of roast dripping into it. "Will it be one pork chop or two you'll be wanting?"

"Well, if I've got to keep this up I'll need the strength. So I'd better hae twa chops and a wee slice o liver."

"Just the one slice of liver?" Rachel asked mockingly.

"Aye, I'm nae wantin' to be greedy. And here, Rachel, ye wouldnae mebbe hae a bittie tomati or ingan to be gaun wi it?"

"Naw, no the day, Johnny son," Rachel responded sweetly. "But once I've sold what we cannae use, I'll get you all the garnish you'll ever want."

Johnny jumped from his chair, grabbed Rachel by the arms and birled her around so that they were facing each other. "Sell aff aw whit we cannae yaise? Naw. naw, Rachel, ye cannae dae that."

"Why for no?" Rachel demanded as she pulled herself free.

"Cos I swore to Father O'Hara that if I did go in wi' yon sergeant I'd hand in twa pork chops and a couple of slices o liver to the Chapel Hoose on my wey to work the morn!"

CHAPTER 3
ISOLATION

When yet another row began between Mam and Dad, Hannah felt the fear seep into her. There was simply no way she could stop her throat muscles tightening and her stomach churning. The rows were so frequent and violent now that she knew it was just a matter of time before something dreadful would happen.

Although only going on eleven, Hannah was very astute and was sure that the deterioration in Johnny and Rachel's relationship had started when that bent sergeant had bullied her father into stealing the food from the Cold Store. It was true the family was now better fed and enjoyed the benefits that arrived when Rachel sold the excess food on the black market – but it was all at the price of her father and mother drifting apart.

The sergeant had grown increasingly bold and greedy – every week demanding that more food be stolen. Naturally tongues wagged; and eventually someone (and Hannah suspected it was Johnny under the guidance of Father O'Hara) wrote an anonymous letter to the Chief Constable. Suddenly the sergeant was assigned to desk duties under the strict supervision of his Inspector and his replacement at the Cold Store proved to be an incorruptible God-fearing Presbyterian. Unfortunately Rachel had reached the same conclusion as Hannah and when the family found themselves back in grinding poverty, all the harder to bear after the luxury of plenty, Johnny's name was perpetually on the receiving end of Rachel's caustic tongue.

The row of two hours ago had resulted in Johnny storming out of the house. Hannah knew she had to get everybody to bed before he returned. If not, Rachel would do what she was expert at – restarting the argument from where it had broken off. The added problem that night was Rachel's insistence on getting everything ready for the morning. She was viciously chopping sticks for the fire on the glory-hole's stone floor when the door opened and Johnny entered.

"And where the hell have you been?" demanded Rachel, who knew full well that Johnny had either been at the chapel speaking to Father OHara or down bleating to his mother.

"Doon at ma Maw's."

"How is Granny?" asked Hannah, who was desperate to defuse the situation.

"Fine."

"Aye, so she should be. After all, she managed to offload you on to me."

"In the name o heaven, Rachel, gie it a rest," protested Johnny wearily.

"Oh, life a bit hard for you then?" said Rachel with heavy sarcasm. "No easy now for the bairns either. Aye, Carrie was just wondering when she ..."

"No on aboot haein' pork chops again?"

"Naw. Nor egg and chips," said Rachel advancing threateningly towards Johnny. "She was just wanting a piece – ye ken, some bread and jam. But I told her – you had to be an orphan to get bread and jam for your supper."

Johnny had the grace to blush and step back before uttering, "I'm *entitled* to dae whit I like with ma ain pocket money."

"Entitled? Now there's a funny thing! Our Hannah here she was wondering why the nuns are *entitled* to six loaves of bread tomorrow for the orphans – two from you, two from your mother and two from Ella – when *she* won't be entitled to even a crust in the morning." Rachel stepped forward again and Johnny backed away to the wall.

Hannah's large, soulful blue eyes widened in fear and she began to twist the tresses of her blonde hair with growing agitation. "But, Mam, I didn't ..." she began to protest – but Rachel turned and silenced her with a warning glare.

"It wasnae ma faut the sergeant gettin' moved." said Johnny, trying once more to put distance between himself and Rachel, this time by edging sideways.

"The sergeant is no the half of it," replied Rachel, menacingly swinging her hatchet in the air.

"Please, Mammy, let me take the axe," begged Hannah tearfully. "It should be in the glory-hole. It really should."

"Maybe it should or … maybe …"

Johnny flinched as Rachel brought the axe closer to his face. "Are you mad or somethin', wumman?" he croaked.

Rachel was now so near that when she spoke Johnny could feel the spray of her breath as it hit his face. "Mad? Of course I'm bloody mad. You callous swine! Why, oh why, do you always put everybody and yourself before my bairns?"

"I dinnae!"

"But you bloody well do. All hail-fellow-well-met with the Union lads. The humble benefactor to your church's bleeding orphans. And you know I just will not tolerate anybody, especially you – their useless father – taking the food out of my bairns' mouths." Rachel shook the hatchet again. Johnny began to lower himself to the floor in a bid to protect himself. "Aye," said Rachel in exasperation, "I should put this in your thick skull but know something?" She now pulled his chin forward with her left hand. "You're not even worth swinging for."

Johnny sighed with relief and Rachel continued. "As a matter of fact, why the hell do you not just get out of here and leave us to fend for ourselves." Wearily she let the axe drop and Hannah scrambled to pick it up and put it safely away.

Johnny took a moment or two to recover and when he did he nodded before saying, "Aye, I think ma gettin' oot o here wid be for the best."

"For whose best?" demanded Carrie, who had got out of bed when the raised voices had awakened her.

Without another word Johnny started to pack his few belongings into a pillow case – his work clothes, shaving brush and razor. Then he went into the bedroom and took his Home Guard greatcoat off the bed where Alice and Paul were sleeping. But before leaving the house for the very last time, he hesitated, wanting to look at his children yet being unable to look any of them in the eye. All he could mutter was, "Can ye no see? I just cannae tak ony mair? It's a maitter o time till she does for me." With that he stepped into the stair and out of their lives. Rachel kicked the door shut behind him as if to confirm the finality of the deed.

"Why didn't you stop him, Mam? Dad leaving us means we'll be … destitute."

"Destitute?" shouted Rachel. "Know something, Hannah? I think you read too many books."

"Mebbe she does," said Sam thoughtfully. "But yin thing's for sure. If she means we're gonnae be poor – even poorer than poor – then I'm thinkin' she micht be richt!"

****

The next eighteen months were indeed hard on the family but they all pulled together. Rachel seized any paid work she could get. At one time she had four jobs simultaneously, though all naturally carried meagre wages. She was washing stairs, cleaning houses, working early shift in the local bakery and doing the back shift as dispense barmaid at the Queen's Hotel. The older children likewise pitched in. Hannah found work after school in the shop that recharged the radio accumulators while Sam and Carrie, lying about their age, took milk and newspaper delivery rounds.

They were just beginning to feel that they could cope and were anticipating that life would get better when six year old

Alice, the youngest of the family, became ill. Very ill indeed. She would cough and cough – and then cough again. After a long silence there would come a long whoop – a dreadful sound that none of the children had ever heard the like of before. The whoop would last so long that it would cut off Alice's breathing and her face would turn blue. Whenever that happened Rachel would dash over to Alice and lift her up tenderly. She would then put the index finger of her right hand down Alice's throat and hook out the horrible green phlegm that was choking the life out of her child. Once the phlegm was removed Rachel would put Alice on to her shoulder and rhythmically pat her back, murmuring gently, "There, there, my dear. It's all right."

At those times there was nothing Sam, Hannah or Carrie could do except stand, stare, gulp and pray – "Please, God, make Alice breathe again." And God had always answered their prayers; but even so their little sister would lie there like a limp rag doll and huge silent tears would roll down her cheeks.

The only other thing that Rachel could do for Alice was to put the kettle on the cooker, along with her biggest pot filled with water, and let them boil furiously. The scullery then became a steam chamber that brought some relief to Alice's breathing. On this occasion, however, after one of the severe coughing fits they were all certain she would never breathe again and Rachel screamed, "For Christ's sake, Alice, don't die on us. If you do, I'll kill you stone dead myself, so I will."

Hannah was so frightened, she yelled, "Mam, what Alice needs is a doctor."

Rachel wheeled round on her. "D'you think I don't bloody know that?"

"Then why are ye no sendin' for yin," demanded Sam, picking Alice's doll up from the floor. Just for a moment he held it tight to his chest before gently tucking it in beside his sister who was now propped up in the old easy chair in one corner of the scullery.

"Look, Sam," explained Rachel, her voice cracking with sobs. "Don't you understand that before a doctor puts his foot over the door I'd need to cross his palm with silver? And because I haven't been able to work for ten days now I've only got one sodding penny left – and I need that for the gas."

"But surely, Mam, a doctor'll come when a bairn's as ill as Alice," argued Hannah.

"Listen, all of you, and listen good – not only will they no come but they'll no even let the hospitals take the sick bairns in either," Rachel retorted, clattering the empty soup pot into the sink and filling it again with water. "Oh aye, that'll be the day – when a doctor docsnae demand his half-crown first."

"Some bairns get takken in," said Sam quietly, leaning over to turn off the tap his mother had forgotten about.

"Aye, at twelve oclock at night. It's only at midnight that they take in the sick bairns no doctor has seen."

Rachel carefully poured some of the water from the pot before lifting it out of the sink and replacing it on the gas ring. She didn't strike a match though because the gas wouldn't light without another penny going into the meter. "Dear Lord," she said looking tenderly on Alice who was now fast asleep. "Do I use my last penny now? Or wait till she gets bad again?"

All her life Carrie would remember the long silence broken only by Alice's rasping breathing. No one spoke. They were all terrified of what would happen to Alice if there was no steam to help her breathe.

After what seemed an eternity, Rachel sank down on a chair and lifted up the bottom of her apron to mop her face. Trying hard to control the panic that was racing uncontrollably through her tormented mind she eventually announced, "Right. There's nothing else I can do – at eleven o'clock tonight I'll take Alice down to Leith Hospital."

Hannah looked at the clock and swallowed hard. "But Mammy," she said fearfully, "it's only four o'clock. Eleven o'clock is years away. Alice needs help now!"

Ignoring Hannah, Rachel went on: "Aye, I'll take her down to the hospital and stand in the queue along with all the other paupers." Here she lowered her voice to a whisper, "And I just hope, I do, that they'll take Alice in." She hesitated and sniffed loudly before gulping, " ... as a ... *charity* case."

"But how'll you get her there? It's at least a thirty minute walk away," asked Hannah, who knew that six year old Alice was so ill she was quite unable to walk there. And she also knew full well that, much as Rachel would want to, she couldn't possibly carry Alice all that distance.

Rachel shook her head and bit her lip. The time ticked slowly by and the children felt almost deafened by the silence that pervaded the room. Then a slight smile began to appear on Rachel's face and a brightness sprang into her eyes as she jumped from her chair and ran from the scullery into the bedroom which lay completely empty except for the old pram that Rachel had pushed her five children in. She'd meant to give the pram to poor Mrs Wilson upstairs but there was something about it, with its battered old hood and wobbly wheels, that reminded her of happier days – those times when Alice used to be propped up at the top end of the pram and Paul, legs dangling over the side, deposited at the bottom, while Carrie and Sam hung on to the handles – those long-gone days when Hannah skipped up the road in front of them all and lack of money had been her only worry.

Rachel wheeled the pram out of the bedroom and into the scullery. "Right now!" she said emphatically, "We'll give it a real good wash, dry it, put a pillow and blankets inside and, if Alice curls up her wee legs, that's how we'll get her down to the hospital."

Hannah grinned before asking, "Will I put the last penny in the meter then and light the gas again?"

Rachel nodded. "Aye, let's go full steam ahead."

Relief soaked into Carrie. She sidled over to Alice, lifted up her clammy hand and kissed it. "Everything's going to be fine noo, Alice. Our Mammy's her old self again."

Sam, who was also awash with relief, sniffed and pushed out his chest. "Ye're bluidy richt, Carrie. Oh aye, we mightnae win this blinkin' war but at least noo we'll hae a fighting chance."

At exactly eleven o'clock Rachel lifted Alice and wrapped her in a blanket, remembering to raise the pillow before laying her gently into the pram. Hannah opened the outside door to let her mother out. Rachel paused for a second. "Now," she whispered, eyeing each of her children in turn. "You know you are *not* to answer the door to anybody." Then, looking straight at Sam, "And don't *you* do anything you shouldn't do, while I'm out."

Carrie, Hannah and Sam all nodded. Rachel turned to go but halted again. "You do all understand, don't you, how important it is that nobody knows I've left you alone?"

"But how'll anybody ever find oot?" Carrie bleated. "Most people don't even ken Daddy's left us."

Rachel shook her head in annoyance. "Look, I've enough to worry me this night without you reminding me about your blooming useless deserting father."

Hannah opened the door further and, as quietly as possible, Rachel wheeled the pram into the street where she had to face the ferocity of the stormy night. She bent her head towards the relentless gale that buffeted and shrieked all around her. For a moment she felt quite astonished that nature could be so cruel.

Midnight was chiming when Rachel reached Leith Hospital. Inconsequentially she recalled that it had been built as a memorial

39

to the gallant men of Leith who had laid down their lives in the First World War. Her late arrival was due in part to the furious wind that had repeatedly driven her back one step for every two she'd taken. Sheer exhaustion was beginning to overtake her when she was greeted by the hospital porter as she pushed open the door.

"Needin' ony help, Rachel?" he asked, taking the pram from her.

"No me, Tam, but my youngest is," Rachel said as she blew hard into her hands in an effort to put life back into her frozen fingers.

Then her words were drowned out by Alice's racking coughing.

"Here," Tam blurted out. "Never you never mind sittin' in that queue. Just get the bairn out of the pram and follow me."

Stiff with cold, Rachel awkwardly lifted Alice and staggered forward, almost letting her fall. Tam grabbed Alice from her and raced ahead up the stairs into the consulting room.

The Night Sister, in charge of admissions, looked up, "Is there a problem, Tom?" she enquired icily.

"This bairn's in real bother, Sister," Tam replied.

"Maybe so, but careering around is hardly going to help. Decorum, Tom! Decorum at all times is what we must have in this hospital!"

With pursed lips Sister rose and took Alice from Tom. She was about to lay Alice down on a trolley when Rachel entered. "You are the mother?" Sister asked in her clipped tones.

Rachel nodded, controlling the urge to take Alice back into her arms.

"Well, I'm just going to put her on the trolley here so that I can examine her," said Sister, sensing Rachel's panic and melting her tone somewhat.

One look at Alice had Sister recognising that Alice needed

medical help urgently. Without displaying emotion, she called to one of the staff nurses to help her. It was then that Alice began to cough, whoop and choke.

Swiftly Sister lifted Alice, laid her on both knees and gently yet firmly patted her back. Then she turned the child over and placed one finger in her mouth. Rachel flinched and gasped. The Sister was hooking out *three times* as much phlegm as she had ever been able to do.

"Isolation Ward for this one, Nurse," Sister announced, placing Alice into a nurse's waiting arms.

"Isolation?" gasped Rachel as she grabbed hold of the Sister.

Before answering, Sister removed Rachel's hand from her arm. "Yes," she nodded. "Your child has whooping cough, possibly with severe complications. First thing in the morning she'll be transferred to the City Hospital. All infectious diseases have to go there."

Rachel shook her head in disbelief once she realised that Alice was to be transferred to isolation. "Please, could I see her once more before you take her?" she pleaded urgently.

"No," replied Sister firmly. "But this is her number: five, one, three. Now do you know you can either consult the *Edinburgh Evening News* or listen into the BBC six o'clock bulletin on the radio?"

Rachel looked blank.

"Look, when you hear you child's number being called out, a message will also tell you how she is progressing."

"Are you saying I won't be allowed to see her?" Rachel croaked.

"Yes. I'm sorry, but there is no visiting unless a child's life is in imminent danger."

Sister was about to end the conversation but, seeing Rachel's obvious distress, she added, "You see, my dear, visiting is so upsetting for the children. It has them crying for home. Much better for them to get quickly used to the hospital routine. Then they settle down and recovery is much quicker."

Rachel stared long and hard at Sister. How could this woman – who had never given birth, never nourished a child at her breast – possibly know that to take a child away from its mother was the cruellest thing that anyone could do? A child who is ill needs its mother, Rachel argued to herself. Needs to be reassured. Not left alone and frightened in a hospital ward tended by strangers. Rachel knew all this because her own mother had been taken from her. She could vividly recall the clinical setting of the Poorhouse Orphanage where she had spent the first four years of her life. That Poorhouse where it was useless to cry for attention because no one had time to give you any.

Lost in these memories Rachel hadn't noticed the nurse had left the room with Alice. Once it dawned on her, she made to run and snatch Alice back. Sister instantly barred the way and looked directly into Rachel's eyes. The warning stare told Rachel what she didn't want to admit – that Alice was very ill and needed the expert medical attention that Rachel now knew she couldn't possibly provide.

When Rachel arrived home she wheeled the soaking wet empty pram into the stairwell. Her hand lingered on the handle and scalding tears sprang to her eyes before she took the front door key from her pocket. Once inside, she became aware that Carrie, Sam and Hannah were all waiting up for her. Immediately they clamoured to know what had happened and in graphic detail she told them everything – even those memories of the Poorhouse that had stayed with her while she trudged home. These confidences frightened Hannah and terrified Carrie.

****

Carrie had been sitting hunched up in the corner for half an hour or more with an open library book on her knees. In all that time she hadn't turned a single page or noticed that the book was upside down. She'd been thinking how frightened, really terrified, she had been every day since Alice was admitted to hospital. For three weeks now she'd been haunted by the threat of having to face the loss of Alice. She knew that would be even worse than the loss of her Daddy had been. What would she do if someone told her that Alice had … ? No! She would never say that word. To say that might make it happen. Especially now that she knew, because her pal Bernie had told her, that deaths always happened in threes in the same street. Why, she wondered, did old Mrs Baird and Jimmy Burns have to die right now? Carrie nodded to herself and gave a slight smile as she thought: maybe Bernie was wrong and maybe Captain Hyde would count even although he had lived in the private houses across the street. And if he did count that would be the three which would mean that Alice, her darling Alice, would be safe.

"Carrie," said Hannah, brusquely breaking into Carrie's thoughts. "Mam's trying to tell us something important and you're not listening."

"Did you say something, Hannah?" Carrie muttered absently, letting her book clatter to the floor.

Hannah shook her head in exasperation. "You can go on now, Mam. She's stopped daydreaming."

"About time too," said Rachel emphatically. "Now you all know I haven't been at work since the week before Alice went into hospital?"

"Aye, because you had a right bad dose of the flu," said Sam.

Rachel eyed each of the children in turn. She knew that they knew it was more than flu that had been wrong with her. This time her recurrent depression had been blacker than ever and she'd taken to her bed. She had lain there, simply drifting to and fro between merciful oblivion and unbearable distress. She'd hardly been able to lift her head off the pillow for more days than she could remember. All she could recall was that the children had taken it in turns to lift a cup of water or sweet tea to her parched mouth. It was the thought of what might happen to the children that had finally made her face life again.

Nevertheless, five weeks had passed without any money coming in and … Her thoughts were interrupted when a fit of coughing overtook her.

"Oh, Mam," Hannah cried, "You're just no well enough to go back to work yet."

"And you dinnae need tae," Sam shouted. "Carrie and me hae been pinching tatties, tumshies and onything else we can find in the fairmers' fields and sheds. So we'll nae stairve."

Rachel shook her head. "Look, what I have to tell you is this." She took a deep breath before announcing, "We're goin' to be evicted on Tuesday!"

"Evicted?" Hannah and Carrie chorused.

"Ye mean pit oot on the street?' Sam said in horror.

"'Fraid so. You see, I didn't have the money to pay this month's rent." Rachel turned away from the children to look out of the scullery window.

"But they allow you one month," Hannah interjected.

"That's true. But I couldn't pay last month's either," Rachel continued, beginning to wipe over the table with a damp cloth.

"But why Tuesday? I mean, that doesnae gie us much time to find the money," protested Sam.

"To tell you the truth, it was to have been this Thursday but it's not Christian to toss poor beggars out just before Easter."

"Surely, you're not saying that all their charity rolls away on Easter Monday," Hannah snapped bitterly.

Rachel nodded.

"But this is oor hame," said Sam angrily. "You fought to get it for us. We've all slaved to keep it – so there just has to be somethin' we can dae."

"'Fraid not," Rachel said wearily.

"But, Mam, if we're evicted, where will we go?" asked Carrie tearfully.

"A Home," Rachel replied.

"Like that one you were once in?" queried Hannah.

Rachel dearly wished now she hadn't told them about the orphanage. No one had ever heard her condemn the orphanage. There were just too many children and not enough resources. Feeding, washing and beating the fear of God into the children was all they could achieve.

She'd been lucky though, because her mother's friend had petitioned the board when Rachel reached her fourth birthday. Anna had pleaded to be allowed to foster Rachel and they had readily agreed, providing Anna took Gabby, Rachel's father, to court for her maintenance.

Auntie Anna had always assured Rachel that she'd have taken her immediately Norma, her mother, had died were it not for the fact that she'd already taken in her brother's three motherless bairns. And Rachel accepted that caring and providing for Bella, Jimmy and Rab had made quite it impossible for her to take on an infant too.

As to Gabby providing maintenance – some hope! Rachel still cringed with shame as she remembered all too vividly how every Friday night Auntie Anna would sigh and mutter, "Hoo that Orphanage Board expects *me* to get yer ne'er-do-well faither to come up with yer keep when *they* couldnae, I just dinnae ken?"

While Rachel was reminiscing, Carrie had started to have a tantrum – screaming, kicking, jumping and throwing anything she could lay her hands on up in the air.

"Carrie!" her mother yelled, grabbing hold of her and shaking the girl until she stopped. "What the hell d'you think you're up to?"

"I just don't want to go into a Home. I've got to be here when Alice comes home. And she'll come here because this is our home. She knows we're here and that we're all waiting for her." Carrie broke away from Rachel but spun around and continued at the top of her voice, "It's been three weeks since you took her away. You'd no right to take her. No right at all, Mammy! I'm the one who pushed her pram and took her to school. She always waited for me, every day, so we could walk back together. I've *got* to be here when she comes back."

"Look, Carrie, it'll be all right because Alice'll go into a Home along with you," her mother reasoned, trying to pull Carrie towards her again.

Far from pacifying Carrie this only served to make her scream louder and kick out. "No! No! No! We're *not going* into a Home. Alice isn't going. Paul's not going. Sam's not going. And I'm not going."

"And what about me?" Hannah asked. "Am I the only one that has to go?"

"You can do what you bloody well like, Hannah," sobbed Carrie, "You're so smart you should be able to take care of yourself."

"That's enough of that, my lady," warned Rachel as she managed to grab Carrie again. "Haven't I spent the last few months getting you all to speak properly and here's you talking like a guttersnipe. Now, just calm down. All of you."

Rachel let go of Carrie and walked over to the mantelpiece. She looked at the Dresden shepherd and shepherdess standing there and felt a hot flush of remorse suffuse her. "Don't worry. Don't panic. I'll think of something in the end. I always do," she said to herself reassuringly.

Carrie's eyes too were now on the ornaments that she loved

so much. For all their poverty and deprivation she reckoned she was as good as anybody else as long as those ornaments adorned the mantelpiece. She truly believed that they possessed some kind of magical power that would eventually make things better for them all. "You're not thinking of selling my ornaments, Mam?" she nervously questioned.

Rachel's eyes remained fixed on them. "No, Carrie, selling them would be the last card in my hand."

"But if it means keepin' this roof ower oor heids, then why no?" demanded Sam.

"Cos they're the only link I have with your Granny. I told you, didn't I, that my mother was Jewish. Married out of her class and her religion, so her family would have nothing more to do with her."

"No wonder, when you look at Granddad," growled Hannah.

"Upper middle-class your Granny's people were," said Rachel, pulling herself up.

"Aye, and that's a richt big help."

"What d'you mean, Sam?" demanded Carrie.

"Just that we've got bugger-aw to eat the nicht but that's okay, cos we're better class than the folks next door who're nae doubt stuffin' their gobs wi' egg and chips and no gettin' chucked oot on their erses next week."

Rachel ignored Sam's outburst and went on: "When my Mam was having me, she caught TB and they took her off to the Poorhouse Infirmary in Seafield Road. I was born there and was just a few months old when my Mammy died. Just afore she died my Dad married her."

What Rachel didn't tell the children was that Gabby, her father, had been too drunk to stand or repeat his marriage vows and her mother, Norma, too weak. Nor did she explain that her mother's last wish had been granted and that, by marrying Gabby, she had removed the stigma of illegitimacy from her precious daughter.

"Anyway," she continued, "one day, a woman – some far-off relative of my mother's – came to the door and handed me these ornaments. Said she wanted me to have them because – just like you, Carrie – my mother loved looking at them. No! Selling them would be like selling my own mother. They're my heritage. All my hopes and dreams are in them.

CHAPTER 4
SOLUTIONS AND PROMISES

The following evening, Rachel was getting ready for work and combing her hair in front of the scullery mirror. "Oh no!" she gasped, leaning closer to get a better look, "These just can't be. But they are! Blooming grey hairs. Grey hairs! At thirty-eight? Surely I'm far too young for grey hairs." She was about to pull out one of the invaders to get a closer look when she was distracted by muffled sounds from Sam. "You saying something, Sam?" she asked.

"Just that I dinnae suppose us going wi' milk and papers does onythin' to get us oot the mess we're in?"

Rachel shook her head, realising that premature grey hairs were the least of her worries right now.

"Not really. But I'm glad of the ten bob I get from you each week." She sighed. "But let's face it. There's no way it even pays for what you eat."

Sam nodded and blushed deeply. Rachel knew he was regretting having supped the tinned milk and having taken two pieces of bread spread with dripping after she'd rationed them all to one each.

She went over to Sam and gently ruffled his shock of ginger-tinted blond curls. "Don't you worry, Sam. I'll take care of things. I've got things in hand and I'm sure it'll all be ..." She broke off and smiled, leaving her hopes only half-said.

For Sam though, the threat remained. If his mother didn't get the money they needed, they were all fated to be taken into care. The thought made Sam bite his lip so hard that it drew blood.

Rachel had turned back to finish her grooming and didn't witness his distress. She turned to face him. "Now, tonight I want you all to stay here in the scullery," she said firmly. "That means no one is to light the gas in the living room. That clear?"

49

"Is that an Easter thing – no having a light in the living room?" asked Sam, as he took the bread from the bread tin and realised there was only enough for one slice each.

"No, it's not. And when Carrie comes in, you see to it she *stays put* in the scullery."

Sam nodded.

"Now remember the rules, Sam. No trouble. No fighting. No answering the door to anyone. No one is ever to know I leave you alone at night when I go out to work."

"Why're ye always sayin' that, Mam?"

"Cos you're all under sixteen years of age, Sam. That means they'd say I was neglecting you so you could be put in a Home," Rachel warned, picking up her coat.

"So what? If we get kicked oot on our erses on Tuesday we'll land in yin onyway," Sam retorted.

Two hours had gone by before Carrie reached home. She had stopped off at Bernie's so she could read the final gripping instalment of the serial and she hadn't been disappointed. Oh no! The ending was even better than she had imagined, with that horrible upper-class woman, who'd inveigled the hero into promising to marry her, being hurled off the cliffs at Kinghorn. Her death meant the hero could come back and rescue the true love of his life, that poor sick overworked damsel in the manse. Promised her, he did, that she'd now live in a mansion – Carrie was certain it had two bathrooms. He'd also pledged to her on bended knee that she would never again have to scrub floors to buy food. No, she would have maids, not just to scrub the floors but to massage her back as well. Finally, the hero swept up the fragile maiden in his arms, dashed down the stairs, two at a time, and they both disappeared off into a golden sunset.

Carrie had followed the story eagerly in the *Red Letter* for six weeks and the ending left her toes curling in ecstasy. An unaccountable sensation permeating her whole body, worked strange stirrings in her that she couldn't even acknowledge: stirrings that made her flush guiltily.

Whenever she opened the door into the house, however, her temperature plummeted. "Oh, bother," she exclaimed. "Would you look at that fire? It's freezing outside and it's banked up with wet dross. Not a bit of heat'll come out of it the night."

Sam stood framed in the scullery doorway. "Weel, ye dinnae hae to worry aboot it – cos we're aw to bide in the scullery the nicht."

"Why?" demanded his sister, pushing past him.

"Dinnae ken. But what I do ken is it's dried egg for the tea and seein' ye're so guid at scramblin' things ye're to switch them up."

Hannah, who had been through in the bedroom, came to join them in the scullery She closed the door firmly and signalled to talk quietly. "I've an idea," she confided. "You know, Carrie, that you've to go across to Mrs Gracie to find out where Alice's number comes on the hospital list?"

"She's surely not on the danger list again, is she?" In her alarm Carrie almost spilt the dried egg mixture that she was measuring into the bowl.

"No. I think she's still fine. It's just that once you're done scrambling the eggs the three of us have to sit down and think what we can do to get money for the rent."

"But I'm only good at asking people for rags, empty bottles and jam jars."

"That's right. So after tea I think you and Sam should both go out scrounging."

Before Carrie could reply, a loud cackle from Sam rang through the scullery and he blurted out: "Dinnae talk such shite, Hannah. It's a fiver we need."

"I know that. That's why I think we could make it."

"Mak it? But ye only get a penny for a jam jar." Sam gestured at a jar labelled 'Lipton's Fine Apple and Raspberry Jam'.

"Aye. So that means Carrie would only need to get – how many, Sam?" Hannah paused as she started to butter the bread.

"Well, there's twa hunner and forty pennies in a pound; so hoo aboot twelve hunner? An' I dinnae think that there's that mony bluidy jam jars in the hale o Leith – full or empty."

"Oh!" was all Hannah could say before opening the door to call Paul through for his tea.

Paul and Sam were only just seated before she began again. "Look, I think that we can do it – and we will. But if we start off saying things like … "

"Twelve hunner jam jars?" interrupted Sam.

"… we'll never make it," Hannah continued, ignoring Sam's observation. "And you and Carrie are real good at hawking. So after tea I think you should at least try"

"And what're *you* going to do?" demanded Carrie, as she shared out a flat yellow omelette among four plates.

Hannah rolled her eyes in mock horror. "Surely you know it's against the law to leave a child under sixteen alone; so I will have to make the sacrifice and stay in to look after Paul."

Carrie swung the empty pan to and fro dreamily. "See? When I'm big – I'm going to have a Mars bar all to myself. Real blankets instead of coats on my bed. And every night I'll have toast dripping wi' butter for my supper. And I'll eat it while I'm reading my *Red Letter.* "

Sam was filling his shoes with cardboard soles and took a long look at the big holes in his shoes before commenting. "Aye! An' I'll be playin' centre-forward for the Herts."

The twins started out, Sam dragging his guider and Carrie with a couple of sacks tucked under her arm.

"Right, Carrie, noo we're oot in the main street I think we

should split up."

"It's dark, Sam," whispered Carrie, looking around for a patch of light. "Look, could we no ask Dad for help?"

Sam stopped his make-shift guider by putting his foot down on the pavement to stop it rolling. "Daddy? Dinnae tell me you havnae got it intae yer thick skull yet that yon eejit has gone aff to find himsel' and has got lost." He paused. "Look, I ken his daein' a runner has made life awfae tough for us. It'd be great if he'd help but let's face it, hen, – he's no gonnae."

Sam then spoke more to himself. "A Christian he is noo. A pillar o the Chapel. So the only wey we can get the money to pey the rent ..." he hesitated before emphasising, "... is to *steal* it."

"Steal it! You mean rob a bank?"

"Aye. But richt noo they're shut, worse luck."

"Oh, Sam, I could never steal money. And Sam, if you rob a bank you'll land in ..." Now it was Carrie's turn to hesitate.

"I ken," interrupted Sam, "a Hame with bars on the windaes."

"No. In the burning fire aneath the floorboards," sobbed Carrie before turning away. "I'm away to see what I can find to sell."

"Aye, awa ye go then," Sam called after her. "And remember. It's at least a bleedin' fiver we need."

Carrie nodded and thought: "I wonder if Jesus felt as bad as I do when they nailed him to the cross. Good Friday it is today – for everybody but us." She pulled her scarf tight around her neck and shivered.

Sam dragged his guider into the entry and parked it in the stairwell. The clatter alerted Hannah who shot out of her chair and on to her feet. Before opening the outside door she thought she'd better hide the book she'd been reading. So she reached up and popped it behind the soap powder on the scullery shelf.

"Oh, goodie! I see you've got somethin'," she said with relief as she took one of the two bags that Sam was holding. "And you know it's all thanks to me and my continual praying."

"Eh?"

"Yes, that's what I've been doing ever since you left – praying. And God has answered our prayers."

"Aye, just like he answered his ain laddie's and left him hingin' aboot aw day," sneered Sam pushing past his sister.

"Sam Campbell! That's blasphemy," Hannah gasped.

"Naw. It's the hale truth. Oot aw night in the pissin' rain I've been and what has yer prayin' got us?" Sam's feet lashed out at the bags. "Nowt that'll bring in a tosser. Just a bag of coke aff the railway line an' some rolls an' buns that were getting' chucked oot o the store."

"That all?" Hannah asked taking the coke to store it in the glory hole.

"Well, to be truthful, I *did* get something else." Sam grew excited "A guid place for us all to hole up in if we do get kicked oot."

"What?" Hannah exclaimed.

Sam was looking down at his shoes. "See these, Hannah? My shoes are like paddlin' pools. Aw flippin' sodden. An' it's supposed to be the bluidy spring."

Hannah was about to speak when a high-pitched scream and a great thump on the outside door sent them both rushing to open it. There, prostrate on the doormat, lay Carrie.

"What on earth has happened?" asked Hannah, as she tried to dodge the apples, onions and potatoes that were rolling around the landing.

"Some eejit went and left that guider sticking out, that's what's happened," sobbed Carrie "And I've just tripped over it and broken my leg."

"Never mind yer bleedin' leg, ye blind bat," said Sam, pushing the guider further into the stairwell and then picking up one of the sacks that Carrie had let drop. It clinked. "An' I hope you havnae broken ony of thae bottles? Because that really would bring tears to ma een."

After picking up every bit of the fruit and vegetables, the children took themselves back into the scullery. A limping Carrie staggered over to a chair. Sam stared hard at her dripping wet hair and swollen blue fingers. Without a word he lifted a towel and began to rub her hair dry. "Ye look like a droookit rat that's 'scaped aff the Titanic," he sniffed.

"A drookit rat?" she snivelled, "I'll be lucky if I don't die of pneumonay."

"Cut out the dramatics, Carrie," Hannah commanded. "You're a wee bit wet and cold. So what?"

She started to look into the bags Carrie had brought in. "More importantly, what did you get?"

"Well, there's the chipped fruit and vegetables that we've just picked up."

"That's mair chipped noo," chuckled Sam.

"And a bag of rags I left in the coal bunker. But they won't fetch much. Not many woollens."

"That all?" Hannah exclaimed, her tone insinuating that Carrie was worse than useless.

Carrie blushed. She didn't like being accused of letting the family down. "No," she quickly defended herself. "There's four empty beer bottles in that sack."

"Only four?"

"To be truthful I did get eight but …"

Sam stopped rubbing Carrie's hair. "Ye greedy wee pig. You went and sold the other fower and bocht a bag o chips for yerself, didn't ye?" he accused, thumping her on the back.

"Ouch! That was sore, Sam. And I didn't buy any chips," Carrie protested.

"Then what happened to the other four?" asked Hannah.

Carrie gulped before whimpering: "Look, I met a wee squatter lassie. Her mother had gone off for a good time with some GI. The wee lassie was out in all that rain looking for somethin' to eat and no only for herself but her two wee brothers an aw."

"Oh, Carrie," sighed Hannah, bending to count the bottles in the sack. "It's nice to help people. But we need all the help we have for ourselves right now."

Carrie's lip trembled as she bowed her head for a few seconds. Then suddenly she looked up and her eyes were sparkling. "But I also got a half-crown from Granny!"

"You didnae tell Granny aboot the mess we're in?" said Sam in alarm.

"Course not. What more could she do? She already gives us half of her five shilling pension. Poor Granny. I'm that sorry for her."

"Sorry for Granny?" Hannah asked, unable to hide her concern.

"Aye, how do you think she feels about our Dad leaving us. He's her son after all. The poor soul beggars herself to make it up to us."

"Did she say anything about him?"

"No, Hannah. All she ever says is that she's had nine bairns and only three are still living. Now she wishes it had only been two."

Hannah and Sam exchanged glances but said nothing while Carrie went on. "She just asked me when I went in if there was something up? Like Mammy flinging me out again for setting up cheek. I just said no. And if there *was* anything wrong we could easy fix it ourselves."

"That richt? Then hoo aboot tellin' us hoo?" demanded Sam as he went to light the gas under the kettle. "Whae's for tea?"

"Me," sighed Carrie. "And is there any bread for toast?"

Sam shook his head.

"But there are some nice stale rolls that Sam got."

"Nice stale rolls, Hannah," grumbled Carrie, taking a roll from Hannah and tearing it apart in the hope that the inside was soft. It wasn't. "You know, some day I just know we're going to be rich. I said that to Granny and she said, 'Aye that'll be right. When our boat comes in'."

Hannah sighed "So you didn't get much to help either, Carrie?"

Her sister shook her head and went on gnawing at the roll.

"But I did get something to help us," Sam exclaimed. "A place to stey."

"You don't say!" said Hannah while she warmed the teapot. "Now where exactly is this place?"

"Doon the road in Craigentinny. You ken the auld army camp that's noo been taen ower by the squatters."

"Oh, Sam, that squatters' camp is worse than a pigsty," wailed Carrie. "We just couldnae take Alice there when she comes home."

"And I couldn't stay there either," exclaimed Hannah, banging the filled teapot on the table. "I'm going to be a doctor or a missionary and I've never heard of any folk like that living in a squatters' camp."

But before Carrie or Sam could answer her, a loud knock came to the door and a decidedly drunken voice called out. "Open up! Open up! Open up in the name o the bluidy law."

All three children looked in consternation at each other. Without saying a word they joined hands, crept out of the scullery and sidled along the living room wall.

"The law," squealed Carrie as the door was hammered again.

"Should we open up and see who it is?" whispered Hannah.

"No," replied Carrie. "You know what Mam says – we're not to open it to anyone." Then she gasped. "And what if it's the rent man wanting his money?"

"Rent man? You're cuckoo, Carrie. That lot hardly work when they hae to, so there's nae bleedin' chance of them comin' oot on a blinkin' holiday," quipped Sam in a hoarse whisper.

The hammering came again. Louder this time. And, while the children huddled closer together, the voice thundered, "Open up, I say. Open up. It's yer Granddad and I've got sweeties for you."

Hannah and Carrie collapsed against the wall with relief. Sam pushed them aside and opened the door cautiously. In reeled Gabby, their grandfather, who in his youth had been an articulate, handsome and debonair lad, but now – thanks to fifty years of abusive drinking – was little more than a shrunken shambles of a man.

Gabby had just recovered his balance when he tripped over his own feet and did a pirouetting stagger across the room before collapsing in a heap on the floor. While this impromptu display was going on, the children just stood and stared in astonished silence. But when Gabby half rose and spluttered, "Some pissin' weather we're haein'," they all had to stifle a giggle.

Carrie was the first to stop laughing. She felt instinctively that she should help her grandfather to his feet but the stench of alcohol, mingled with the stink from his unwashed body and hair, made her retch and turn away.

Trying to focus his bleary eyes, Gabby squinted first at Hannah and then at Sam before his gaze finally came to rest on Carrie. That brought a crooked smile to his face and without uttering a sound he fished around in his pocket and brought out a bag of sweets which he shooggled noisily before handing them out to the children. "Bluidy lucky ye are," he warbled. "Ah hae jist laid hands on some of ma Post-War Credits the day and I've backed a couple of winners forbye."

"How much have you got?" Hannah asked sweetly, taking a

single sweet.

"Nane o yer bluidy business, Miss Smarty-pants," snapped Gabby. "And yer snobby bitch o a mither's no getting ony o my thirty-five pounds neither. So there."

Wide-eyed and gaping, the three children all looked at one another. Eventually Hannah said, "Our Mam's very hard up and you owe her, Granddad. You know you do."

"What we're saying, Granddad, is this," explained Carrie, taking a big breath before helping him to his feet. "Could you no see your way to giving her a wee loan?"

"Naw I couldnae. And why should I?" grunted Gabby belligerently.

"Cos she's yer ain dochter and she's skint," replied Sam.

"Some dochter," sneered Gabby. "D'ye think I dinnae ken thon uppity bitch disnae want me comin' up here an' giein' her a showing-up? Worst thing I ever done was lettin' that bleedin' sufferin' get influence her."

"What suffering get?" asked Carrie, looking apprehensively from her Granddad to Hannah and Sam.

"The blethering skite means Mammy's auld freend Eugenie, the suffragette. No a sufferin' get like him," Sam whispered back.

"Uh-huh," was all Carrie said as she began to pat her grandfather's arm, and gently crooned, "And Mam *does* like you coming up here, Granddad. It's just that she doesn't like you being an alcoholic."

"Al-co-ho-lic?" thundered Gabby, staggering about the room. "I'm nae al-co-ho-lic. It's just that I'm partial to a dram or twa."

"Aye, and he's no drunk aw the time neither. It's just that he gets less and less flipping sober," remarked Sam ruefully.

"See you?" Gabby snapped, aiming punches that Sam had no difficulty in dodging. "Ye're a razor-blade mooth just the same as yer bluidy mither." Gabby turned to Carrie and wheedled, "Come on, hen, help us through to the lavvy."

Once Carrie had complied meekly, Hannah asked, "Is he safely in the bathroom?"

"Aye, and I shut the door on him."

"Look," Hannah whispered. "He's got money and we need some of it."

"Money? He's a millionaire," Carrie gasped. "I've always dreamed of being rich but a Granddad with thirty-five pounds – that's scary. Really scary."

"Be quiet, Carrie. We've got to think of a wey o partin' Granddad from his dough," said Sam, scratching his head as he tried to figure out a way of doing just that.

"That's easy," said Hannah. "We steal it."

Carrie yelped before breaking out of the circle. "Steal it! Look, Hannah, stealing money is different from us finding tatties in a field that need dug up and apples needing shaken out of a tree."

"You think so?"

"I do, Hannah, I do! Because, as you know, stealing money is breaking God's commandment and Jesus isn't too keen on it either."

"But it's just like the food and coal that Sam and you found," Hannah argued before becoming aware that Sam wasn't listening. "Are you still part of this family, Sam?"

"Aye."

"Right then. Now listen, both of you. I'm convinced that Jesus knows it's a fiver we need and that's exactly why he sent Granddad up here to visit us. Now d'you think you can get the money away from him, Carrie?"

"Me?" shrieked her sister, looking aghast at the others.

"Yes! Surely, if he's to be robbed by anyone, it would be kinder if it was his favourite." Hannah smirked. "That's you,

Carrie. Isn't it?"

"Don't talk rubbish," said Carrie. "But I *will* do it cos when I took Granddad through to the bathroom I looked in on Paul. Lying asleep like a wee angel, he was. Only thing is that Alice isn't there beside him. But she soon will be when I take the money."

"Dinnae, Carrie," interrupted Sam. "See, when you start on like this ye're the only yin that can mak me want to greet. But ye're richt. We hae to keep this roof ower oor heids for Paul and Alice's sakes. There's nae wey they could survive in a Hame. They're just too wee."

Just before Gabby reeled back into the scullery, Carrie started to write out an IOU.

"Surely you're not going to put that in his pocket?" exclaimed Hannah.

"No. I'm going to put it behind the gas meter."

"You're what?"

"Come on, Hannah, you know that's where we keep the pawn tickets and when we have the money we go and take them out and get our stuff back. It's just the same with this IOU. Yes, when I have the money to pay Granddad back, I will," Carrie replied solemnly as she got up and hid the IOU behind the gas meter.

"Ye're no the full shillin', Carrie, so ye're no," began Sam, but Hannah broke in before he could go on.

"Sssssssh! Here he is."

Gabby duly appeared bearing a half-bottle of whisky in his hand. Unscrewing the top, he lifted the bottle unsteadily to his mouth and took a long hard swig before dragging his hand across his lips.

"Drink up, Granddad," Sam encouraged, pulling up a chair.

"That I will, son," and with that he took another long swig.

"Here's tae us an' wha's like us. Damn few and ..." Gabby didn't finish his recitation. Nor did he sit down on the chair. Instead he began gradually to sink to the floor. The bottle dropped from his hand and the pungent liquid seeped into the worn faded linoleum.

"He's asleep," pronounced Hannah.

"Deid drunk, ye mean," said Sam, giving Gabby a kick with his foot.

"Whatever. But it's safe now. So go on, you two."

"And what'll you be doing, Hannah?" asked Carrie.

"I'm going to sit beside Paul naturally. We don't want him waking up in the middle of all this." Hannah flounced out of the scullery, leaving Sam and Carrie to exchange glances.

"Right," said Sam at last "Let's get started."

"But, Sam, I'm scared. What if we get caught?"

"Then they'll just hing us."

"Hang us?"

"Just joking, dopey! Ye dinnae get hung at twelve. They jist birch ye wi' a cat o nine tails."

"What!" shouted Carrie, backing away.

"But dinnae worry. It doesnae break yer neck; it only taks the skin aff your erse."

Carrie jumped again when Gabby let out a loud snore. "I suppose," she remarked stoically, "that whatever's going to happen to us *will*."

"That's right. And we've just got to save oor hame. No maitter whit."

Carrie and Sam dropped to their knees and began cautiously crawling towards Gabby. Sam went on one side and Carrie the other. Sam signalled to Carrie that they must roll Gabby over. So they pulled and pulled but he just wouldn't budge.

"Ye'll need to push while I haul," Sam whispered, but he now saw that Carrie was trembling and was quite unable to do anything. "Get a grip, Carrie," he urged through his clenched teeth.

Carrie took a deep breath and then shoved at Gabby with all her might until he slowly rolled over. In his coat pocket her first find was the bag of sweets. She shoogled it joyously before picking one for herself and then popping a second into Sam's mouth.

"Look, dopey, I cannae haud on much longer. So will ye get a move on?" pleaded Sam

Carrie furtively searched all of Gabby's outside pockets, but all she found was another half-bottle of whisky, a couple of broken biscuits, a twist of Bogey Roll tobacco, a box of Swan Vesta matches and, finally, a clay pipe.

"Try his inside pockets," urged Sam, tightening his grip on Gabby's coat.

Carrie obeyed and immediately her hands curled around a small wooden cylinder. She was about to take it out when Gabby suddenly roared, "Thievin' bastards! Thievin' bastards! I'll get even wi ye aw!"

The unexpected outburst startled Sam so much that he instantly let go of Gabby whose body now firmly crushed Carrie's hand.

"Sam, I'm stuck," she wailed, realising that Gabby had lapsed once more into a drunken stupor.

Sam made a grab for Gabby's coat again but his grasp slipped repeatedly before he managed to haul Gabby over and allow Carrie's hand to break free.

"Sam! Sam! See! See! I've got it! I've got it!" Carrie yelled triumphantly, brandishing the cylinder with its bundle of crisp fivers rolled around it.

Hannah, who had heard Gabby's shouts, now came running in. She snatched the money from Carrie and began to unroll one five-pound note after another.

"What d'ye think you're doing?" Carrie demanded angrily.

"Getting the money for Mam."

"But we only need a fiver. You've taken two. Now – there's three in your hands!"

"If we leave any he'll just drink it. And we could do a heck of a lot with all this," moaned Hannah, waving the fivers in the air.

"No, Hannah! We only take *one fiver*. The rest goes back," Carrie replied decisively, as she grabbed the cylinder and money.

"But – ."

"But nothing! Our rules are always that we only take what we need to get by. Besides, Jesus knows exactly what we need, so to take more would be letting him down."

"Besides, Hannah, Granddad mightnae miss yin fiver," Sam suggested. "The state he's in, he'll think he either drunk or gambled it. That wey he'll no caw in the polis."

"Does that mean I'll no get the birch?" asked Carrie, rubbing her buttocks.

"Aye," said Sam, nudging her playfully with his shoulder. "Cos I was just kiddin'."

"You were?"

"Aye. Did ye no ken they stopped birchin' the hell oot o bairns years ago?"

With great satisfaction, Carrie handed one large five-pound note to Hannah. She rolled the rest around the cylinder again and fastened them with the elastic band but before she could put them back in Gabby's pocket he let out another great roar and screamed, "Bastards! Bastards! Bleedin' thievin' bastards."

Sam and Hannah scampered from the room followed quickly by Carrie, who only just had time to drop the wooden cylinder by her grandfather's side.

Rachel emerged from the side entrance of the Queen's Hotel

where stinging ice particles of sleet assaulted her face.

"Some night, Rachel, and you've missed the last bus," Duncan the doorman informed her.

"Aye, well. Lord Strathcannon drinks to all hours so the bar must bide open till he drops," Rachel responded, pulling her coat collar around her face.

"Aye, but surely they gave you somethin' for your inconvenience?"

"Five bob for a taxi," Rachel chuckled.

She had just sallied forth when the doorman called after her, "Good. And the next one that comes along is yours."

Rachel waved a dismissive hand and without turning round called out, "Dinnae be daft, Duncan. Me take a taxi when five bob'll feed my bairns for two days?"

"But lassie, you've miles to walk."

"Och, I'll dae it in about two hours."

"But see this weather. No tac mention there's a rapist on the loose."

She was now too far from Duncan for him to hear her reply, "Oh, if that was all I had to worry me, Duncan, I wouldnae caw the Queen my auntie."

It was after two in the morning when Rachel reached her front door but before taking the key from her bag she slipped off her shoes. As quietly as possible, she let herself in and crept through the living room into the scullery where she tripped over something solid. "Sam's blooming guider, I bet," she muttered rubbing her shin. "Told him so often, I have, not to bring the thing inside."

She ran her hand lightly over the obstacle. "Good heavens," she thought. "It's a human being and from the stench I know it's my own father."

Fumbling her way to a chair, she struggled to her feet, sought for matches and lit the gas. As the eerie blue and yellow flame lit the room it did nothing to temper her disgust at the sight of her sleeping, drunken father. "Well, well!" she said philosophically as she nudged him with her foot. "Wonder what brought you here tonight? Wanting something, no doubt, cos you sure never ever gave anybody anything – but heartache."

It was only when she pulled her foot away that she noticed the wooden cylinder with the five-pound notes wrapped around it. A puzzled expression crossed her face as she unrolled and counted them. After a moment's reflection, she opened her handbag and slipped one of the notes inside before replacing the re-rolled money by Gabby's side. Only then did she allow a quiet smile of satisfaction to light up her face.

Five minutes later, she was calmly seated, drinking a cup of tea, when Hannah came into the scullery and thrust a five-pound note into her hand. "Where the hell did you get that from?" Rachel exclaimed, banging down her cup and grabbing at her daughter.

"Er, er, er," stammered Hannah while she tried to dodge her mother's grasp. "Carrie stole it from Granddad for you."

Rachel dashed immediately to the bedroom and dragged Carrie out of bed and into the scullery. It was hardly surprising that the commotion wakened Sam from his sound sleep. Jumping out of bed, he decided at once that he too should be part of the drama now unfolding in the scullery.

"I keep asking you what's wrong, Mammy?" Carrie whimpered. She wondered perhaps if she was still dreaming about the end of the *Red Letter* serial.

"*This* is what's wrong!" Rachel screamed, brandishing the fiver.

Carrie didn't wait for her mother to continue. She guessed she was in for a right good leathering – one that her mother would say she had asked for – but she knew she hadn't. Flight was the only option, so she bolted from the scullery and into the living room.

Sam too realised Carrie was in deep trouble. Without hesitation he sprang forward and yanked the front door open for his sister. But just as Carrie leapt out, Hannah kicked the door shut, trapping Carrie's hand. The resulting screams sent blood-curdling waves of shock through each of them and they cringed when the door was re-opened to display the terrifying picture of red blood gushing from Carrie's hand. "Mammy, Mammy," she bleated piteously, "I'm dying."

"Ye're a richt bleedin' ass, Hannah," Sam accused his older sister. "She was only tryin' to mak a getaway and noo ye've broken her airm."

"It's all right, Sam," sobbed Carrie, shaking her hand in the air. "My arm's not broken but see – my whole thumb is and the nail's hanging off." Her sobs then reached a crescendo before she ruefully announced: "That means I'll never be able to write for the *Red Letter.*"

Hannah squirmed away from Sam. "I was only *trying* to keep her in, Sam; I mean, what would the neighbours think?"

"The neebers? Weel, as they dinnae bluidy live wi' us, I really dinnae gie a shite what they think." Sam spat at Hannah and rammed his clenched fist into her face.

"Why on earth did you do that?" Rachel yelled, making a grab for Sam.

"Cos she asked for it."

"Never did," sniffed Hannah, trying to stem the flow of blood from her nose.

"That's enough from all of you," said Rachel. "Come on now, Carrie, get on your feet and stop bubbling," She took Carrie to the fireside. "Quick, Sam. Fetch the matches from the scullery and get this gaslight lit."

Sam scurried into the scullery and duly brought through the

matches and lit the gas.

Carrie's mutilated thumb then became the focus of their combined attention.

"Some mess it is. You'll need to go to the hospital in the morning and get it seen to," pronounced Rachel, wrapping a towel round Carrie's bleeding hand. "And why, can you tell me, did you do it?"

"Oh Mam. We need to keep our house. I just couldn't bear it if Alice and Paul ended up in a Home. And I'm sure Jesus knew how I felt and that was the reason he sent Granddad here the night."

A bemused smile crossed Rachel's face before she said. "I meant, why did you run away from me?"

Carrie was about to answer when she glanced at the mantelpiece. A still more strident scream escaped her mouth.

"What is it? What is it? Is there more than your thumb hurt?" demanded Rachel frantically.

Carrie nodded her head to the bare mantelpiece. The shepherd and the shepherdess were gone! "That's why you wouldn't let us have a light in here the night. You didn't want me to see the rotten, stinking thing you've done," Carrie howled, pulling away desperately from her mother.

"Carrie, I *had* to sell them today," sobbed Rachel. "Surely you can see that keeping the roof over our heads was more important than a couple of china dolls?"

"They weren't just china dolls. They were *my* ornaments. My beautiful ornaments. I loved them. I want them back. Please, oh, please."

"And we *could* get them back, Mam," Sam argued. "We could yaise Grandad's fiver."

Rachel shook her head. "No, we can't. You see, the dealer that bought them from me had a customer who was desperate for them. And with us bombing the hell out of Dresden at the end of the war there'll be no more." Rachel hesitated, thinking, "Oh please, Carrie, try and understand!" Then she reflected, "Got four pounds ten shillings for them, I did. But then I would, because they're so valuable."

No one spoke aloud. There was nothing to say that would pacify Carrie and the only sound that filled the room was her uncontrollable sobbing.

Eventually Rachel, her face etched with fatigue, croaked, "The ornaments are by the bye. None of you must ever steal again. It's wrong. And if ever we do need to steal again it will be done by me and me alone."

"Does that mean you're going to put Granddad's money back?" asked Hannah.

"Course not. I was ten shillings short for the rent. But now, not only do we have enough, but thanks to me having more respect for Gabby's liver than he has, there's also enough for next month's rent too."

"There is?" Hannah cried as she looked at Sam who was smiling broadly.

"Aye," continued Rachel with a wink. "And a wee bit left over for luxuries like a warm coat and shoes for Alice, ham ribs and cabbage for tea the night and a clootie dumpling on Sunday."

Hannah and Sam beamed. But even the thought of ham ribs and cabbage and clootie dumpling wasn't enough to lift Carrie's spirits. She was still staring at the bare mantelpiece and pitiful sobs still racked her thin frame.

When Sam became aware that Carrie was so upset, he stopped grinning and went over to her. Putting both arms around her, he pleaded, "Stop greetin', Carrie. Please! Ye ken hoo ye brek my hert, so ye dae." And as he brushed his lips over her hair he murmured, "I promise ye, I dae, that if ye stop bubblin' an' thole it, I'll get them back for ye."

"When, Sam?" Carrie sobbed, lifting her eyes to his.

"I dinnae ken exactly when. But what I dae ken is – that some bluidy day I will."

CHAPTER 5
THE ART OF SURVIVAL

"Crippled for life. That's what I'll be after all this," Carrie moaned, as she scrambled after the tractor to pick the potatoes that the digger relentlessly threw out to her.

Sam turned to look at his sister. He shook his head and sighed. "Look, Carrie," he said in exasperation. "I telt ye hoo to dae it yesterday. Get stuck in efter the tractor's past and pick the biggest tatties. It's easy to fill yer basket that wey."

"Easy? I never should have listened to you. You said it would be jammy, like picking the rasps and strawberries in the summer."

"But tatties are ten times bigger, so they're much easier to pick," Sam argued back with increasing impatience.

"No, they're no. And you cannae eat raw tatties to keep you going. Nor make jam neither out o the ones you smuggle home." Carrie picked up a potato and threw it at her brother

"Naw, but they make braw chips," Sam laughed, making a flying dive to catch the potato and then tossing it high into the air.

Carrie wearily sank down on the earth before bleating. "Sam, I just cannae go on. I want to go home."

"Why?"

"Cos I'm flaming freezin'. Soddin' soakin' an' screaming hungry," she yelled through her cracked sobs. "Worst of all, my back's broken and I'll likely never straighten out again."

"That aw?" mocked Sam.

"No, it's not aw," she retorted, hot tears spilling down her cheeks. Carrie wiped them away with her muddy hands and whimpered: "I want my Mammy."

Sam tutted as he helped her upright. Then he wrapped his arms about her and rocked her back and forth comfortingly. "C'mon noo, Carrie. It's okay." He began to wipe the rain from her hair but suddenly pushed her away and warned urgently. "Sssh! Stop greetin'. That bluidy fairmer's on his wey ower."

"Hey, ye twa," the farmer shouted when he was still twenty feet away. "Ye didnae get a week aff the schuil just so ye can skive. So get liftin' they tatties. And afore ye start, it's no bucketin' rain. It's only drizzle ye're haein' to work in."

Sam and Carrie both nodded but the farmer strode close up to them and shook his fist in Carrie's face. "And Missie, if you dinnae manage yer bit the day – dinnae bloomin' bother comin' back the morn."

Sam said nothing but sprang to help Carrie fill her basket. "Just keep goin'," he whispered. "And remember that we'll baith get three and a half quid. Nae countin' the bag o tatties we tak hame wi' us every nicht," He squinted at her. Tears were still running down her face. "Hoo aboot – if I no anely dae my ain bit but half of yours as weel?" he coaxed.

All Carrie could do was brush her hand across her dripping nose and nod.

"That's richt. And we're hauf wey through. Only Thursday and Friday to go efter the day," said Sam encouragingly, as he took a piece of rag from his pocket and spat on it before wiping Carrie's face.

An Irish family who were working alongside them had all stopped howking by now. They stared long and hard at the two children before the mother asked, "You no got a pair of mittens for her, son?"

Sam shook his head as he pulled his sister's collar up and tucked it in round her neck.

"Here then. Take mine," the woman said, pulling off her own mittens and handing them to Sam. "Sure, me own hands are well enough seasoned. Hard as that blessed farmer's heart, so they are."

These acts of compassion served to make Carrie's tears run even faster. However she did manage to push back her damp curls before looking down at her mud-caked hands, scowling when she saw that her nails were all edged in thick black mourning as if to match her mood. Without a word she lifted her right hand to her mouth and blew on her white bloodless fingers while managing a half-smile for Sam and the Irish woman. It was the best Carrie could do to convey to them that she was determined to soldier on.

Two weeks later, at the end of October, winter set in. Wind, rain and sleet arrived; and finally the snow came – the snow that would fall and lie for weeks and weeks well into the spring of 1947. Always there would be fresh snow falling on top of packed ice. Always the wind would whistle and howl, chilling every bone in your body to the marrow.

"You know, I'm beginning to wonder who won the blasted war," Rachel raged as she shivered.

"What d'you mean, Mam?"

"What I mean, Hannah, is – I thought things would've got a lot better by now. Seeing we won. Not worse like they are."

Rachel was at the coal bunker in the scullery and flung it open with such force that the lid bounced off the wall. "Pass me the torch, Hannah," she said, bending over to see down to the very bottom. "Never mind. I don't need any blooming light to tell us we havenae even any dross."

"But we must have a fire for Alice. We mustn't have her getting sick again."

"You know something, Hannah," Rachel retaliated venomously, lifting her head out of the bunker. "You're a real genius at telling us what our problems are. Pity you're no so clever at coming up wi' the bloody solutions."

Slightly embarrassed, Hannah made herself scarce by slinking off into the living room.

"Right. We just have to find some coal or something to burn. Bloody Hannah's right, Alice just has to be kept warm," Rachel muttered to herself before shouting to Sam who was out in the stairwell fixing his guider. He had built it himself – and, like Sam, it had a mind of its own.

"Was that you shoutin' on me, Ma?" Sam asked, wiping his hands on a towel as he came in.

"Aye. You were saying they're selling briquettes down at the Coal Depot just past the docks?"

"Aye, just aside the railway station at Lindsay Road they're sellin' them, richt enough."

"Well, how'd you like to take your guider and some of your tattie-picking money and go down to buy some?"

"Weel, I wouldnae, cos ye've got to stand in a queue for at least three hoors."

Rachel looked piercingly at Sam. Her eyes glinted a stern warning to her son, who had been quite truculent ever since she'd been down to school to tell his teacher, Miss Stock, to stop coaching him for the Heriot's bursary he so longed for.

Miss Stock had been absolutely furious and explained how it would be such a wonderful opportunity for Sam; that his fees to the prestigious school would be met until he was eighteen; and that when he was ready for university they might even help him there too. All Rachel would have to provide was a blazer and his bus fares.

"That all?" Rachel said bitterly, as she turned to walk away from Miss Stock. "Well, rides on the bus, my dear, are luxuries you may be able to afford, but not us."

What Rachel couldn't understand was why the teacher didn't realise that if Sam did go to Heriot's, he'd have to give up his morning milk job – ten shillings a week that the family simply couldn't do without. Yet if there was any mother who wanted her bairns to go to a posh Edinburgh school it was her. Hadn't she already had to cope with dashing Hannah's hopes of sitting for a bursary – Hannah, who was brighter than Sam? Folks would tell her she must be right proud to have two such bright bairns. Proud, aye, but broken-hearted because their father didn't pitch up with any keep for them, so that good schools, even with bursaries, were way, way beyond their means. But Rachel did promise herself, there and then, as she waited for Sam's response, that she would make sure that he got a good trade. It would be a struggle even getting him through that but she would do it for him, one way or another. Oh aye, one way or another, she'd make it up, as far as she could, to Hannah and Sam.

"I'll gae if Hannah gangs wi' me,'" said Sam reluctantly, willing her to send her precious Hannah with him.

Sam's face fell though when Rachel shouted, "Carrie!"

"I've an idea," Carrie said, jumping from one foot to another.

"Your heid's aye runnin' on wheels," Sam replied. "An' I hope to heavens this time ye've thocht of somethin' that'll get us oot o this blinkin' queue."

"Well, no exactly out o the queue," Carrie went on chirpily. "But how's about we take turns to stand here and that'll let us go round the corner to Admiralty Street to see Granny for a heat?"

Sam shook his head but then he began to make clucking sounds with his tongue.

"And just remember, Sam," Carrie wheedled, when she saw him weakening. "Granny aye has soup on the fire. A big black pot of yummy soup."

"Aye, an' she ayeways has big slices of plain breid to dunk in it." Licking his lips, Sam decided, "Richt. Ye first. But dinnae be ower lang. I'm stairvin'."

Carrie's backside landed twice on the icy pavements so she

decided to walk instead of run to her Granny's. But when she did finally reach 35 Admiralty Street, she bounded up the worn wooden stairs two at time. Until, that is, she reached the dark landing – the dark landing where Spring-heeled Jack had sprung down and grabbed children, to whisk them away, never ever to be seen again. Or so the story went, as Carrie had been told it again and again by her mother.

A door creaked open as Carrie crossed the landing to the next flight of stairs. She froze. Footsteps shuffled. Carrie began to whistle loudly and then called, "Granny, Granny, it's me. I'm coming."

"Aw it's just ye, Carrie hen? Comin' to see yer granny, are ye?" the neighbour called out.

"Aye, Mrs Burgess. Didnae ken it was you. Thought it might be – Spring-heeled Jack."

Mrs Burgess chuckled. "Wish'd I was. Oh aye, maybe a couple o springs on my heels would help my auld rheumaticky legs get up and doon they stairs."

Carrie just giggled at Mrs Burgess' comments. At her Granny's door, she knocked before opening it.

Like all the doors in 35 Admiralty Street, this door was always unlocked. It wasn't simply that everybody trusted everybody else in the stair: it was just that nobody there had anything worth stealing. Yet Carrie wouldn't remember much of the poverty, squalor and stench of that condemned slum, with its scampering mice and cockroaches. Nor would she recall the bug-deterrent red lead paint that covered the floor and three feet up the wall of her Granny's bed-recess; nor the ramshackle dresser, that held everything Granny owned, but whose doors had to be jammed shut with cardboard wedges because it stood on a steeply sloping floor. Yet Carrie would always remember the wardrobe, rammed tight against the foot of the bed, whose mirror welcomed you when you opened the door, and the white, starched valances that skirted the brass-knobbed big bed where she had often cuddled into Rosie. Then there was the two-seated linoleum-covered fender-stool where she and Sam had sat to warm themselves and listen to Granny's stories, the small wooden stool that Sam saved his pennies in, the battered alarm clock that would only go when face down and the wally dogs that adorned the sloping mantelpiece. But her most treasured memory would be of Rosie, her grandmother, whom she never noticed had become bent over with arthritis and was now weary of the struggle of just staying alive.

Once inside the darkened room, Carrie was glad to see Granny was sitting by the fireside, dressed in her floral wrap-over pinny. The hairpins that held her bun in place had been removed and she was busily grooming her hair.

"Hiya, Granny."

Rosie turned. "Carrie, love," she said delightedly, "Whatever brings ye oot on a sic a day?"

"We've no coal for the fire so we've come to buy briquettes at the coal yard."

"Whae's we? You an' Hannah?"

"No. Hannah doesnae stand in queues – only Sam and me. Anyway we decided … because it's a really long queue. Three hours, Granny."

"That lang?"

"Aye, so as I was saying, we decided I'd come up first for a wee heat here and Sam would keep our place in the queue." Carrie looked over to the range and smiled when she saw, sure enough, that the big black pot was over the fire. "What's in the pot, Granny?"

"Noo, what would ye like to be in the pot?" said Rosie, sitting up and lifting the lid to let the aroma waft over Carrie.

"Soup. Some hot bubbling soup."

"Weel yer luck's in cos that's just what's in it. And ye'll get yer share in a meenit or twa, when it's ready." Rosie lifted a wooden spoon and stirred the soup before sitting down again.

"Could I brush your hair while we're waiting, Ganny?"

"Brush my hair?"

"Aye, I'd love to brush your hair. We're no allowed to have long hair. Just short back and sides."

"Why?"

"Cos Mammy says, long hair ends up getting nits and poggies and we're not allowed to have them neither."

Rosie chuckled as she handed over the brush and Carrie began with long, sweeping strokes to brush her grandmother's hair. Soon the hair was free of tugs and began to shine. Rosie sighed. "That feels guid, Carrie. Really guid! Noo I'll just put the plaits in and roll it back up."

While Rosie arranged her hair, Carrie sat watching with a feeling of unease creeping over her as she noticed that her Granny's china-blue eyes, the deepest blue Carrie had ever seen, were now growing rheumy. The chill of that discovery was soon replaced though by the warm glow that swept over her when she realised that, no matter how dimmed her granny's eyes became, she would always be there for her – as she had been last week when Carrie and her Mammy had had one of their many rows. That time it was because Rachel had forbidden her to go anywhere near the Carnival that had arrived at Leith Links.

That particular row had resulted in Carrie running out of the house and vowing never to return. But after pouring out the whole story to her Granny about how desperately she wanted, only once, to go down the helter-skelter, Rosie had let Carrie warm herself by the fire and had given her some soup before sending her back home. Carrie would always remember Rosie's words as they parted.

"It's in naebody's interest for me to hae a row wi' your Mammy. She'll hae cooled doon by noo. So ye go richt hame and it'll be aw richt. Never fear."

Carrie never told Granny what terrible things Rachel said – that Rosie was a drunken, snuffing old bitch. And Carrie knew her Granny liked her snuff. She was often sent to the newsagents for a quarter-ounce poke of it. On the way back Carrie would open up the poke and have a wee sniff at it herself. She cackled at the thought of being so daring and remembered the big sneeze that would invariably follow. Carrie also knew her Granny didn't drink. Not now, at any rate.

"Granny," Carrie asked, quietly, "Is it true that you used to drink?"

Rosie took a deep breath and exhaled ever so slowly. "Aye," she admitted. "I drank at a time in my life when I couldnae cope. Couldnae tak ony mair, so help me."

"What was so awful for you, Granny?"

"Yer grandfaither, Andra, God rest his soul," Rosie said, crossing herself, "was a stoker on the steamships. He'd be awa for years at a time, so he would. He'd leave me an allotment – part of his wages, that is. But he was nae different from ony ither men. Naw, naw, my share was far less than what he kept for his ain pooch. I just couldnae manage, so I took a job in the Roperie to mak ends meet. In the hemp bit I was. Making ropes for the big boats."

"It's an awfy dirty place, that Roperie, Granny. My Mammy says that people who work there are all dirt-common."

"Listen, lassie," Rosie interrupted. "Onybody that gaes oot to work for their livin' is respectable. And there are some richt guid folk work in that Roperie. Onyway, I was tellin' ye, while yer grandfaither was at sea I had took a job that seared yer lungs. But I needed it to keep your Auntie and Daddy that were at schuil. Nae to mention wee Paul and the other bairn I was cairrying. Weel, yin day I went into work at eight. I'd put wee Paul into the Tolbooth Wynd Nursery just efter seven and that let me work through till six at nicht."

"That was a long working day for you, Granny."

"Aye, was it. But at six I cam oot and went to the nursery to pick up the bairn. Just eighteen months auld, Paul was." Rosie stopped to take out a piece of rag from her pocket to dab her eyes. "Handed him to me, they did. Cauld and stiff."

"Oh Granny, are you sayin' they never came to your work and told you that he was ill?" Carrie gasped, flinging her arms around the old woman.

"Naw. They didnae bother in they days aboot folks like us. They thocht we'd nae feelings. Factory fodder. That's aw we were to them. Just like the beasts o the fields."

Rosie sighed and Carrie stayed silent.

"I mind," Rosie began again, more to herself than to Carrie. "Aye, I mind takkin' him in my airms. Openin' my shawl and haudin' him close to me. Tryin' I was, to warm him up. Bring life back to him."

Rosie stopped and dabbed her eyes again. Carrie gently climbed up on her Granny's knee and put both arms around her neck.

"When I got hame to this hoose," Rosie continued in her distinctive Irish lilt, "my guid sister, yer great-auntie Anna, that fetched up yer Mammy and looked efter your Auntie Ella and yer Daddy for me – she took wee Paul frae me. Washed him, she did, and got him ready for buryin' in the paupers.

"Next week, the bairn I was cairryin' came early. Lang afore her time she was, that's for sure. Never breathed. Naw, wee Jeanie never breathed a breath." Rosie hesitated and shook her head before going on. "Efter that, I just needed somethin' to blot oot aw the misery. Ye see, oor betters were wrang. We dae hae herts and mine was sair wrung." Rosie stopped again and clicked her tongue before adding dreamily, "Red Biddy dulled the pain. So, aye, I was a drunken disgrace for a couple o years. Faw doon into the gutter, I would. Glad enough I was, to be in a senseless stupor."

"How did you manage to stop drinking, Granny? Our grandad, Gabby, can't do it. Mammy says he really *is* a drunken disgrace," Carrie interjected.

"Weel, when Faither Kelly came to be priest at Star of the Sea he picked me richt oot o the gutter yin day. Didnae kick me like the nuns yaised tae. Took me to the Chapel Hoose he did and talked things ower. Telt me, he did, that drinkin' wasnae the wey oot and I should come back to my faith cos Christ was waitin' for me. An' he said that Christ gave his blood to forgie me onythin'. An' somehow, Carrie, the guid Faither got me on the wagon and we made it."

"You never touched a drop from then on?"

"Couldnae exactly say that. Naw. Naw. I did slip aff a couple of times but Faither Kelly was ayeways there to pull me back on board."

Rosie shook her head again before putting Carrie off her knee. Lifting up the poker she vigorously stirred the fire. Flames leapt. Logs crackled.

"Is that him that's still in St Mary's Star of the Sea?" Carrie asked, wondering if she had been put down because the soup was ready.

"Aye, a fine man. Kens the names of aw the bairns in Leith."

"Aye, even us Proddies."

Rosie smiled. "Mind ye, even though I've been dry for years, there are still them that like to mind hoo I let awbody doon." Rosie hesitated before whispering, "Just like yer Daddy's daeing noo."

"Could I get my soup now, Granny? Sam'll be waiting," Carrie deliberately interrupted before hearing anything bad being said about her Dad.

"Richt enough and he's turnin' into a braw lad, is oor Sam."

"Tallest in the class, he is. And Granny – know something else? – Sam can pee further up the school wall than any other laddie. Just a shame he's got dropsy now."

"Dropsy?" Rosie exclaimed. "Oh no! Hoo did he get that?"

"Well last Monday he was puttin' the morning rolls into bags to deliver to his customers when he dropped one on to the dirty floor. Manager told him to bucket it. So every morning now he has dropsy – drops a buttery for himself an' a bran scone for Paul. Never drops anything for me or Hannah though."

Rosie shook her head in mock horror. "Dearie, dearie me, my hert was sair wrung for yer Mammy when Sam didnae get sittin' for the bursary."

"But it was Mammy stopped him."

"Aye, I ken," Rosie said with a nod. "That was because she couldnae dae onythin' else. But it must hae broke her hert. Oh aye, aw she's ever wanted was for ye aw to dae weel. Dreams, she does, of ye being doctors, lawyers and whatever. Puir soul, when her dreams for Sam and Hannah were comin' true, she couldnae find the blinking bus fares." Without another word Rosie stood up and started to dish up Carrie's soup.

As soon as the blue and white delft bowl was placed in front of Carrie she began to drool. She was in such a hurry to sup the scalding liquid that she spluttered some of it over the clean newspaper that Granny always covered the table with. Once finished she immediately stood up. "Got to give Sam his time off now," she said.

Before she left, Rosie asked, "Is that thin coat aw ye've got to stand in that lang queue wi'?"

"Aye, but I'll be all right, now I've had your soup, Granny."

But Rosie took down her own black woollen shawl from the nail on the back of the door, wrapped it around Carrie and fastened it securely with a hairpin from her newly-groomed hair.

"Noo aff ye gang, my dear," she said, opening the door.

Carrie hesitated. "Granny," she said, reaching up to peck Rosie's cheek, "I don't care if you did drink long ago. You're the best soup-maker in all the whole wide world now. And what matters to me is that you aye keep some for me."

Rosie turned away. She didn't want Carrie to see the tears springing to her eyes. "Here, lass, I'm forgettin'," she said, hurriedly, lifting the steaming marrow bone out of the soup pot and laying it on to a plate. "On yer wey past tak that ben to Mrs Burgess, and mind an' tell her I've only boiled it the once."

Carrie looked puzzled.

"The docks hae been rained aff for a fortnight, lassie," Rosie explained. "That means there's nae sae much grub aboot. So we aw hae to stick thegether this winter or we'll nae survive it."

CHAPTER 6
CHRISTMAS GREETINGS

The snow that had started falling at six o'clock, when Carrie left home to do her morning paper run, had now developed into a raging blizzard that swirled and eddied about her as she made her way to school.

She had the comfort however of knowing that the door would be opened when she arrived at the school. The weather had been so harsh for the past five weeks that the children had not been expected to line up in the playground or huddle together in the sheds. They went instead straight into their classrooms whenever they arrived. And it was not unusual for Hermitage Park School to grant more than one half day off in a week that winter. Many of the children attending Hermitage Park were judged to be needy and therefore lacking the suitable clothing or footwear to withstand the elements.

As she trudged along, Carrie became aware that someone was following her. Then she was greeted with a "Hiya, Carrie. Here, d'ye think we'll get anither halfie the day?"

"Don't think so, Jean, seeing we got one on Thursday and Friday last week and it's only Tuesday today."

"Aye, but that doesnae maitter if the weather's really bad. And it's worse the day than it was on Friday," argued her classmate, Jean Watson.

"*I* know that," Carrie emphasised with more force than was needed. "But it's also Christmas Eve, so we'll be getting out at half past two anyhow."

The next thing the girls knew was a shower of snowballs thudding into their backs. Jean ran into school screaming but Carrie bent down and seized a fistful of snow which she firmly pressed into a ball and fired it into the ring-leader's face. Before John Ellis or any of his gang could retaliate, Carrie bolted for the school steps but as she reached the door she heard a voice call out: "Hey, where're ye goin'?"

Pulling up hard she retorted, "Into school, Sam. Where else?"

"Weel, come ower here first and gie's a haun."

"You're not really expecting me to help you to humph that milk into the classrooms?" Carrie spluttered with indignation.

"Naw. I need ye to haud they twa Kola bottles while I fill them wi' milk. Then I'll bunk them in the jannie's office and tak them hame later."

"But that's stealing."

"Naw, it's no. It's bein' thrifty, cos aw the really puir bairns are hardly ever at schuil the noo. So their free milk would just go to waste if I didnae find a yaise for it."

"You're turning into a right spiv, Sam."

"Am I? Weel see, the nicht, when ye reach ower to pit some o this milk on yer parritch, I'll cut the fingers aff ye, so I will," snorted Sam as he filled up the Kola bottles.

Carrie said nothing but raced away into the school building.

She was pleased to see that she was into class before Sheila, the girl she shared the double desk with. That meant she could get herself to the far end of the seat and tuck her feet underneath the radiator. While her hands and feet were gradually thawing, Carrie's thoughts turned to Sheila. Though her best friend at school, Carrie hated the fact that Sheila had been lucky enough to get herself born to a forty-seven year old mother – which meant Sheila had a jammy life because her three elder brothers were all working. Not only could her mother afford Wellington boots for her daughter but she could buy slippers for her to change into when in class. "How come you have such an old Mammy?" Carrie had once asked her.

"I'm a gift from God," Sheila had said. "You see, women my Mammy's age don't get babies the way your Mammy got you."

"You mean your Mammy and Daddy didn't … " Carrie had screwed up her face and gulped, "… do what we never ever must do till we're married and even then we're not supposed to like it?" Carrie stopped reminiscing when Sheila sat down beside her.

"Hi, Carrie."

"Hi, Sheila." Carrie kept her hands on the radiator.

"Will you help me off with my wellies?" asked Sheila, taking off her pixie hood and shaking it.

Carrie wanted to say she was heartily sick of helping Sheila off with her wellies but thought better of it. After all, Sheila might have an apple for her play-piece, a Canadian Macintosh Red, and she might offer Carrie a bite. Reluctantly she lifted her hands from the radiator and eventually, after much heaving and pulling, managed to remove the boots. "There you are, Sheila"

Instead of thanking Carrie, Sheila wrinkled up her nose and bawled, "Your hair is stinking, Carrie Campbell."

"It is not! It was washed last night."

"Yes, maybe, but with Derbac, I bet. Smell mine." And Sheila waved her hair under Carrie's nose. "Mine was washed with Dreen Shampoo. I've got such long hair a bottle only lasts me once."

Carrie delicately lifted one of Sheila's gleaming, beribboned ringlets to her nose. The perfume of roses assailed her nostrils. If ever she was able to afford a bottle of Dreen she was sure she'd be able to get at least three washes out of it because her own hair was so short. For months her hair would smell so sweet. She was still dreaming of the perfumed suds when Miss Stock, their teacher, came into class and shouted, "Carrie Campbell, please put Sheila's hair down at once."

Carrie was taken aback. It wasn't like Miss Stock to speak to her like that. She was certain Miss Stock had a soft spot for both Sam and herself. She knew that in Sam's case it was because he was always top of the class and should have got to sit for the bursary. In her case it was probably because she had a squint in both her eyes and wore glasses – glasses that were forever getting broken. That meant Carrie had to sit at the front, in the dunces' row, to be able to see the blackboard.

While Carrie was recovering from the shock of the rebuke, Miss Stock had gone on to say that, since it was Christmas Eve, the class would get through their work quickly and in the afternoon could play games. Lifting her desk lid, she took out the class register and began to check each child's name from the alphabetical list. Sheila meanwhile fished in her bag and pulled out, not the cosy slippers, but a shiny pair of split-new, black patent leather, ankle-strap shoes.

"Where on earth did you get those?" gasped Carrie.

"Remember we wrote letters to Santa Claus last week?"

"Aye," Carrie replied. "I've been writing to him for three years now and he's never even sent the Mars Bar I asked for, never mind the ankle-strap shoes."

"Well, he sent me my shoes early so I could wear them today," Sheila explained as she fitted on the gleaming shoes and waggled them from side to side so Carrie could get the full effect. "And know something else, Carrie? My Mummy says I've been such a good girl that I'll be getting everything else on my list."

"*Everything?*"

"Aye, and we're to have chicken and trifle, with a red cherry on top, for our dinner tomorrow."

"A chicken dinner and nobody's ill?" muttered Carrie, who was still unable to take her eyes off the gleaming shoes.

"Yeah. Oh here, I nearly forgot. My Mummy plucked the hen last night and was wondering if your Mummy would want the feathers?"

Carrie's head shot up. "Look, Smarty. If I'm not getting any of your blinking chicken you can stuff your feathers where the monkey stuffs its nuts."

Before Sheila could speak, Miss Stock looked up and wagged her pencil in their direction. "I'm trying to take the register and you two are talking. Now I'm not going to warn you again."

"I'm sorry, Miss Stock, it wasn't me. I was only trying to be nice to Carrie," Sheila simpered unctuously. "But now I'm going to move to the end of the seat as far from her as I can get."

"Thank you, Sheila. I would really like you to do that."

Miss Stock closed the register and put it tidily away in her desk before proceeding. "Boys and girls, now that the register call is finished, all stand. Bow your heads and we'll commence our devotions with a prayer."

After the prayer was finished Miss Stock went to the piano and had launched into the opening bars of "Away In A Manger", when Sam dashed through the door.

"You're late again, Sam Campbell," Miss Stock said without missing a note.

"I ken, Miss. I was helping the jannie."

"Perhaps you were. But right now," Miss Stock replied, lifting her hands from the piano and pointing to the far end of it. "kindly stand there until we finish our morning service."

"But, Miss," protested Sam, looking down at his feet. They were newly shod in a pair of running shoes that one of his lady customers had given him out of pity for the holes in his shoes. Her son's old spiked track shoes would do him a turn. And so they did. They were brilliant for running through the packed frozen snow – but what would happen now that he'd have to stand for twenty minutes on the worn wooden floorboards of the classroom?

Sam looked pleadingly at his teacher who seemed unaware of his problem. Then he looked at Carrie. She was about to speak but Sam signalled to let things be.

Miss Stock went on with the Christmas service. After the class finished singing "Away in a Manger", she read the Christmas story – how Mary and Joseph went all the way to Bethlehem and what happened when they arrived at the inn. Sheila raised her hand and snapped her fingers. "Yes, Sheila, what is it?" Miss Stock asked.

"Please, Miss, it's just that I don't like sad stories, so could Mary and Joseph please get a bed at the inn this Christmas?"

Carrie started to snigger.

"Something amusing you, Carrie Campbell?" asked Miss Stock.

"No, Miss. I'm very sorry, honestly I am, but Mary and Joseph will *never* get a place at the inn."

"And why do you think that?"

"Because they're poor, so very poor, Miss, that they'll never ever get a warm bed for the baby Jesus – and Santa Claus will never bring patent leather, ankle-strap shoes neither."

Miss Stock seemed about to correct Carrie but then she noticed Sheila's gleaming new shoes peeping out from under the desk, so she merely announced that they would finish the service with the singing of "Still the Night".

Miss Stock finally closed the piano lid and then motioned to Sam that he could now go to his seat but with the nails in his running shoes firmly embedded in the floor poor Sam was well and truly stuck. All he could do was swing backwards and forwards, to the huge merriment of the whole class – all except for Carrie, who felt a warm flush of shame spread over her whole face as tears sprang to her eyes.

Realising what had happened, Miss Stock did her best to pull Sam free. The more she pulled him forward, however, the further the nails dug in.

Eventually Sam whispered. "The jannie will ken what to dae, Miss." And indeed the jannie *did* know what to do. First he undid Sam's shoe laces and lifted him free. Then, with the help of a screw driver, he levered the shoes out of the floorboards and presented them to Sam who proudly offered his cheering audience a deep bow before swaggering to his seat.

Miss Stock tutted loudly before announcing, "And now that Sam's pantomime is quite over, we will all settle down to our mental arithmetic. Everyone take out your slates and slate pencils."

Carrie heaved a sigh of relief because she was always happy doing mental arithmetic. When you were poor you simply had to know how to count every penny. Last night, for instance, she'd worked out just how many beer bottles at twopence, jam jars at a penny and messages at threepence she would have to collect or do to get one shilling and eleven pence.

She needed that amount because she was now having swimming lessons at Docky Bell's swimming baths down in Great Junction Street. Her mother had given her Hannah's old costume. Hannah had got it in turn from Ella Preston whose two elder sisters had worn it. Josie, the oldest, had been a big girl – so big that everybody called her Desperate Dan in knickers. And if that wasn't enough to put the swimming costume out of shape, it had originally been knitted in stripes by Mrs Preston, using odd bits of wool. The result was that, when Carrie jumped into the water for the second time, her sodden costume had flown up and smacked her on the back of the head. The class had all howled with laughter – just as they laughed at Sam today. Carrie silently vowed that no one would be laughing at her or Sam when they came back to school after the Christmas holidays. Somehow she would have a proper bathing costume and Sam would have proper shoes or wellies.

"Are you all ready? Or would you like some more time, Carrie Campbell, to sit and dream?" Miss Stock asked rather tartly.

Carrie nodded and held her slate pencil poised.

"Four plus fifteen minus one, divided by three."

Carrie promptly scratched a "6" on her slate.

Miss Stock began again. "Five times six, minus ten, divided by five."

Again Carrie began to write down the correct answer when she heard a "Psst!" from her left. Sure enough, Sheila was trying to attract her attention. "Come closer, Carrie," she mouthed. "I need a copy of your answers."

Carrie shook her head. She was already listening to Miss Stock calling out the next sum.

"But you know I can't count! If I get more than five sums wrong I'll get the belt."

Carrie smiled sweetly at Sheila.

"What's wrong with you two?" demanded Miss Stock who was now aware of the interaction between the girls.

Carrie jumped to her feet. "Please Miss," she said, snapping her fingers, "I broke my glasses yesterday so I'm not hearing very well. So may I change seats, please?"

"Very well! And I don't care whether you can see or hear, just so long as you two get as far away as possible from each other," Miss Stock announced firmly.

Sheila could see that Carrie was smirking as she gathered up her things and began pushing past her, so with unfeigned delight she whispered, "Not only have I got posh ankle-strap shoes – *and* chicken and trifle for dinner tomorrow – but I'm the only one in class that's going to get a Christmas card from Miss Stock."

Carrie could never really explain what happened next. All she knew was that somehow she seemed to jump in the air and land with a thump on Sheila's shiny new shoes, resulting in howls from Sheila and a grim-faced Miss Stock inviting Carrie to spend the next half hour in the corner facing a blank wall.

Having completed her two evening newspaper deliveries, Carrie was very glad to arrive home. As soon as she opened the door, however, her whole body quivered when she looked at the fire. It was piled high with spitting potato peelings and the remains of an old shoe. There were no flames – not even a flicker. Just a listless smouldering that would do nothing to thaw out her frozen fingers and depressed spirits.

Only yesterday she'd complained to her mother about the fire and the lack of heat coming from it. Rachel had been quick to explain that there was no shame in being poor – but there *was* in being dirty. So the fire, such as it was, mightn't give them much heat but it would warm the water so they could all get washed – washed, that is, in the washing tub. Oh yes, in all the years they'd lived at Learig Close, not once had there been enough hot water for a *real* bath. That was another of Carrie's dreams – a wash in the bath where you wouldn't have the water taps digging into your back and your knees tucked underneath your chin.

She was still staring at the fire and dreaming of a hot steaming bath when Rachel broke into her thoughts by calling through from the scullery. "That you, Carrie?"

Carrie made no answer but advanced slowly into the scullery. The gas light was lit and was giving out a greenish-yellow glow because the mantle, thanks to Sam heading a ball in the scullery, was broken once more. Its ghostly flickering lit up the room sporadically and when it suddenly flared Carrie was confronted by a sight that resulted in her screams echoing melodramatically around the room.

The noise so startled Rachel that she dropped the porridge spoon and spun round to face Carrie. "What is it? What's wrong, hen?" she asked anxiously.

"Oh, Mammy," Carrie wailed, pointing to the bunker. "Please don't tell me that that horror there is our Christmas dinner?"

"And what's wrong with sheep's heid?"

"Everything. Oh, Mammy, don't you realise I *hate* sheep's heid?" Carrie spluttered through her sobs. "And I *hate* being poor. I want to be rich. To have a Mars Bar all to myself. A tin of condensed milk, a loaf of bread to spread it on. A pair of shiny ankle . . "

"Aye, aye," Rachel interrupted, "And I want to tap-dance on the moon but I'll have a long wait, will I no?"

Still sniffing, Carrie tried to squeeze cautiously past her mother.

"Is that your shoes squelching?" Rachel asked. Carrie nodded as she brushed a hand under her dripping nose.

"Did you not cut out new cardboard soles for them last night?"

"No. D'ye no mind? You were showing me how to turn the heel of a sock."

"Aye, and a right waste of time that turned out to be. Here," said Rachel, handing Carrie some cardboard, a pencil and a pair of scissors. "While I finish the tea, you cut yourself out some new soles for the morn."

Reluctantly, Carrie sat down to do as she was bidden but began to girn as drops of melting snow trickled down her face. Only when she realised that her mother was taking no notice of her moaning did she start to cut out the soles. She had just finished the first one when she decided to broach the subject that was on her mind. "Know what? Sheila Cameron has new ankle-strap shoes."

"That so? Well, *her* mother maybe knows where this month's rent is coming from, while I don't."

"But, Mammy, I do everything right and isn't God supposed to reward you when you do? I've even joined the Band of Hope."

"Aye, cos they've the best Christmas party," commented Rachel dryly as she dished up the runny porridge.

"*And* I've been good at school," Carrie went on, ignoring her mother's cynical remark.

"Carrie!" said Rachel with growing impatience, tapping the

spurtle on the table. "What exactly are you trying to say?"

"Just that Sheila does nothing right. She's a dope. Yet she gets new shiny ankle-strap shoes and here's me, who's done everything right, cutting out cardboard soles."

Rachel leant over towards Carrie and whispered confidentially into her ear. "Aye, but it isn't any old cardboard, Carrie! It's the very best corrugated I could lay my hands on. So just get on with it, will you!"

At six the next morning Carrie rose promptly to go out and deliver the Christmas papers – in Scotland there were always newspapers on Christmas Day. She had just pulled on her jumper when Sam asked, "Whit are ye daeing, dopey?"

"Getting ready to go and deliver the papers. And *you* should already be away to the store to deliver the milk and rolls."

"Naw. Naw. We're nae goin' oot till efter nine the day."

"After nine?" Carrie protested indignantly, "But I'm hoping to be home long before that. Home before all these bloomin' bairns come out with their doll's prams, bikes, skates and ankle-strap shoes that Santa has left them: that rotten pig, Santa."

"Forget Santa bluidy Claus. We'll mak oor ain Christmas cheer."

"How?"

"By no goin' oot till efter nine."

"*After* nine? But why?"

"Cos it's Christmas and they'll aw be feelin' charitable. So we hae to knock on every door and haud on to their paper or their milk until they stump up wi' the Christmas tip."

Carrie made twenty-five shillings in tips that day, thanks to Sam's good thinking. However Sam did even better by coercing two whole pounds out of his customers. And since it was Christmas he didn't need to have dropsy. The Store Manager gave him a bag containing ten rolls, four bran scones, a bag of broken biscuits and a two-pound jar filled with nine chipped eggs.

When it was time to go back to school in January, Carrie had completely forgotten about her row with Sheila. The money she and Sam earned in tips had made life a lot easier for the whole family.

On Boxing Day, Rachel went straight to her friend Roman and had him sole and heel all the family's shoes: then she bought two bags of coal, one of which was of chirles. As a result the whole family was happily seated around a blazing fire while they listened to the church bells ringing in the New Year of 1947.

Sam was busily toasting bread on a long fork in the louping flames. Each of the family in turn got a hot slice of toast that had been liberally spread with best butter. The feast was washed down with the mandatory New Year nip of ginger wine – judged suitable for children. An added bonus, according to tradition, was that the family would be sure of a whole year of good luck, since they had been first-footed by a tall, dark, handsome man bearing gifts – coal, bread, money and shortbread.

Back at school, Carrie was still basking in her New Year memories when Sheila came in and plopped down beside her. "Please, help me off with my wellies, Carrie," she pleaded.

Carrie obeyed. Once the boots were off, Sheila began fishing in her bag and this time she brought out her cosy slippers. Thankfully the ankle-strap shoes that had so irked Carrie had been left at home. As Sheila started to put on her slippers, she remarked to Carrie, "Your hair's stinking again."

"Yeah," Carrie replied. "I washed it with Derbac soap last night and the rest of me was scrubbed with carbolic."

Sheila grimaced. "Surely your Mammy knows that Dreen shampoo is best for your hair and Pears soap is the right thing for your face."

Carrie just smiled proudly.

"My Mum says," Sheila went on smugly, "I could've been Pears Baby of the Year if she'd put me in for it."

"That right?" was all Carrie responded before changing the subject and asking, "Did did you have a nice Christmas?"

"Wonderful. And you?"

"Great it was." Thinking of Christmas reminded Carrie about the Christmas cards. Neither she nor anyone else in the family had got a single one. "Here, Sheila," she asked, "did you really get a Christmas card from Miss Stock?"

"It wasn't a Christmas card. It was a letter," simpered Sheila.

"A letter?"

"Aye, a letter just to say that the school were very pleased that I hadn't left and gone off to Gillespie's Ladies."

"But you *couldn't* go – you didn't pass their entrance exam," Carrie reminded her.

"I wasn't very well the day I sat that exam. My Mammy said so," Sheila retorted in pique. "But the letter said I had been one of the best pupils they've ever had here. A credit to the school I am. And they would have been so sorry to lose me but they knew that when I go on to secondary school in April I'll do very well there too."

Carrie said nothing. Sam had come into class late again but thankfully this time Miss Stock didn't make him stand by her desk. "Happy New Year, Miss," Sam beamed as he sailed past Miss Stock.

"And a happy New Year to you too, Sam," Miss Stock chuckled, taking note that he was wearing his recently repaired and well-polished shoes.

When school was finished for the day, Carrie approached Miss Stock. "Miss," she said, "I'm sorry to bother you but Sheila got a letter on Christmas Eve and I would like to have one the same."

Miss Stock shook her head.

"But I deserve it more than her, Miss."

"But you don't, Carrie," Miss Stock said, as she rose and began cleaning the blackboard.

"But I do," argued Carrie.

"No you *don't*. You have to qualify for one of those letters." Miss Stock turned to face Carrie, "and you, I'm pleased to say, do not."

As soon as Carrie arrived home she went straight into the scullery where Rachel was busily making the tea. "Your favourite tea the night, Carrie. Egg and chips," she announced, breaking an egg into the frying pan where it spat and sizzled.

"Good," replied Carrie. "But, Mam, I've got to talk to you first. Got to tell you what that stinking school has done."

Rachel half-turned towards Carrie but held on to the handle of the frying pan. "Done to you? Whatever are you on about now?"

Carrie poured out the story of the letter. To her amazement, her mother only shrugged and said, "If that's the way they feel about it, don't let it bother you." Rachel then drew herself up to full height before adding, "You know full well that you come of a better class than Sheila. And that's all that matters."

Carrie began to cry. "But, Mam, you don't understand. I simply *have* to get one of those letters. I deserve it. And I *do* qualify."

Rachel finished frying the eggs, placing one on each plate along with some chips and a dash of tomato sauce. Meanwhile Carrie's wails were growing louder and louder.

"Oh, Mam," Hannah pleaded, "could you not go and get her one of those blinking letters before she drives us all mad?"

"Tell you what," Rachel conceded. "I've got to come to school tomorrow to see why that bitch of an Infant Mistress hasn't put

Alice back into her own class now she's made up for what she lost while she was in hospital. And once I've done that, if I've got time, I'll pop in and see Miss Stock."

The following afternoon Carrie was writing her essay when a knock came at the classroom door. Raising her head, she was delighted to see, through the glass panel in the door, that her mother was standing in the corridor. She smiled broadly to herself as Miss Stock made her way calmly out of the classroom to speak to Rachel. When the door opened again, Carrie was pleased to hear the teacher and her mother laughing and her mother saying, "Thank you so much, Miss Stock. You've been *most* helpful."

Once the door closed again the rest of the afternoon dragged for Carrie. She thought the lessons would never end but when they eventually did she sprang over to Miss Stock's desk and said, "Miss, my mother came up to see you today – so have you got a letter for me?"

Miss Stock shook her head. "I'm afraid you're not getting one, Carrie. You see, you don't qualify and I explained to your mother why you don't and she's very pleased about that."

Carrie's eyes welled with tears as she thought, "My Mammy's a traitor."

Ignoring Carrie's distress, Miss Stock continued, "And when you come into class tomorrow I don't want you to mention the letter again. Just forget all about it."

Miss Stock then stood up from her chair and opened the tall cupboard. On the top shelf stood a large jar of boiled sweets. The jar had first been placed there back in 1940. All classes in Edinburgh schools had one such jar and the regulations stated that, should the school be hit by a bomb, each child was to receive three sweets from the jar. Sam had always asked what good the sweets would do you if your head was no longer attached to your body. But that was the rule – or so the children at Hermitage Park School were told.

Carrie wasn't thinking about such things as she watched Miss Stock climb on to her high chair and take down the jar of sweets that had lain there unopened for seven years. Miss Stock then opened the lid carefully but, since all the sweets were by now fused together, she had to chisel three of them free.

The regulation three sweets were then proffered to Carrie who was now sobbing openly. She shook her head and tucked her hands tightly behind her back. "No, Miss, I haven't been hit by a bomb. So I don't need the sweets;" she blurted out as tears cascaded down her face. Then she wailed even more loudly: "All I wanted was a letter."

Miss Stock shook her head wearily and laid the three sweets on her desk top.

Carrie shot into the scullery as soon as she got home. Rachel looked up and smiled, "You're finished your papers early. The macaroni cheese will be another wee while."

"Never mind the blooming macaroni," Carrie cried bitterly. "I didn't get a letter. And you knew how important it was to me."

"Aye," said her mother coolly, taking a loaf out of the bread bin. "And let me tell you, Carrie, I don't like the tone of your voice."

"Mam, don't you realise I just *have* to get one of those letters. And I *do* qualify."

"No you don't," Rachel answered as she began to saw the bread as thinly as possible.

"Look, Mam," Carrie yelled. "It's like this. If I don't get one of those letters I'll commit suicide."

"And if you do get one of those letters it's me that'll commit suicide," Rachel retorted, waving the bread knife in her daughter's puzzled face.

Carrie's tantrum stopped abruptly and she drew her head back from the threatening knife. "Wh-why?" was all she could splutter

It was then that Sam piped up. "Oh, Carrie, surely ye're nae sae daft that ye havnae worked it oot that the blinking letter was a last warning to Sheila's mither."

"Last warning?" exclaimed Carrie.

"Aye," chuckled Rachel, "Three weeks is all Sheila's Mammy has to get her head cleaned up. And if she doesn't get rid of all the nits and poggies – then off comes, no' just the bonny coloured ribbons, but all the bonny black ringlets as well!"

CHAPTER 7
HOLIDAY QUALIFIERS

That harsh winter seemed to go on forever for the Campbell family but spring eventually did manage to push its way in and, as the ice melted away, so did Rachel's depression. Her thoughts and those of the children turned to summer. "Jammy days" lay ahead – days when life was bound to become easier.

Chalky White, the next-door neighbour's boy, was one of the lads with whom Sam shared the delivery of the Leith Provident Store milk. Chalky's dad had been killed in the war and his Irish mother, as Sam would say, was hardly the sharpest knife in the drawer. Hard-working she was but no matter how she tried she was no miracle-worker with bits and pieces, like Rachel.

Sam was always telling Chalky that Rachel and Jesus had a lot in common – for they could both feed a multitude out of nothing. Chalky was indifferent to that. He didn't care that his mother was a bad manager and couldn't cook well. After all, there was always the chippie and, thanks to Sam being his best pal, he would always have at least the price of a bag of chips when he was hungry. However, there was one thing Sam had that Chalky really envied – his guider. Now that the war was over, Jaguar and Ford were churning out cars again but there was nobody who could make a Rolls-Royce guider like Sam.

Sam's latest model had been built with nothing but the very best. It had Silver Cross perambulator wheels and a coffin-top rosewood base which was fully upholstered with offcuts of maroon Wilton carpet. The finishing touch though was given by the white nylon guide-ropes that British Ropes' experimental base in Leith didn't know were missing. For all the plush finery this was a working guider, the family lifeline. There was nothing too dirty or too heavy that Sam couldn't carry on it – bags of coal or logs of wood from trees that had been blown down. Bags of tatties when he and Carrie went tattie-howking, And every Saturday morning it was cleaned up and refurbished, ready to serve as the market stall where Sam did his buying and selling.

It was, as he explained, his "Johnny-aw-thing" stall. Goods that folk didn't know they had lost could be found there. In October you could buy tatties there – the excess that the family didn't need. His special customers, for a couple of bawbees more, could even buy a recipe card which read: 'Ten ither things ye didnae ken ye could dae wi' a forpet of tatties'.

However the tattie-selling came to an abrupt end when Sam discovered that, if he was on the harbour at Granton when the trawlers pulled in on a Friday afternoon, he could get one of the trawlermen to exchange a pauchle of fish for a bundle of kindling wood. And it didn't take much persuasion for Sam to get Rachel to make scrumptious fish cakes out of the family's leftovers. Every Saturday morning, Sam could be heard shouting: "Fish cakes! Secret recipe! Made by the best fishcake maker in the world! Buy a half dozen for the price of six!"

The fish cakes were such a success that Sam soon had regular clients and the cakes were often sold before they were made. However, the tatties were soon used up and as Rachel had to find full-time employment again she simply hadn't the time to help Sam with his money-making schemes.

School had just finished for the Easter holidays and Sam and Chalky were both busy in the stairwell fixing Sam's guider when Chalky remarked, "Soon be my birthday, Sam."

"Nae soon. It's only April and ye were born in May," Sam answered, without looking up from the guider wheels he was furiously scrubbing.

"I ken that. But see hoo yer sister Carrie is ayeways dreaming o gettin' things? Well, so do I."

"If it's a birthday present ye're anglin' for, we dinnae hae birthdays in oor hoose. Naw. Naw. Nae presents. Nae cards. Ye just get a year aulder."

"Naw, I'm no expectin' a present from ye. I was just wantin' to say – I dream o haein' a guider like yours, yin day."

"Dinnae dream aboot it! Just get your finger oot and knock yin up," advised Sam tersely as he finished polishing the spokes of the wheels.

"I'd dae just that, but I'm no handy like ye and yer faimily. I ken ye aw could mak soup oot o auld claes," said Chalky, waving his ham fists under Sam's nose.

Sam blew out his lips before replying. "Weel, we've made soup oot of maist things but I cannae mind of us ever takin' aff oor claes and firin' them in the pot."

Both boys giggled and then a silence fell between them which gave Sam time to look intently at his friend. Life had been even worse for Chalky, Sam thought. Not only had he no Dad; he hadn't even a Mam as good as Sam had. Finally he shrugged and said, "Tell ye what. We'll gang ower the road to Walker's timber yaird and get some wuid. Then we'll rake aroond Johanson's junk yaird, doon in Salamander Street, for some wee pram wheels."

"Great," gurgled Chalky, "And yince we've got aw them things, will ye help me bang a guider thegether?"

Sam nodded his assent.

It took Sam and Chalky a whole week to find or borrow the materials they needed to bang the guider together. And because Chalky was all thumbs it took another week for Sam to assemble it. They had barely finished when Chalky said, "Thanks, pal. Wish you were goin' with me on the Puir Bairns' Holiday Treat."

"The Puir Bairns' Holiday Treat? What the devil's that?"

"Och, Sam, dinnae tell me ye dinnae ken that the do-gooders doon at the Leith Rotary hae raised money to send really puir bairns, like me, awa to Rothesay for a holiday?"

"Rothesay? Doon the watter in the West?"

"Aye. They're sending us there seein' the winter was so bad."

"Here, I was bluidy cauld an aw last winter and I could dae wi' a holiday tae. Never had yin, so I hivnae," Sam retorted. "Only ever got a wee dauner, wi' a juice bottle filled wi' water and a couple o jammy pieces, doon tae Portobello beach when the sun was shining," Sam sniffed pessimistically. "And maist times, by the time I got there the bluidy sun had taen the huff and went back in again."

"Weel, in that case why d'ye no go doon and ask they blokes that are dishing oot the trips to Rothesay if *ye* can have yin an aw?"

"Think I just micht dae that."

"Great. So aw ye hae to dae is gang doon to the Methodist Church Hall on Friday nicht and mak them believe ye're as puir as me."

Rachel managed to persuade the hotel manager to give her a job back in the Queen's Hotel but he would only give her constant late shift. That meant starting at four in the afternoon and sometimes she wouldn't be home again until two in the morning.

That day, after scouring the house and preparing the children's tea, she lay curled up on the settee having forty winks, dozing peacefully in that part of sleep where you're neither sound asleep nor fully awake yet in a comfortable snug haze, with the troubles of life far behind. Suddenly a sharp tapping at the window jolted her into reality. "Where am I? What's that?" she cried out. The tapping at the window continued so she rose, went over and cautiously lifted the window.

"Have you heard the latest?" whispered Grace Stoddard, her neighbour, as she looked all around to make sure she wasn't overhead. "Bunty up the stair is awa again."

Carrie, who'd been warned by Rachel to keep quiet so that

her mother could have her nap, had been quietly reading a book but now pricked up her ears. "Bunty's away again?" she said to herself. Then she thought, "What a load of rubbish. I saw her just an hour ago."

The next thing Carrie overheard was her mother asking, "When d'you think she'll be better?"

"Well," said Grace, looking furtively about again. "I think she's at least two months gone."

"Again?" Carrie thought. "Rubbish! If she's two months gone who was it I saw just an hour ago?" She couldn't hold back any longer. "Mam," she cried, "I saw Bunty Green just..... "

Rachel drew her head back inside. "See you, Carrie?" she snapped. "You're too fond of talking about things that shouldn't be talked about. Now, just haud your wheesht." Rachel's head disappeared out of the window again. This time the gossip was about Aggie Glass having a throw-back black bairn. One she wished to hell that *she* could have thrown back – with people saying it was more than a coincidence that she had just finished befriending a homesick black G.I.

Finally, Grace went on to speak to Rachel about what she had really come for. "Rachel," she wheedled, "my Susan has a wee bit put by. Saw a nice skirt in the store windae, she did. But she's used up aw her clothing coupons. You wouldnae hae ony spare, would ye?"

"Och, I'm really awfae sorry, Grace," Rachel responded, "but mine are aw used up too." She hesitated and then went on. "But here. Hold on a minute. I think I ken where I could get you some."

"But will they no be pricey?"

"No, just one and sixpence each."

"One and six each?" Grace gasped. "But the last yins ye got for me were only one and three."

"Aye but as you know, Grace, everything is aye going up,"

laughed Rachel – but the smile died on her face when she looked beyond Grace and saw her father, Gabby, staggering along the road.

He was blethering as usual, to anyone daft enough to listen. Right then, Gabby was spouting about how it was a pity Hitler had lost the war before he'd sorted bloody Rachel out.

The next thing to upset Rachel was Gabby doing a sort of double somersault over the hedge and into the garden. Luckily, at that very instant, Sam appeared round the corner on his guider. His first action was to park it carefully; then he peered with interest over the hedge at his grandfather lying prostrate among the daffodils. Sam was strongly tempted to leave him there to rot but Rachel gestured to bring him indoors. The commotion and Rachel's slamming down of the window alerted Carrie, who rushed into to the garden in time to help Sam with their grandfather.

"Just ye help me get him on tae the guider," Sam ordered. "Then haud him there while I pull him up the path."

Once laid firmly on the guider, Gabby continued his tirade about Hitler and the Gestapo sorting Rachel out. "And what maks ye think bluidy Hitler and his henchmen could hae sorted my Mammy oot?" Sam demanded sternly.

Before Gabby could speak he half fell off the guider but was hauled roughly back again by Carrie. Then he spluttered, "Weel, him and ten Panzer divisions just micht hae put the bluidy wind up her."

Carrie was never quite sure what happened next. All she did know for certain was that Gabby was catapulted off the guider and into the entry. Then there came a loud crack as his head came into contact with a concrete step. "Aw dearie dear," was all Sam said. "We've no even been invaded by yer pals and here's you endin' up a bleedin' casualty."

Once they had Gabby back on his feet and inside the house,

Sam judged this would be a good time to ask his mother about the holiday. Rachel, still fuming about the showing-up Gabby had given her in front of Grace, only muttered, "Holiday, what holiday, Sam?"

"The yin they're sendin' aw the puir bairns awa on. Chalky's goin' and I thocht I'd ask if I could gang wi' him."

"Right enough," Rachel conceded, "Chalky's a poor soul so you'd better go with him or we might never see him again."

Before Sam could thank her, Gabby interrupted drunkenly, "Holiday? I've never been on a bluidy holiday."

"That so?" Rachel spat vehemently at him. "Well, if you haven't, it's your own bloomin' fault. Cos you sure have gambled and drunk enough, not only to have paid for a cruise on the Queen Mary, but to buy the whole bleeding Cunard Shipping Line as well."

Sam and his guider whizzed down Restalrig Brae. Faster and faster they went. Faster than they'd ever gone before. Sam squealed with delight and flung his legs high in the air as the guider wheels swooshed and spun their way down the long brae. He just couldn't believe that Rachel was letting him go on holiday with Chalky. All he needed to do now, to get on that holiday, was to convince a committee of three men that he was really poor enough. To make the right impression Sam had taken great care over his appearance. First he scrubbed himself spotlessly clean and then he attired himself appropriately from the rag bag. His final trick was to kick off his new plimsolls and to fish out a pair of his old well-holed shoes.

Once arrived at the Methodist Church Hall in Great Junction Street, Sam decided he should park his guider discreetly out of sight. Lifting it upright, he carefully concealed it behind the imposing entrance door. To be doubly sure that someone else didn't think they had a better right to it, he removed the steering ropes and stowed them prudently in his pockets.

Satisfied that he had done all he could to secure his Rolls Royce of guiders, Sam began to climb the stone-flagged stairs, to the meeting room. He was only halfway up when he stopped to smooth down his ragged jumper and truculent curls.

Opening the door at the top of the stairs, Sam was surprised to find himself in a hall so big that everything echoed. The voices of the men on the committee at the far end of the room – and even the hushed whispers from the queue of hopeful children – all resonated around him.

Waiting patiently, he watched the large clock on the wall tick away a whole hour. He was beginning to wonder if his turn would ever come when at last he was summoned forward. Taking a deep breath, he strode confidently through the room to stand to attention in front of the table.

There he immediately rehearsed his battle plan. He intuitively knew that he had to figure out which of the benefactors he should make eye-contact with. That strategy had always worked well in the past – for Sam was a master at making direct eye-contact and then using his quick wit and ready smile to cajole anything out of anybody.

However, the three men seated there were impassive. One in particular, a small hunched man with steely grey eyes, a true Holy Willie, made Sam feel like squirming.

"Name?" this little man demanded just as Sam was deciding that the chairman was the man he had to court.

"Samuel Campbell, sir," Sam answered demurely and the man dipped his pen into an inkwell and scratched the name down on a piece of paper which he meticulously blotted.

"Where do you reside?" was the man's next question.

"Reside?" Sam queried dubiously.

The man sighed. "Live."

"16, Learig Close, sir."

"Am I hearing right? Did you say 16 Learig Close?"
Sam nodded. "Yes, sir."

The small man then leaned towards his two colleagues and they began whispering amongst themselves.

Sam shifted uneasily from one foot to the other and the clock ticked loudly. From time to time the men would scrutinise Sam as if he were some sort of alien – perhaps a creature just landed from the moon.

"Now, Samuel. As I understand it, Learig Close is a very affluent street. All privately-owned homes," the chairman of the group eventually said gravely.

"Naw, naw, sir," Sam replied, reverting to his mother tongue. "Just on yin side. The ither side, the far side, belangs to the Corporation. I bide in a Corporation hoose. Same stair as my pal, Chalky White, whae ye've already gien a holiday tae."

The small man leant over and picked up a pile of papers. Leaf by leaf he checked through them until he came to Chalky's application. Again Sam shifted from foot to foot and the clock ticked loudly as the three men huddled together to scan the form.

Once the form was laid back in the pile, the chairman asked, "Now son, tell me this. How many reside, I mean live, in your house?"

"Mammy, me, my wee brother and my three sisters."

"Your father?" the mean man asked.

Sam shrugged his shoulders.

"No doubt killed in the war – like your friend's father?" the chairman suggested.

"Naw. He was a conchie."

"A conchie?" the Chairman asked looking for guidance from his two colleagues. "What's a conchie?"

The small mean-looking man seemed only too happy to inform the chairman that a conchie was a conscientious objector.

"Ah," the Chairman said, "That means he's in prison."

"Naw. He's no in prison," Sam interrupted. "He just went oot to find hissel yin day and never cam back."

Now it was the mean man's turn to say, "Ah!" and then continued, "You mean he has deserted you?" He lowered his voice before muttering, "And I'm beginning to understand why."

"That's richt. He left us; and my Mammy cannae earn enough money to keep us." Sam, who was sure that things weren't going his way, babbled on. "And we were near evicted for arrears last Easter. But we'll be all richt noo cos Mammy's oot o hospital."

"Which hospital was she in?" the chairman asked.

"The Morningside yin."

The men coughed and looked meaningfully at each other.

Sam realised he should have said that Rachel had been in the City Hospital with something respectable like leprosy or the Black Death. People were always full of sympathy for somebody in the Royal Infirmary or the City Hospital, no matter what was actually wrong with them. But they thought that people who landed in a mental hospital were all bad. They were folk who couldn't, or more likely wouldn't, pull themselves together. Sam had lost count of how often he had taken a swipe at someone when they asked, "Is your mammy in the Loony Bin again?"

It was true Rachel suffered from terrible depressive bouts but she would never be mad, so far as Sam and his siblings were concerned. They knew that when she was well she was the best mother any family could have. Even when she had to go into hospital she'd warn them not to let anybody know they were all alone in the house. She'd coached them well in the art of survival.

"Have you anything else to say?" demanded the small mean man, who was tired of waiting for an answer. "I mean, is there anything further you wish to tell us to support your" – and he coughed – "blatant application?"

Sam, like Rachel, never gave in easily. He racked his brain for something else to say that would have him reach his goal of a holiday in Rothesay with Chalky. He looked down at his feet. "I gang wi' milk and rolls," he added brightly.

"Most commendable," said the chairman with a smile.

Encouraged, Sam added: "And my shoes are aw holed," he said, balancing on one foot and lifting the other so that the committee could see the holed sole and down-trodden heel. "I've to put cardboard soles in them every nicht, so I dae."

All three men were still looking at him intently. He knew the chairman was waiting for him to say something more. Something that would swing the decision in Sam's favour. He bit his lip and his eyes began to twinkle. Without uttering a word, he kicked off his right shoe, to expose a holed sock. "See, sir," Sam beamed. "I've big tatties in my socks."

The chairman nodded and smiled before turning to consult with his colleagues. Sam grew apprehensive when he noted that the mean little man's face was starting to take on a look of triumph. He knew that meant that he was sure to be turned down. Deciding he had to do something very quickly, he blurted out, "And please, sir, there's somethin' else ye should ken."

"And what's that, son?" the chairman said encouragingly.

"Just that my ither socks, that my Mammy's gonnae wash, hae big tatties in them an' aw."

The mean man immediately jumped up. "Just a minute, did I hear you say you have *two* pairs of socks?"

Sam nodded. "Aye, but baith pairs hae big tatties in the heels and the taes."

A cruel smile of satisfaction lit up the mean man's face as he sat down. The chairman shuffled his papers on the desk before saying, "I'm sorry, son, but as you have *two* pairs of socks we deem you not poor enough for a holiday."

Sam looked up at him. "No puir enough?" he stammered as deep outrage flamed upwards from his belly to his head.

Without a further word he turned on his heel and strode defiantly up the hall. But as he opened the big creaking outer door he turned and shouted back at the men: "No puir enough for a holiday, am I? Tell me this then. Hoo bluidy puir dae I hae tae be?"

CHAPTER 8
ALL STRAIGHTENED OUT

Carrie awoke suddenly and listened intently. What time was it? For the past week, only sounds had given her any idea of whether it was morning or night. For seven days now she had been blindfold and kept in this bed. For seven days she'd only occasionally been allowed to move her arms and legs. The hardest thing for Carrie, however, was not being able to move her head. It had been kept immobile by two sandbag-like pillows on either side of her face. Food had been fed to her in liquid form through a straw.

In her imprisonment all she could do all was think. That day she was wondering if anybody understood how frightening it was to be blind and her memory flew back to the day she had to go down to Leith Hospital after Hannah had caught Carrie's thumb in the outside door. The doctor had terrified Carrie when he looked at her thumb and announced it would have to come off.

Carrie had screamed, "Mammy. Mammy! Come quick and save me."

Rachel, who had stayed behind in the waiting room, at once bounded into the treatment room. "What's going on?" she demanded, pulling the doctor away from Carrie.

"Oh Mammy, he's going to cut my thumb off," Carrie wailed before the doctor could speak.

"Surely you're not?" shrieked Rachel in absolute horror.

The doctor had smiled. "No, no. All I'm going to do, is this." And he tore off the thumb-nail that was hanging by a shred. Once the nail was completely removed he snapped his fingers. A nurse jumped to attention and gave him some swabs – two of which he used to stem the bleeding from Carrie's thumb and the third to wipe away her gushing tears. "Dear, dear. What *have* we here?" he asked, taking Carrie's chin in his hand and gently rocking her head from side to side.

"I try to keep her in glasses. I really do. But she's forever getting them broken," Rachel said defensively, taking Carrie's glasses out of her pocket. The glasses, as usual, had pipe cleaners attached to them where the legs should have been.

"Not the spectacles," the doctor remarked thoughtfully as he took the glasses from Rachel's hand and placed them on Carrie's face. "I mean her strabismus."

"Strabisms? Strabisms? What the hell do you mean by strabisms?" Rachel almost shouted in sheer panic.

"No need to worry, Mrs Campbell. Strabismus is the medical term for a squint," the doctor replied with a reassuring smile.

Carrie's face had fired. She'd always hated that her eyes were so different from everybody else's. Why, she wondered, did they always have to look in different directions from each other?

The doctor tut-tutted and swung reflectively from side to side in his chair. All the time he kept looking into Carrie's eyes. "Tell you what," he said at last to Rachel, "I'd like you to make an appointment to see a colleague of mine, Mr. Luke. He's an excellent ophthalmic surgeon. Could straighten these." He hesitated before adding, "Those ... er ... squints."

Rachel was amazed. "Are you saying Doctor, that something could be done about Carrie's eyes?"

"Yes indeed," the doctor responded, patting Carrie's cheek. "No sense in leaving such a pretty girl with such unattractive strabismus."

Carrie's thoughts were suddenly interrupted by the nurse asking, "Are you awake, Carrie?" Carrie nodded. "No, no. Don't nod your head. You *must* keep it still. I'll bring you a drink in a minute."

Unthinkingly, Carrie nodded again, but quickly blurted out, "Sorry."

The nurse patted her hand. "It's all right. It'll soon be Tuesday."

"Tuesday," Carrie sighed wistfully as the nurse left her side. Tuesday was to be that happy day when the bandages would be removed and she would have straight eyes. No more being called cock-eyed by the bullies in the playground. No more being afraid to meet someone new. No more being the ugly one. No! On Tuesday it would all be different and she just couldn't wait to see it all happen. Tears began to choke her when she thought, "Maybe I'll be very lucky and see properly again on Tuesday – but what about Sam?" Carrie's thoughts raced back to the night before she had come into hospital.

Rachel had been washing the outside of the windows. It hadn't seemed to matter that she had washed them the very day before. What *did* matter was that it had rained through the night, which meant the windows had lost a little of their pristine sparkle.

It was when Rachel had climbed the stepladder to wash the outside of the bathroom window that the trouble started. The top half of the window was of clear glass; not opaque like the bottom. And when Rachel peered into the bathroom through the clear glass she screamed. The ladder, the pail of water and herself had all crashed to the ground when she jerked backwards in shock.

Sam, who had been in the bathroom, made a dash for the outside door. Rachel had been quick to pick herself up though and, just as Sam tried to dash out of the entry, Rachel firmly barred his way. Without a word she slapped his face with the chamois leather and roughly hauled him into the house. Still without a word she seized the carpet beater, that was conveniently at hand, and began laying into Sam.

Hannah, Carrie, Paul and Alice all looked on in consternation. Naturally their mother beat them from time to time when she said they were asking for it. But *never ever* had she thrashed any of them as she was beating Sam now.

"What's he been up to?" asked Hannah, catching hold of Rachel's raised hand as she was about to whack Sam yet again.

"I'll tell you what the dirty wee bugger was doing!" Rachel yelled, rounding on the others. "Trying to make himself go blind, that's what he was up to."

"I wasnae," Sam protested indignantly, rubbing his painful backside.

"Oh, my bonny lad, but you were," Rachel insisted. "And any idiot knows that sort of thing will make you go blind."

Carrie looked from Sam to her mother. She was completely confused. "Paul," she whispered to her younger brother, "what on earth was Sam doing that was so awful?"

Paul shrugged his shoulders. "Dinnae ken. Aw he said tae me was that he was off to polish his conkers."

"What did you just say, Paul?" Rachel demanded grasping him by the collar.

"Nothin', Mammy," Paul stuttered as he tried to wriggle free. "Just told Carrie, I did, that Sam said he was goin' to polish up his conkers."

To Paul's relief, his mother released him and turned on Sam again. "You like polishing up your conkers, do you?" she spat venomously in Sam's face. "Well, let me tell you this, my lad: If *ever* I catch you at that again you'll no need to wait to go blind because I'll blind you myself." With that, Rachel gave Sam another great whack across the backside. Turning away, she let the carpet beater slip from her hand, sank down on the easy chair and lapsed into deep thought.

There was complete silence for a minute. They all waited for Rachel to say or do something. Eventually she got up and strode into the empty bedroom. "Sam," she called. "From tonight on you'll sleep in here with Paul. You have never *ever* to sleep with the girls and me again. Is that perfectly clear?"

Sam nodded.

"But, Mam," protested Hannah, who had followed her mother into the room. "There's no bed in here. And we haven't got a spare one to put in it."

"And besides," Carrie had butted in, "we've always slept three up and three down in the one bed."

Rachel gave an exasperated grunt as she came back to the living room and faced Sam again. "That's right. But from now on they'll share a palliasse in that room till I find them a bed."

As she lay on her hospital bed Carrie had wondered how Sam and Paul were faring sleeping on their palliasse – until last night, when Hannah had visited and told her that Rachel had got the single bed she needed for Sam and Paul. She'd bought it, Hannah said, on the never-never.

Creeping footsteps near her bed alerted Carrie. "Who's there?" she whispered.

A calloused hand took Carrie's. She smiled, needing no answer. As soon as her fingers had gripped the hand she'd felt the deep gouges made by the knives that were used in the Roperie. "Granny," sighed Carrie. "I'm so happy to see you."

"Ah, dearie, but ye cannae see me." Rosie chuckled.

Then another voice spoke sneeringly. "Aye, and on Tuesday I'll be proved richt and she'll never see nae mair."

Carrie bristled from head to toe. Auntie Ella was with Granny – Auntie Ella whom Carrie had vowed to hate for ever and ever after she found out that her Dad, Johnny, was now living in Ella's house.

It was true enough that Auntie Ella had had a hard and sad life. All her three bairns had been still-born. And her man had died last year with TB. But, Carrie argued to herself, all that bad luck didn't give Auntie Ella any right to be jealous of her Mammy just because she had five healthy bairns. So jealous indeed was Auntie Ella that when Carrie and Sam had been born she'd gone straight out and adopted identical twin boys. Nice enough bairns, Mark and Tony were. Even Rachel admitted that. But what really angered Rachel was that Ella wanted them to be Rosie's favourites and her bairns to be pushed aside.

Even Carrie had noticed that when she visited Rosie, and Auntie Ella was there with her boys, Granny would pay more attention to Mark and Tony than she did to Sam and herself. Once, when Auntie Ella had left, Carrie had asked her Granny why she liked Mark and Tony more than herself or her brothers and sisters.

"Och, lassie, ma Ella's had a hard row to caw," Rosie answered. "And I'm pleased she's adopted twa braw bairns that were needin' a hame. But as to me lovin' Mark and Tony mair than aw o ye?" Rosie laughed with scorn. "Naw. Naw, lassie! Ye're ma ain flesh and blood. It's agin nature for onybody to love ither folk mair than their ain blood line."

Carrie now knew how true that was because each week Granny handed over a half-crown to Sam or herself to take to Rachel. She would say, "Noo, tak it to yer Mammy alang with this," and she would produce bread or margarine or even a tin of Spam. "But remember. Never a word to yer Auntie Ella." Sam, of course, was indignant that Granny was, as he put it, shit-scared of Auntie Ella and was always wondering what Auntie Ella would say if she ever found out that Granny saved pennies for Sam in the little wooden stool that read, "Our Wee Boy is no fool. He keeps his pennies in the stool".

The little stool that stood on the mantelpiece belonged to Granny's youngest son, Davy. Uncle Davy wasn't, and never would be, married, so he stayed with Granny. Sam and Carrie knew that it was his wages coming into the house that helped Granny to be so good to them. And Uncle Davy was always so pleased to see Hannah, Sam, Carrie, Paul and Alice. When he backed a winner he would often fill up the stool for Sam. Not only with pennies but with tanners too.

"Did you no hear what I said, Carrie?" Auntie Ella demanded.

"No," squeaked Carrie, who, like her Granny, was terrified of Ella.

"Well, what I'm sayin' is: on Tuesday when they tak aff the bandages and we find oot that ye've been blinded for life, we'll look efter ye."

Before Carrie could speak, a voice retorted angrily. "You, look after my bairn? That'll be the day!" Carrie heard a loud crack as a newspaper Rachel had been carrying was smacked across Ella's face. "And," Rachel continued, "I suppose this piece in last night's *News* by your useless brother, my hapless husband, was your idea as well."

The paper was snatched from Rachel's hand by Rosie who started to read aloud from it. "Notice is hereby given by Mr John Campbell that he will not be responsible for any debts incurred by his estranged wife, Rachel Campbell, residing at 16 Learig Close." Rosie let the paper slip from her hand to the floor whimpering, "Whitever dis this mean?"

"Mam," Ella replied, "it means that she forged oor Johnny's signature tae tak on debt. And we're no haein' it."

"Aye well," said Rachel hotly, "if I was like you, having Johnny's wages keeping a roof over my head, I wouldn't need to forge his name to get a bed for his son, your legal grandson, Rosie. Aye, Carrie, did you know that? That your father provides for her Mark and Tony while you go hungry."

"My brother's a guid man and he needed a hame."

"He's got one. One that he's never chapped the door of in three bleeding years."

Ella snapped back, "Aye, because you're mad. And ye're doubly mad noo he's back in the fold leadin' a guid Catholic life. Ye should be real proud, Carrie, that your Daddy's noo a member o the St Vincent de Paul. Arranging trips to Lourdes for the sick and readin' to the blind, he is."

Rachel sniggered. "Reads to the blind, does he? And what about Carrie here? He doesnae even come into the hospital to visit her. Never mind read her a blinkin' fairy story."

"My brither's quite richt to lead his ain life noo. Your marriage, that you trapped him intae, wasnae in oor chapel – so it's no recognised."

"Are you insinuating my bairns are bastards?" Rachel interrupted.

Ella gulped. Her hands curled. Her eyes bulged. "In the eyes of oor church," she began, but before she could go on Rachel had leapt across the bed and grabbed her by the throat. But, as luck would have it, the ward Sister had been alerted to the fracas and dashed up to pull Rachel away before she could silence Ella for ever.

Having separated the two, Sister firstly straightened her cap, which had unprofessionally gone awry in the struggle, and then, smoothing down her apron, demanded that all visitors present leave. And immediately at that. "Failure to do so," she warned, "will result in my summoning the constabulary and having you all charged with breach of the peace."

Once everyone had gone Carrie began to sob, wishing she was not only blind but deaf as well. At least she thought they had all gone until a hand sought hers.

"Don't cry, Carrie. On Tuesday you won't be blind. I've prayed for you every day and every night."

"I'm not crying about Tuesday, Hannah. I'm crying about today. Why did they have to make such a scene?"

"It must have been so awful for you, Carrie. Mammy will be so upset about it. And it wasn't really her fault."

"I know. Auntie Ella's such a bitch."

"Aye, and Daddy's nothing but a selfish hypocrite."

"But what I don't understand is why Mammy needed to forge his signature."

"She couldn't get the bed on the never-never without doing that. Women on their own can't get tick."

Carrie nodded. "I'm glad then that she did forge his signature – I really am."

"You are?"

"Oh yes, because if that bed stops Sam going blind then it must have been the right thing to do." Carrie's hands were now feeling around the bandages on her eyes. "Believe me, anything's better than oor Sam being blind."

"Oh, good grief!" Hannah suddenly interrupted. "If you thought Auntie Ella and Mammy having a rammy was humiliating, just listen to that!"

"But it's only the Salvation Army Band and singers. They play here every Sunday."

"I know that – but listen to who's leading the choir."

Carrie half sat up and then she let her head fall back on the pillow as a very drunken solo rendering of Leith's very own hymn, *Will your anchor hold in the storms of life?* resounded through the ward. It was the voice of her inebriated grandfather, Gabby!

CHAPTER 9
RED LETTER DAYS

It was now three months, to the day, since Carrie had been able to stumble up the ward towards a tearful Rachel. Every night after Carrie's operation her mother had lain awake, haunted by the unanswered question that would not let her eyes close in merciful sleep: how could she live with herself if Carrie had indeed been blinded?

"Mammy, Mammy!" Carrie had cried as she staggered into Rachel's arms. "See my eyes. They're straight! Both of them.'"

Rachel swallowed hard and peered at Carrie's eager face. Her eyes were indeed straight and Rachel became aware, for the first time, that Carrie had been blessed with eyes of the deepest violet that she'd ever seen. How on earth, she wondered, had she failed to notice the exceptional beauty of these eyes? Two oval eyes that were now dancing with delight.

Carrie herself was equally delighted that Hannah's prayers had successfully undone Auntie Ella's grim prophecy of disaster. She too was able to look in the mirror and see her own straight eyes. Indeed, for two whole days after she arrived home from hospital, Carrie lost no opportunity to take up lengthy residence in the bathroom. She would just stand there staring at her reflection in the cracked mirror. Then she would turn her head this way and that, making certain that she had indeed been transformed from an ugly duckling into a swan.

Delighted as Carrie was with this miracle, she was well aware – because Bernie had told her – that bad things always came in threes. Auntie Ella and Mammy having a punch-up in the hospital was certainly one. Hearing Granddad in his drunken rendering of *Will your anchor hold in the storms of life?* was the same. And since neither she nor Sam had ended up blind, another disaster would undoubtedly have to follow.

Consequently, the day after Carrie came home from hospital this disaster to end all disasters was revealed when Bernadette chapped on the door and asked Rachel if she could speak urgently to Carrie. Carrie immediately joined Bernie out in the stair and because the shock was going to be too much for Carrie, Bernie suggested prudently that they sit down on the bottom step.

"What is it?" Carrie whimpered.

"It's Ruth. She's going to Canada. Emigrating."

Carrie's hand flew to her mouth. Ruth, Bernie's elder sister by ten years, was going to emigrate? Surely it couldn't be. That would mean Bernie and Carrie wouldn't be able to get big sister's copy of the *Red Letter* to read when she was finished with it. On top of that Carrie knew full well that Canada was such a very backward and unsophisticated country that they would probably never ever have heard of the *Red Letter* so Ruth couldn't even send it on to them from there. "Whatever will we do, Bernie, if we never ever get to read those wonderful, terribly exciting serials again?"

Bernie just shrugged her shoulders. "Wish we were as rich as that Mrs Stivens up in Restalrig Circus. Imagine that, Carrie. Not just able to afford the *Red Letter* but *Secrets* and the *Red Star* as well."

Carrie sighed. She delivered those magazines to Mrs Stivens every week but couldn't imagine anyone reading all of them in one week. Not properly anyway. Carrie's eyes widened suddenly. That was it! Instead of delivering the *Red Letter* to Mrs Stivens along with the morning paper she'd deliver it with the evening paper. That would allow Bernie and Carrie to read the serial on their way to and from school and during dinner break.

"Listen, Bernie," said Carrie. "What d'ye think of this brilliant scheme?"

"Sounds smashing," agreed Bernie.

The enterprise worked beautifully for three months – until

the morning of the great snowfall. That was the morning when Carrie got up earlier than usual to deliver her papers. She was intensely excited because it was the day when she'd be able to read the final episode of "Jungle Passion" which had been building to a climax for the past five weeks.

The tension in both girls had by now reached fever pitch. Would Murdo Bruce, (of course a direct descendant of Robert the Bruce) be able to disentangle himself from the snare of that Sassenach hussy? The smart besom who was holding him to the promise that she declared was made to her when he was delirious with tropical fever. The two had been on safari when he was struck down with a mysterious ailment and once he regained consciousness Lady Antonia Atholl Forbes was seated by his bed with a triumphant smile on her face. And if Murdo did indeed escape the clutches of this *femme fatale*, or if God graciously intervened and Lady Antonia was struck dead by a bolt of lightning, would Murdo be in time to prevent Flora, the true love of his life, from leaving on a ten-pound assisted passage to the Australian outback?

That day, when Carrie opened the entry door, she was greeted by a swirling blizzard. Commonsense dictated that she should go back inside and wait for the storm to pass but the compulsion to know exactly what would happen in "Jungle Passion" was more important to her than her own safety. After battling through the snow to the newsagent's shop, however she became alarmed when the proprietor, Mr Dagleish, said, "Nae magazines for ye to deliver the day, Carrie."

"What?" exclaimed Carrie

"Aye, the train from Dundee is snowbound on the ither side o the Forth Bridge."

Carrie gasped in dismay. What was she to do now? She simply had to know what had happened to Flora and Murdo.

But the newspapers from London and Edinburgh were still

there to be delivered. Carrie was only halfway through her task when she dimly saw a figure, its head swathed in a towel, floating eerily towards her. "Caa – aa – aa – rie," a distorted voice rang out. Carrie froze. Was this some sort of ghost? It certainly sounded like one. "Caa – aa – aa – rie," the voice called again. "I couldnae wait ony longer. I need to ken."

Carrie sighed as relief swept over her. "Well, I'm sorry to tell you, Bernie, but the answer is they're still on the blinking train."

"Dinnae tell me I got oot o my bed and battled through aw this snaw and the magazines didnae get through?"

Carrie nodded despondently.

By eleven o'clock the snow had stopped falling and the sun had broken through. Looking out of the schoolroom window Carrie was reminded of a scene in "Holiday Inn". Thinking of that film, she wondered whether she and Bernie would ever get to Hollywood and make Ginger Rogers look clumsy? Bernie had been getting tap-dancing lessons for over a year now and would show Carrie all the steps afterwards. Until last week, that is, when Bernie realised that Carrie, who'd never had a dancing lesson in her life, was a far better dancer than herself. Poor Bernie had been quite upset when Miss Lightfoot, her dancing teacher, had apparently forbidden Bernie to show Carrie any more steps. Evidently it was very dangerous for someone, who wasn't properly trained, to show someone else the dance steps. So dangerous indeed that they would probably catch polio and end up in an iron lung. And Bernie certainly didn't want that for Carrie. Oh no!

When Carrie arrived at the shop to pick up her evening papers, Mr Dalgleish, was smiling broadly. "Wells Fargo got through, Carrie."

"Eh?"

"What I'm saying is – that the train with the Dundee magazines got through at dinner time."

"Oh good."

"Aye, so now you can get this *Red Letter* delivered to Mrs Stivens with her evening paper."

Carrie shakily took the precious magazine into her hand and held it tightly to her bosom. For a moment she was tempted to hide it in her school books and deliver it the following night but then, she reasoned to herself, while her hand lovingly stroked the magazine, that was a long time away. What if Mrs Stivens, who always went into the shop on Wednesdays to pay her papers, asked why her *Red Letter* had not been delivered?

She was still pondering the problem when Bernie approached her. Carrie told her what had happened, adding that it looked now as though they'd never be able to find out what had happened to Murdo and Flora. Bernie sniffed and blew a raspberry. "Here!" she said, grabbing Carrie's arm. "Ken hoo my Mammy cleans the chapel and then brings the half-burnt candles hame?"

"Aye, cos she cannae really afford your tap-dancing lessons an' that means she's no got a penny left for the gas after Tuesday."

Bernie ignored Carrie's sniping. "'Weel, hoo aboot me giein' you twa of they candles and some matches? Then you can tak the *Red Letter* hame and read it in the lavvy. And the morn I'll find oot what happened in the story afore ye deliver it to Mrs Stivens."

Carrie grinned. Her straight and violet eyes twinkled and a wicked little smile curled round her lips. "Suppose I could, Bernie," she drawled. "Specially if Miss Lightfoot changed her mind about you showing me the dance steps."

It was half past five when Carrie got home. She had just opened the door when Rachel called out, "That you, Carrie? You've been some time."

"Yeah, Mam. I'm just goin' to the lavvy."

"Toilet, Carrie! How many times do I have to tell you to speak proper? The only job *you'll* get talking like that is gutting fish."

Carrie ignored her mother's remarks and once safely in the bathroom she took the *Red Letter* magazine from under her jumper and lit the candle before installing herself comfortably on the toilet seat. Soon, however, the story unfolding had her knees knocking. She became so excited that she had to stop momentarily and use the toilet she was sitting on. She flushed it and was ready to start reading again when Rachel shouted, "Tea's up."

This caused a dilemma for Carrie. It was Tuesday and because last Tuesday it had been only beans on toast for the tea that meant it would be Carrie's favourite tea this Tuesday. Egg and chips. Carrie was tempted to read just to the bottom of the first page but then she remembered that if Sam got to the table first he'd be dunking his chips in her egg and at least four of her chips would end up in his greedy gob. Needs must. So Carrie slid the magazine under the bath before blowing out the candle and racing through to the scullery.

Sam was already at the table with a small head peeping out of his V-neck. It was Tiny, the puppy Sam had found wandering in the street three months ago. Carrie looked at her plate. The egg yolk was burst and Sam had twice as many chips on his plate than on hers. "You greedy big pig," she spat, picking a chip off Sam's plate and dunking it in his egg.

Sam made a grab for the chip – but Carrie had swallowed it. Undaunted, he took another chip off Carrie's plate and smirked. "Hae ye forgotten, dopey, that ye promised to help me feed wee Tiny here?"

"Aye, wi' my mince and tatties. No wi' my egg and chips," wailed Carrie, as she remembered the night Sam had brought in the wee dog.

Carrie had just been discharged from hospital that day back in December. Sam had been doing her paper round while she'd been away and, according to Sam, he'd found the wee dog sitting on his guider when he came out of a stair. It had been shivering and whimpering so what else *could* he do but bring it home. Sam was clapping the little dog when he asked Rachel if he could keep her. Rachel threw him a scornful look. Hannah and Carrie both knew she'd say, "No, we haven't enough food to feed ourselves, never mind a dog," so in unison they sang out that they would willingly help feed the dog off their own plates. Rachel shrugged her shoulders. "Well, suppose it might stop you clapping something else." So the little dog had come to stay at 16 Learig Close.

It came as no surprise to Carrie when Hannah told her that the little dog had been the runt of a litter from the dog breeder down in Links Place. Sam seemingly delivered a bag of kindling there every week and, learning the little dog was about to be given swimming lessons in a pail, he'd asked the breeder if he might have her. A hard bargain the fellow drove. Sam would now be delivering the kindling free for a whole year – and, since the wee dog was not up to the breeder's standards, Sam was never to tell to anyone where the wee dog had come from.

By now Carrie had finished her egg and chips. She clapped the wee dog, got up from the table, laid her plate in the sink and was making for the door when Rachel asked, "Where are you off to?"

"Just away to the lavvy – I mean toilet, Mammy."

"Something wrong with you, like?"

"No, Mammy," Carrie replied, edging closer and closer to the door.

"Then in that case you won't need to go. And you can get on with washing the dishes. It's your turn."

Carrie grimaced but came back and began washing up the

tea dishes while her mother did the drying up. Rachel had just finished when she called out, "Did you mind to go into Harrison's the day, Sam?"

"Aye, but he didnae hae ony spare newspaper. So I cannae cut ony up for the lavvy."

Carrie sniffed. "You know something? We're the only folk I know that go to the fishmonger's and *ask* for old newspapers. Everybody else *gives* them their old papers."

"That, Carrie," said Rachel emphatically, stretching up to turn off the gas, "is because *they* can afford to buy newspapers, or even toilet rolls, but we can't."

Carrie had just got into the living room and was waiting for Rachel to light the gas there when she replied, "See me? When I'm big I won't wipe my backside with newspaper. I'll be so rich I'll have a toilet roll all to myself. An Izal toilet roll at that."

Rachel sighed. "Right. But till then will you just sit down while I show you how to turn the heel of that sock you've been knitting for the last six months."

Carrie's face fell. "But I was just going to the lav – I mean, toilet, Mam."

"Look! I asked you five minutes ago if there was anything wrong with you and you said no. So is there?"

Carrie blushed deeply. "No."

"Good. Because there are five other folk besides you, in this house and they like to use the toilet too. So as you've been there in the last hour you'll just wait your turn and not go again till you're ready for bed."

An hour and a half later there was even less of the sock than there had been when Rachel had started to show her how to turn the heel. Somehow Carrie simply could not master the four wires and so ripped-down wool was now wound all around wee Tiny.

"See my wee dug," Sam cried out in delight when he realised

Tiny thought it was all a game and had joined in, frantically pulling the wool this way and that until she was completely entangled.

"Here, Sam, come and help me get your pup out of this guddle," Rachel muttered irritably as she picked Tiny up.

"Just hold on, Mammy, and I'll get the scissors and cut her oot."

"Am I hearing you right, Sam? Did you say, cut her out? Waste the wool?" Rachel fumed. "No, no! No cutting. We'll have to unpick it, knot by knot. That way Carrie can start knitting it up again."

A full half-hour was to pass before Tiny was finally disentangled from the wool. And when at last the dog was free Rachel sighed, shook her head, announced it was high time they were all in bed and went over to turn off the gas.

"Is it all right for me to go the lav – I mean toilet, Mam?"

"Aye. But know something Carrie? If you hadnae been born at home I'd have sworn somebody had given me the wrong bairn."

Once Carrie had settled herself securely in the bathroom she fished out the candle and matches from under the bath. The soft candlelight imparted a romantic glow and Carrie sighed with eager anticipation as she reached for her *Red Letter*. Her hands shook as she searched for the vital page. Then a cry of dismay escaped her. The page and the next one were gone! Panic seized her when it dawned on her what had happened to them. Paul and Sam had used them as toilet paper. "Good grief," she moaned. "Whatever am I going to do?"

All the time she'd spent trying to turn the heel, her mind had visualized herself drifting luxuriously to sleep knowing the climax of the story – discovering that delicate Flora was at last the blushing bride of Murdo, and about to experience all the bliss of her wedding night. Now, because of the disaster, Carrie would toss and turn all night wondering how she was going to explain the mystery of the mutilated magazine.

Next morning Bernie was understandably furious when Carrie was unable to tell her the ending of the story. Carrie was equally put out because Bernie didn't seem at all concerned that her friend could be in deep trouble. What made matters even worse was that Bernie just stomped off when Carrie whimpered, "Whatever *am* I going to do?"

To blazes with Bernie! She would just deliver the magazine with its missing three pages to Mrs Stivens with her morning paper. After all, Mrs Stivens might not follow the serial and therefore not notice that the last three pages of her magazine had been ripped out. Carrie squirmed with embarrassment as she remembered how she herself had had to rip out the third page when the shock of what happened to the magazine resulted in her having an attack of diarrhoea during the night.

When Carrie arrived at the newsagent's to collect her evening papers, Mr Dalgleish was waiting for her. He motioned sternly with his finger for her to come to the counter. His tongue, as usual when he was angry, was hanging out and was licking his bottom lip from side to side like a pendulum. "Mrs Stiven's been in and she wants to know what's happened to the back of her *Red Letter*?" he thundered.

Carrie hesitated. All night she'd rehearsed what she was going to say but realised the story about Tiny eating the magazine wouldn't wash. Nor would the one about some girl who was so desperate to know the end of the serial that she'd robbed Carrie and torn out the last three pages before fleeing with them. She also knew that if she lied she would probably end up in the burning fire underneath the school floor boards. Not only did the minister say that Satan lived there, waiting to devour children who lied or stole, but the headmaster, Mr Green, said so too.

Five minutes later she had confessed all to Mr Dalgleish. He sighed patiently before telling her there was nothing else for it but that she must pay for the magazine – which meant she would be fourpence short in her weekly wages. It also meant she would have to tell her mother because Rachel would be expecting seven and sixpence not seven and twopence. Carrie looked up and pleaded. "But what will I tell my Mammy, Mr Dalgleish?"

"The truth, of course,'" he expostulated. "But before you tell yer Mammy anything I want you to go round and see Mrs Stivens and tell her exactly what happened.'"

After Carrie had seen Mrs Stivens she crept at a snail's pace towards home. During the trudge she thought of running away – but it was macaroni cheese for tea and she was very hungry, starving in fact. She decided though that, if she went into the house sobbing, Rachel would be less likely to bounce her head off the wall. So, taking a deep breath, she opened the door. "Mammy, Mammy!'" she called. "I got a terrible row from Mr Dalgleish because Mrs Stivens reported me for delivering her *Red Letter* late."

Rachel, who was lifting the macaroni cheese out of the oven, turned round. "Are you saying that all some women have to worry about is a comic being delivered late?"

Carrie had now sidled to one end of the wooden bench behind the table. "Mammy, the *Red Letter* is no a comic. It's the best magazine in the whole wide world." Carrie sobbed before continuing in an awesome whisper, "And this week it was the end of the serial."

Rachel banged the dish down on the table, leant forward and yanked Carrie to her feet. If Carrie thought the *Red Letter* was the best magazine in the whole wide world and was also aware that it was the end of the serial then there was more to this business than a magazine being delivered late. "Right, my girl," she yelled. "Out with it!"

Carrie was again tempted to lie but in her mind's eye she could clearly see the hell flames engulfing her. And because she was standing close to the heated scullery wall she could actually feel her flesh beginning to burn. So, when her mother let go of her, the truth tumbled from her mouth.

The tale of woe having eventually ended, Rachel grabbed Carrie again and shook her until her teeth chattered. "Now, just you listen to me, my lady. And listen good. At your age you've no right to be reading a paper as wicked as the *Red Letter* and you're lucky, *very lucky*, that wee Billy up the stairs has bronchitis and his Mammy had just got him to sleep or I'd give you a good doing right now."

"I'm very sorry, Mammy," wept Carrie.

"You will be! *Very* sorry at that. Because I'm going to set the alarm five minutes early for tomorrow morning and you'll get your doing then. And believe me! A Macintosh Red will look pale compared to your backside when I'm done with you."

"Will I set the alarm for ye the noo, Mammy?" This intervention came from Sam who was thoroughly relishing the scene.

"What a good idea, Sam. And while you're at it, set it ten minutes early, because you're enjoying this so much you can also enjoy having your arse warmed first."

"But, Mammy," Sam protested – but was unable to finish because Rachel had turned back to Carrie.

"And is that it?" Rachel demanded.

Carrie shook her head. "No. I had to go round and tell Mrs Stivens what happened." A further fit of sobbing overtook her.

Rachel sighed. "To her magazine?"

"No. In the story, Mammy."

"And what did you say, Carrie?" pleaded Hannah, who hated

family rows.

Carrie's eyes became dreamy. Her voice grew husky. And she spoke more as if to herself. "I just told her that the wicked woman was killed by a bolt of lightning when she was out riding. Mercilessly beating her horse she had been, so God sorted her out. After that, Murdo went quickly to Liverpool and was just in time to jump on the gangplank before it was pulled away to let the ship sail. Luckily Flora had seen him from the rail where she was standing. You see, she'd wanted to get one last glimpse of Britain and when she saw Murdo jump aboard she ran to meet him. He swept her up in his arms and then they jumped overboard together and swam back to the shore. And once they were dried out by a roaring fire, Murdo took Flora back to his house in Corstorphine. Big house it is. And it has *two* bathrooms with an Izal toilet roll in each one of them!"

CHAPTER 10
AIMING FOR THE SKIES

The winter of 1948 melted into spring and spring warmed into summer. A bright June sun streamed into 16 Learig Close through the windows that had been flung open wide. Rachel was on a day off and Hannah was on a week's holiday from her clerking job, and together they were giving the house yet another spring-clean.

They launched into their task as soon as the children left for school. They washed, scrubbed and polished everything in sight. Towels and bedding danced on the washing-line along with the two blankets that Sam had acquired for the family last winter. Had he been at home, he'd have sworn he was scared to stand still for fear he too landed in the second-hand Burco boiler that had quite recently fallen off the back of a lorry into his ever ready hands.

At the time he'd been haggling for the boiler, he was convinced it would save Rachel a lot of work. But he now realised it had become her favourite toy. She never tired of boiling, boiling, boiling – everything that should be boiled and a great deal that shouldn't, with the result that the family washing was now so white that it had become the talk of the street. Indeed Rachel was thrilled when Edna Glass told her that people were actually going up the back lane just to see it flapping in the wind. Now not only would Mrs Anderson in the next stair be remembered when she died for the beautiful washings she'd put out but Rachel too would surely be awarded the same accolade in due course. Or so she told Carrie, who exclaimed, "Surely, Mammy, you don't want to be remembered for just putting out a beautiful washing?"

Rachel hadn't answered. Why should she try to explain it to a young lassie who couldn't even wash her neck properly – never mind wash anything else whiter than white.

"That's me finished black-leading the fireside, Mam. And that's it all done," Hannah announced to her mother, who by now had finished scrubbing and bleaching the wooden bathroom floor.

"Right, get the kettle on and we'll have a fly-cup before they all get here," Rachel shouted back. Thinking of the rest of her children coming home jolted Rachel into reflecting. How, she wondered, had that blasted government the blooming cheek to put the school leaving-age up to fifteen? If they hadn't, Sam and Carrie would be leaving school in three weeks' time and earning money that the family sorely needed. The irony for her, she conceded, was that all of her children were bright enough to achieve the dreams she'd always had for them – dreams that would have taken them out of abject poverty and out of the housing schemes. Out of the labouring-class and back into the middle-class where her mother had belonged and where Rachel felt she and her children should rightly be.

She sighed wistfully. Hannah, the brightest of her children, had so wanted to stay on at school and get her Lower Leaving Certificate. The simple truth was that she couldn't afford to let her to stay on past fourteen. Sam too had been denied his chance at the Heriot's bursary for the same reason. With Sam though, she had the comfort of knowing that, while he might be slightly less intelligent than Hannah, he had what Hannah didn't have – a good dose of animal cunning. And that talent would see him through life and let him reach his goals one way or another.

Rachel's thoughts then turned to Carrie. Ah well, best to forget what happened three years ago. Carrie had passed her qualifying exam well above anyone's expectation – which saw her elevated to a seat next to Sam in class. But so what? Carrie never worked to her full potential – unless (Rachel granted) the subject really interested her. So getting Carrie settled into a good job like Hannah, who was now a clerkess in the Leith Provident head office, was going to be something of a problem.

Footsteps behind her interrupted Rachel's thoughts and she jumped in slight alarm.

"Oh, it's only you, Hannah," she sighed with relief. "See that?" she said proudly, standing aside so that Hannah could admire her handiwork. "All scrubbed and bleached the way I know you like it."

Both Hannah and Rachel took a deep breath but coughed when the smell of bleach and carbolic caught the back of their throats. "I know folks say I'm fussy like you, Mam, but if I'm to be a doctor I really do have to have high standards of hygiene."

Rachel stared down into the cloudy water in the pail. "Hannah," she murmured, "I've looked into the whole business and there's just no way I can afford for you to become a doctor."

Hannah's lip trembled. Tears sprang to her eyes and trickled down her cheeks. "But, Mam, you've always said we should aim for the skies."

"I know, dear, and next year, once Carrie and Sam are working, I might just manage to let you train as a nurse."

"A nurse? Oh, Mam, don't you understand? I've been going to night school to get my Highers so I can get to university one day?"

"Yes. And it'll stand you in good stead."

"I *don't* want to stand in good stead: I want to take out people's adenoids, not wipe their backsides."

"Oh, Hannah, nurses do a lot more than wipe arses."

Hannah snorted indignantly and pursed her lips. "Right then, if you won't let me be a doctor, I'll just lower my sights and settle for being a missionary."

"A missionary?" yelled Rachel in horror as she brushed past Hannah and went into the scullery to empty the pail into the sink. There was a pause, as the murky water gurgled away, before she demanded. "And where exactly are you meaning to be a missionary?"

"Africa."

"Africa? Why Africa?" Rachel asked, wheeling to face her recalcitrant daughter.

"Cos I've been reading all about Mary Slessor and that's where she went to show the native children how to live better."

Drying her hands, Rachel began to laugh disbelievingly and sank down on a chair. "Look, Hannah, if you want to show bairns how to live better, you don't need to bother going all the way to Africa. You just need to go up the stairs to the Sinclairs."

"What d'you mean?"

"Just that they poor bairns up there are living worse than them in Africa. The Sinclairs think a decent meal comes out the chippie, so they do."

Before Hannah could speak, the outside door opened and Carrie waltzed into the scullery, bearing a plate neatly covered with a tea towel. "Mam," she gushed. "You're never going to believe this, but I came second in the class for making these floury scones." With a dramatic flourish Carrie removed the towel to reveal eight perfect scones. "See?"

Rachel rose and picked up one of the scones to examined it. "You only came second?"

"Well, I was first for the scones naturally," Carrie boasted, demonstrating how each scone sprang back immediately she prodded it. "But that bitchy teacher deducted five marks for the mess I'd made, so I only came second all round."

"Aye, and I bet when you finished there was more flour on the floor than there is in the whole of the Chancelot Mills," teased Hannah.

Carrie ignored the barb and all Rachel could do was to fill the teapot with boiling water. "Aye, Carrie, that's you first in History, first in Cooking, first in Keep-fit, first in French. But where oh where are you in Geography and Algebra?"

Carrie laid her plate of scones on the table, picked one up, cut it open and walloped a huge dollop of butter on it. Immediately Rachel seized the knife and scraped off half the butter.

Quite undeterred, Carrie responded: "I was talking to Lottie Glass on my way back from school and she told me her sister Ina has been working three years now and she's never once used her Geography but she's sending whisky all over the world."

Hannah and Rachel looked at each other and shook their heads. "But, Carrie," her mother argued, "Ina only sticks on the printed labels. Somebody else does the typing."

"Maybe so. But she gets real good money just for sticking on the labels the right way up." Without waiting for an answer she bit into her scone. "Here, try one. They're just yummy. Even with hardly any butter on them."

"Look here, Carrie, don't tell me you're thinking of working in a whisky bond?"

Carrie looked up. Her eyes widened in mock disbelief and she let the scone fall from her hand. "Mam, how could you even think that? You *know* how hard I've been working on my tap-dancing."

Rachel's eyes similarly widened. "Tap-dancing?" she exclaimed, through a mouthful of scone.

"Okay, I mightn't be just as good as Ginger Rogers right now but when I get to Hollywood … "

Now it was Hannah's turn to splutter through her scone. "Hollywood?"

"Well, if I don't make Hollywood right away I'll just be a …"

Then a loud knock on the outside door halted Carrie in her tracks. Rachel frowned and Hannah went to see who it was. A big man framed the doorway. Hannah jumped back and her hand flew to her mouth. Surely the rent wasn't in arrears again?

But Mammy did do silly things when she was ill. No, it couldn't be that. Mammy hadn't been to hospital for ages.

"You'll be Sam's sister?" the man said.

Hannah nodded.

"Is your mother in?"

"Mam, there's a man here to see you," Hannah called, without asking the man in.

Rachel came through from the scullery, carefully removing her pinny and wrapping it up. "Aye?" was all she said.

"I was wondering if I could hae a wee word wi' ye aboot Sam?"

"Well, whatever he's done we'll pay for it. Send in the bill," said Rachel, beginning to close the door.

The man stuck his foot in the doorway. "Look, it's nothing like that. It's guid news."

Rachel opened the door again and signalled for the man to come inside. Once the door was closed she ostentatiously shut all the windows before saying, "I don't like all the nosy neighbours knowing my business. Now you're sure my Sam hasn't put a ball through your window or found something you didn't know you'd lost?"

The man smiled. "Naw. Naw. Sam's a guid laddie. Great fitba' player," he said, seating himself on the chair Rachel set out for him. "Him and Chalky White are richt guid players."

"They should be," Rachel chuckled. "They spend every night – light or dark, rain or shine – kicking that ball of theirs to hell and back."

"Well, it's paid aff," the man crowed. "They play for my team – Restalrig Juniors." The man pulled himself up and stuck out his chest: "And it looks as if we'll be takin' the Juvenile Cup this year. Will you be coming to see the gemme, Missus?"

"Mam works all day on Saturdays," Hannah interjected before Rachel could answer. "But Carrie, Paul, Alice and I are all coming."

"That's a real pity, Missus," said the man shaking his head. "You see there's a scout from Gorgie Hearts coming to see Sam. Got a real interest in him, he has."

Hannah and Carrie looked at each other and gasped before raising their clenched fists in delight. Rachel reacted by jumping from her chair and howling, "What?"

The man cocked his head knowingly. "Aye, that's what I've managed to dae for yer laddie. Got a Hearts scout comin' to see him. And, believe me, for I ken these things, they'll snap him up and mak a professional oot of him."

"Here," Rachel demanded, bending her head down so that Hannah could examine it. "Does my head button up the back?"

"What d'ye mean?" said the man, slightly disconcerted by this.

Rachel crossed the room and gave him a sharp poke in the chest. "I'll tell you exactly what I mean," she spat. "I know how these scouts get hundreds o laddies to sign up with promises that they'll come to be football stars. And get into the big money. But you know it doesn't work out like that." Rachel turned and confided to Carrie and Hannah. "Maybe one laddie in a hundred will make it. Now we all know Sam's a pretty good athlete but he's not brilliant – so he'll no be signing for anybody. He's going to get a trade."

"But I'm telling you he *will* mak it," interrupted the man

"Aye, till you throw him on the scrap heap at nineteen or twenty and he's got no trade to turn to."

Carrie and Hannah looked from the man to their mother. They simply didn't know which of them to believe. Sam could kick a ball better and further than anyone else they knew. His dream was their dream – that one day he'd don the maroon jersey.

It was the man who was first to break the silence. "I've spoken to Sam and he's said that ... "

"You speaking to Sam will make not the slightest difference. *I* make the decisions here," Rachel declared firmly, opening the outside door.

"In that case," the man replied, "could ye gie me Sam's faither's address."

Rachel closed the door with a bang. "*What* did you say?"

"You heard me. Aw I want is Sam's faither's address."

Rachel was now shaking. "And what the hell has his father to do with my Sam?"

"Just this, Mrs Campbell. As Sam's legal guardian, he may well see what a golden opportunity this is for the laddie."

"Are you trying to tell me that a man we haven't seen for all of three, no, four years, can override anything I say?" Rachel gasped, sinking down on her chair again.

The man nodded.

"I'm sure he can't, Mam," Hannah blurted out, wringing her hands.

"Oh, but I looked into aw that business afore I came here, and he can, Mrs Campell, I assure ye."

Rachel was still sitting. She slowly shook her head from side to side, then clenched her fists and beat them on her knees while gazing intently at the wall. Three whole minutes passed – three minutes of agonising silence – before she rose and opened the door once more. "I'm sorry I didn't quite catch your name when you came in," she said, in a tone she had learned long ago from Eugenie.

"Henderson. Jack Henderson."

"Well, Mr Henderson, I don't believe I have anything further to say to you!"

The man strode to the door but then turned round to face Rachel. "Let's be fair, Mrs Campbell. I accept that you dinnae want to speak to me aboot Sam's football career. All I want is his faither's address so I can ask him."

"There's nobody here stopping you asking him anything," Rachel chuckled. She knew, and she knew that Jack Henderson knew fine that she knew, that he'd already asked Sam about Johnny's whereabouts and that Sam had stayed mum. "And when you do trace him," Rachel continued sweetly, "could you ask him if he would kindly send on some of Sam's keep because he hasn't come up with one solitary brass bean since the day he walked out of here."

Just then the entry door opened and in dashed Paul and Alice – Paul with Tiny in his arms. "Mammy, Mammy," he pleaded. "Sam's wee dug's no very weel. We found her round the back. She's shivering and cannae walk nor nothing."

"One minute, son, this freebooter here is just leaving," and with that Rachel dismissed Jack Henderson with a curt nod and closed the door firmly on him.

Hannah immediately jumped forward and took Tiny from Paul. "Oh, Mam, she's burning hot and her pads are brick hard," she cried, gently feeling the dog's nose and paws.

"It's not that blooming distemper thing, is it?" queried Carrie anxiously.

Hannah nodded and gulped.

Rachel came over also to press Tiny's pads; then frantically looked about the room before shouting, "Quick, Alice, go and get me that tin of Vaseline from the bathroom."

"What good d'you think that will do?" asked Hannah.

"I'll warm it and massage it into her paws."

Hannah shook her head. "Mam, it's distemper – hard pad."

Rachel turned angrily on her: "Oh, you're so smart now, aren't you? You've no only been studying your Highers at night school but doing a veterinary course as well, I suppose."

Hannah pouted but before she could retaliate they heard Sam parking his guider in the stairwell. All stayed silent, looking from one to the other and thinking the same thing – had Sam met Jack Henderson out on the street?

To their relief Sam entered grinning. Rachel suddenly thought she had never seen him look so tall and handsome. His blue eyes danced, his tanned skin glowed and his ginger blond hair seemed to be curlier then ever. Rachel's thoughts went back to the week before, when she'd felt annoyed at Rosie telling Sam how much he now reminded her of Gabby at that age – tall, strong and athletic. Rachel had often wondered what her mother had seen in her father. Now she could see it exactly; and she could understand why her mother had run off with her father – forfeiting luxury to live in poverty and squalor.

"Mammy," exclaimed Sam, "you're no gonnae believe this, but Jack Henderson, the guy that runs Restalrig Juniors, thinks the Hearts are really interested in me." He stood back and gave a lofty kick at an imaginary ball.

"I know," said Rachel. "He's been here."

"Did he tell ye hoo I'm the guy with the golden feet that's gonnae go to Tynecastle?"

"He did. And I told him to think again – because you're bloody well not."

Sam stopped showing off his footballing prowess. "You what?" he exploded. "But it's what me and my pals are aw dreamin' o and I'm the only yin that's made it."

"Look here, Sam," his mother said, poking vigorously at the fire. "It's all for the best. I'm only trying to make sure you don't get hurt. It's to protect you."

"You think ye want to protect me?" Sam howled, making Rachel wince. "Oh, naw ye dinnae! Ye only want Hannah to succeed. Ye dinnae want *me* to be a success cos ye dinnae like men." Sam now screamed directly into his mother's face. "I ken that. An' that's nae aw. Ye didnae really like my Daddy and that's why ye flung him oot."

Rachel shook her head in despair. "Sam Campbell, how can

you say that? I didn't put him out. He left of his own accord."

Sam's only response was to laugh derisively – which had Rachel realising that she might well lose control of the situation. She retaliated by brandishing the poker at Sam.

"And never once since the day he left has he ever tried to put his foot back in that door. It was me – all alone – that went out to work – and work bloody hard I did – to clothe you and feed you."

Sam guffawed sardonically. "Ye feed me? That'll be the day. It's me that's broke my back to feed the hale crowd of ye."

Rachel knew that what Sam said was absolutely true. Sam was a true Leith keelie – a boy who lived by his wits, a laddie she could always depend on to make a bob or two and keep them all fed. Sam's eyes were roving round the room until his gaze settled on Hannah. "Here, whit are ye daein' wi' my wee dug?"

"Sam," Carrie intervened. "Tiny's ill. Awfae ill."

Hannah shook her head. "She's more than ill now. Look."

Sam took Tiny into his arms and sat down on the settee with her – silently stroking her silky coat in an effort to ease her rasping breath. She responded by putting out her small pink tongue and licking his fingers. Then her little tail gave one last wag, a final salute to her master and friend. Then they all understood that the tiny dog had loved Sam just as much as he loved her. They loved one another for what they were. Each had a need that the other fulfilled. The whole family stood and stared in a hushed silence at Sam and Tiny, aware that Tiny had somehow held on for Sam to reach home before she exhaled her last breath. Carrie went over and sat down next to Sam. "We'll bury her in the garden, Sam," she said. "In my special flower plot. Tiny loved the garden and if you really try hard you'll always be able to see her running there – playing, jumping, barking."

Sam didn't speak. His whole body shook with sobs as he constantly stroked Tiny's lifeless form. Carrie lifted her hand to pat Sam's bent head, while Alice came over and sat down on her knee and Paul hung himself around her neck. Time ticked away very slowly until eventually Sam muttered, "I loved her. I really loved her, Carrie. Oh aye, from the tip of her tiny nose to the end of her tiny tail. Really I did."

Carrie's tears splashed on to Sam's hand as she cuddled him.

Rachel looked long and hard at the four children on the settee before silently turning towards the scullery. Hannah shivered uneasily. There were times, like tonight, when she felt that she was the outsider. She was Mummy's girl. The other four were a band apart and all she could do was to follow Rachel into the scullery. "Don't cry, Mam," she pleaded as she went over to Rachel who sat twisting her hands in her lap. "Sam didn't mean it."

"Maybe not – but he's right," her mother remarked lifting a towel to dry her eyes. "Oh, Hannah, however did this all happen? Why did it all go so wrong?"

"What d'you mean, Mam?"

"Just that all of you are so completely different from other folk's bairns. There's you for a start, aiming to be a missionary in Africa. There's Carrie wanting to tap-dance her way to Hollywood. There's Sam wanting to make his living kicking a ball around Tynecastle."

Rachel hesitated. "And I'm just terrified of finding out what Paul and Alice will want to do. Sure as hell it won't be packing biscuits in Crawfords or bottling whisky at VAT 69 – that's for sure."

"But, Mam," said Hannah so softly that it shook Rachel, "we're only doing what you told us we must do. To think for ourselves. To aim for the skies."

Rachel closed her eyes. Hannah was telling her what she already knew – that she'd brought her children up to think for themselves and have ambition. Now they were doing precisely that, she felt threatened. And they could be heading out of control – or at the very least out of *her* control.

CHAPTER 11
GETTING STARTED

The pawnshop that Rachel mostly patronised was situated in the Kirkgate. You would slink in by the entrance door with a carefully secreted brown paper parcel containing anything – blankets, curtains, candle-sticks, clocks, coats, your man's dress suit – in fact whatever wasn't perishable; and if the pawnbroker thought there was any value in your worldly goods you could sneak out a couple of minutes later by the back door into Coatfield Lane with a bob or two to see you through till Friday.

As Rachel made her way that day in January of 1949 along Charlotte Street and into the Kirkgate, she thought how ironic life was. Here she was on her way to "Uncle's" and she wasn't wanting to pawn anything. That day she desperately needed to buy and was feverishly hoping she'd bump into someone she knew so that she could tell them loudly she was on her way to the pawnshop, not to get money but to bargain for some other poor sod's unredeemed pledge.

She squirmed a little as she admitted to herself that her impending action would appear to most people foolhardy at least. Folk like her sister-in-law, Saint Ella, would think the purchase she was about to make with this month's rent was an obvious sign that she was back to her manic depression. But she was perfectly well and this buy would be an investment – an investment that would mean she'd never again have to scrape around for the four pounds to pay the rent on the twenty-eighth of every month. Indeed she could hardly restrain herself from shouting aloud that her trick had worked and a letter had arrived by first post this morning inviting her to attend for an interview

As luck would have it she'd been scanning the *Evening News* last Friday in a quiet moment at work when she had seen the notice:

Manager required for a respectable pub in the Leith area of the city.
Excellent wages of at least six pounds per week.
Successful applicant must be honest, hardworking, and presentable.
Apply in writing to Box 1643.

Now Rachel knew quite well that they were looking for a man. No woman ever managed a pub. She might run one that her family owned, but not manage one for someone else. Yet the thought of a wage of *six pounds a week* was just too tempting for Rachel, so she chanced her luck and applied in writing to the given box number.

Planning her strategy came to a halt when she reached the entrance to the pawnshop. She looked around and tutted to herself. Why wasn't there at least one person she knew hanging about? If she'd been pawning something, there would have been at least two or three of Saint Ella's clypes hanging about. She sighed, thinking if she only had the time she would have hung around till one of them came by but, being in a hurry, she ran up the entry steps two at a time. Once at the top of the stairs she went straight into the shop and made her way over to the selling counter.

Waiting for attention, Rachel noted that the two members of staff – the male owner and his woman assistant – were closeted in the secluded booths serving those who came in to pawn their treasured possessions. She peremptorily rang the bell on the counter however, and the owner looked up and signalled to his assistant, Betsy, that she should leave her customer and attend to a potential buyer.

"Er, that pony-skin coat over there?" Rachel said casually.

"The yin ye tried on last week to gie yer mind a treat?" chuckled Betsy, pushing her grey wispy hair back and wiping her nose with the back of her hand.

"Aye. You said you would let it go for three pound fifteen."

"Did I?"

"You most certainly did. So let me try it on again."

Betsy, with the aid of a long-handled hook, lifted down the coat from the rail. "Belanged to yin o they actresses that come to the Gaiety, it did."

"So I believe," Rachel replied as she tried the coat on. "You said she was the one that worked with Armundo the magician till he was bowled over by young Chrissie that worked down the stair in the pork butchers?"

"Aye. See, when he saw hoo Chrissie could toss no just yin but a hale string o Bowman's black puddings ower her shoulder and up on tae a hook, he just couldnae wait to let her juggle his equipment."

Rachel buttoned up the coat and flipped up the collar. "Could take it off your hands for three pounds ten." she offered, running her hands over the sleek pelts.

Betsy glanced at her boss who imperceptibly shook his head. "Ken something, Rachel?" she went on. "Ye look a million dollars in that coat so I think we should pit the price up, no doon."

Rachel laughed derisively and began to unbutton the coat. This time her reply was directed towards the boss. "Three pounds ten is all I've got and I know this coat's been hanging on your wall so long that Chrissie has no only done a country-wide tour tossing the Great Armundo's caber but she's been twice in the pudding club as well."

"Maybe so, but it's a business we're running here – no a flipping charity," said Mr Cohen.

"Aye, you tell her, Mr Cohen! And ken this? If she went up the toon she wouldnae get a coat of this quality under four pounds in the second-hand shops there. I mean, even here in Leith, she wouldnae get it for under three pounds twelve and a tanner."

"Done!" said Rachel, banging the money down on the table and starting for the door.

"No want it parcelled up?" Betsy shouted as she got out a

large sheet of brown paper and then cut off a couple of pieces of string.

Rachel turned and fixed her gaze directly at Betsy. "I've waited all my bloody life for a coat like this. So if you don't mind, we'll no bother parcelling it up in blinking brown paper. We'll head straight for the front door with it on us!"

Rachel's hand hesitated on the gate of the imposing Victorian villa. If the rumour she'd heard last night was true then it might be better to forget all about this job interview and stick to being dispense barmaid up at the city's Queen's Hotel. It was true she was sick and tired of getting home at two or three in the morning, but the Queen's was, after all, the most prestigious hotel in Edinburgh and the wee scheme she had going with one of the chefs, who liked a dram or two during his shift, meant she got a share of the food he pauchled. She sighed, thinking that was true enough but there was the fact that Hannah had now been accepted for training – at the Royal Infirmary no less – and the terms of her nursing contract stated she had to live in. That in turn meant that all the care of Paul and Alice at night would fall on Carrie. Rachel came to the conclusion that there was nothing else for it but to ring the bell. After all, the thought of Carrie being in charge of the house till three in the morning was the stuff nightmares were made of.

The maid showed Rachel into a plush, ornate drawing-room that breathed the words *nouveaux riches*. Standing there was Paddy Doyle, a handsome, rather over-dressed, portly man approaching sixty. In her experience most men of his age were either thinking of retiring or – if they were working-class – physical wrecks.

"You're a woman!" he exclaimed before she could introduce herself.

"So it says on my birth certificate," replied Rachel, offering her hand.

Still open-mouthed, Paddy motioned Rachel to the settee and sat himself down opposite her. "I'm sorry, but the job you've applied for is not really for a woman," he began, speaking in a strong Irish brogue.

"And why ever not?"

Paddy sighed. "Look, Mrs Campbell, I'm going into a business I've never been in before."

"Like taking over Myles Dolan's bar on the Broad Pavement?"

"You knew that and yet you've still turned up for the interview?"

Rachel nodded, conveniently omitting to tell Paddy that the story was all over Leith – she'd heard it not only from Gabby, who drank there, but also from her upstairs neighbour, Grace, who had the story from her Tommy who naturally would never be seen in such a den of iniquity. Well, not when sober anyway.

"As you'll know, it's a tough pub that. Aye, the customers there are sailors, thieves, vagabonds, old whores and drunkards."

Rachel silently indicated her agreement to this.

"And what I want to do is bring in a bit of class. You know – some *finesse*."

At that Rachel relaxed and sank back into her settee. She knew that if it was class and *finesse* he was looking for, then he need look no further than herself. As Betsy had noted, she really did look a million dollars in her pony-skin coat, complemented by her high-heeled shoes, leather handbag and her *pièce de résistance* – the jaunty brown hat that she was wearing at a perky angle. No one could deny she was both elegant and classy.

"Aye," drawled Paddy thoughtfully as he scrutinised her. "But if I did give you a chance at the job – and I'm making no promises till I've seen the others – I couldn't possibly pay you *six* pounds a week."

"Why ever not?"

"Because you're a woman!"

"But if I do the job, and do it really well, I need to get the going rate?"

"No, no! You see, there's another barman works there. He'd like the manager's job and if I put you in over him that'll be enough for him to swallow without being paid less than you."

Rachel gave the matter careful thought before answering. "Look, I come with experience of serving toffs. I know how to run a high-class bar. Tell you what: you agree to give me the job, here and now, and I'll agree to come for five ten a week. But as soon as I've proved myself you'll put my wages up by another pound. All right?"

Paddy leant over and shook her hand.

By the April of 1949, Rachel had been working three months for Paddy Doyle. From the first day however, she realised that even if they changed the name from the *Standard Bar* to *The Dorchester* it would always be known in Leith as *Dolan's* and only its unique clientèle would ever cross its threshold.

Rachel had tried barring the very worst customers (including Gabby) from its doors but in the end she had to admit defeat. It pained her to advise Paddy that they would just have to settle for the fact that it was a notoriously disreputable gold mine and accept the class of people who patronised it. Indeed by the end of her first week, despite all her efforts, she knew there was no chance whatsoever of raising its status.

She cherished her Wednesdays off. Those were the days when she could forget about breaking up fights, cleaning up spew, serving Red Biddy to old whores whose minds were now completely befuddled, and checking that Jimmy, the barman, wasn't fiddling the till or doctoring the stock. Wednesdays were the days for family and house: days for cleaning, washing, cooking and getting things generally sorted out. And that particular Wednesday she would be busy in the afternoon getting both Sam and Carrie sorted out with a job.

The Headmaster of Montgomery Park secondary school was allowing all the imminent school leavers time off to find employment and Rachel had arranged with Sam to come home early so that they could spend the afternoon trying to find him a trade.

By the time Sam arrived home, Rachel had his plate of soup already dished up. "Sam," she said, as he began to tuck in, "we've agreed that you want to learn a trade. What exactly would you like to be?"

Sam stared at the gas light above his head. As usual the mantle was broken, thanks to his prowess with a ball. "Well, if ye're still no gonnae let me kick a baw?"

"I'm not."

"Then hoo aboot me gettin' tae be an electrician and pitting electric licht in here?"

By now Carrie had come in and sat down. "Oh, Sam, that would be just great. Imagine it, Mammy, you'd come in and flick down a wee switch and the whole house would be lit up. Even the bathroom."

"Carrie, you wanting to hide in the toilet and read your trashy magazines there is no reason for putting in electric light," snapped Rachel. "Besides, within a year I'll have saved up the money we need to put it in. So, Sam, it's your choice."

"Dinnae ken, Mam."

"In that case we'll just get ourselves down to the Labour Exchange and see what they've got to offer."

When Rachel advanced into the men's section of the Leith Labour Exchange with Sam behind her, a silence fell upon the room. Even Sam could feel the hostility towards his mother for having invaded this male sanctum. Indeed, one man remarked very loudly, "Nae content with runnin' Dolan's she's got the bluidy cheek to come in here to see whit ither man's job she can pinch."

Ignoring both the outburst and the queue, Rachel walked straight up to the clerk who was about to call the next man. "You'd best attend to us first," she cautioned the open-mouthed man. "That way you'll get rid of me and then be able to find out if anybody is daft enough to give blabber-mouth over there a job," she said, pointing towards the man who had had the temerity to try and humiliate her.

"Look, Mister, all I want is a trade," Sam intervened, to demonstrate that he could speak for himself.

The clerk sucked in his lips. "Well, son, we expect you to have reached a certain standard in your education."

"He's better qualified than you," Rachel interrupted, slapping down Sam's Lower Leaving Certificate on to the counter.

The clerk took the certificate and perused it carefully. "Look, son," he said, as he handed Sam back his certificate, "with marks like these, shouldn't you be staying on at school and thinking about a white-collar job?"

Sam shook his head. "All I want is a trade."

"Well, you just might be able to get one. Only problem is there's more laddies wanting trades than there are places. And another thing. The shipyards won't take on any apprentices until after the Trades in July." The man's face brightened. "Hang on though: I do have a plumber looking for a bright laddie right now." The man then began to flick through his card-index box.

"Don't bother with that," snapped Rachel, losing her self-control. "My Sam doesn't shovel his own shit and there's just no way he's going to shovel anybody else's." Rachel made for the door. "Right, Sam, let's go."

"Look," the clerk shouted, "wouldn't it be better for your boy to take a temporary job till he gets into a trade in July? Though most of the laddies who do that get used to having a bob or two in their pocket and don't want to give that up."

Once outside, Sam turned on Rachel. "Mam!" he exclaimed, "ye didnae gie me a decent chance to find oot if there wis a job I could get richt noo."

"Look here, Sam," said Rachel. "I'll tell you what we're going to do. Go over to Henry Robb's Shipyard right now and ask them to give you a temporary job in their office till they can take you on as an apprentice in July."

"An *office* job?"

"Aye, and if you talk proper like your sisters, and stop bloody swearing too, you just might get taken on."

"But Mammy, would that no be me trying to get in by the back door?"

"Oh Sam, surely you know I'd never encourage you to do such a thing?"

Sam and Rachel eyed each other and then without another word they set off walking across the wooden bridge towards the docks. Halfway over Sam stopped. "This is as far as ye go, Mam, cos I hae to go to Robb's on my ain!"

"No, Sam, I'm going with you."

"Naw, Mam, if I'm gonnae work there, I hae to speak up for masel'. Ah'm able to talk for masel' even though it's no the wey ye'd like me to speak. So ye'll just wait here till I get back."

Rachel wanted to argue but Sam's determined look made her realise he'd go his own way no matter what she said. She sighed to herself and stood looking over the worn rails of the bridge at the gurgling, murky Water of Leith that ran below her. The view had always frightened her – as Sam's future now did. Memories of her own past came flooding back and she thought of the many times she had walked over that very bridge with her Auntie Anna. Resting her chin in cupped hands, she wondered what life would have been like if she'd had a real mother – a mother who would have cared for her and protected her. Sure enough, she'd had Auntie Anna and maybe that was as much as she had a right to expect. Then, lifting her head boldly, she stared firmly downwards and vowed that her bairns would never be deprived of a mother's love as she had been. On the contrary, she'd strive to ensure that they'd all reach their full potential; and somehow she just knew that some of them at least would end up in the class that she should have been born into.

The sound of approaching feet made Rachel turn. She hoped it wasn't Sam back already because if so he'd surely have been unsuccessful. A warm smile lit up her face, however, when she saw Bella at her side. Beloved Bella was Auntie Anna's brother's youngest bairn who had also been brought up by Anna. She was just seven years older than Rachel herself and they'd been brought up as sisters.

"Well, are you not a sight for sore eyes? I haven't seen you in weeks," said Rachel delightedly.

"Honestly, Rachel! Sandy and me – we're run aff oor feet, these days."

"Ah well, it's grand to know the funeral trade's no dying."

"Richt enough. By April there's usually less deid customers coming in – but noo that Sandy's got this wee scheme going ..."

"Wee scheme? What wee scheme's that, for heaven's sake?"

Bella looked warily about her before whispering, "Got himself real freendly like wi' yin o the Sisters at Leith Hospital that he fancies. So when onybody dees on her ward and their folk are wonderin' aboot an undertaker she sends them ower the street to Sandy."

"Now, that's a proper dead-end way to build up a business."

Bella chuckled heartily before asking. "But here, whit are ye daein' hingin' ower the bridge with a face as lang as Leith Walk itsel'?"

"Just waiting for Sam. He's away over to Robb's to see about a job and then an apprenticeship."

"Johnny been speaking up for him tae?"

Rachel shook her head. "Johnny? How could he do that?"

"Well, wi' him being sae high up in the Union noo. He spoke up for Ella's twa and they're starting in Bertram's."

"Bertram's Engineering in Leith Walk?"

"Aye. They're just sweeping the flairs to start wi'; but if they dae weel they just micht get the chance o a trade. Mind you, with them no being ower bricht, that'll tak some daeing."

"Och, I don't know. They seem to have the backing of a father my bairns don't have. But at least my Sam can aye say he got his trade by being top of his class and me bringin' him up to speak up for himself."

Bella bristled, realising she'd said too much. Rachel was fuming now and Bella knew she had every right to be. Sam, after all, was Johnny's son and there was Johnny, doing what he was best at – being the Good Samaritan to all but his own.

"Em, does Sam no want to gang to sea like yer ain grandfaither?" said Bella brightly, trying to defuse the situation.

"He hasn't really said. But I know he's quite happy to get a trade."

"So he's got ower the fitbaw thing?"

"Don't be daft, Bella! Of course he hasn't – and he never will."

"And oor Carrie? Is she gonnae dance straight ower to Hollywood?" Bella teased, nudging Rachel with her shoulder. "Or is there a chance she'll stick aroond an' find a real job when she leaves schuil next week?"

"Right enough – she's pretty good at the dancing," Rachel

chuckled, "but not that good yet to tap-dance the whole way over the Atlantic."

Rachel stopped, suddenly aware that Bella was staring beyond her. She turned, thinking Bella was seeing Sam coming back; but it was a dirty, drunken old man staggering on and off the pavement that was holding her attention.

"Some folk never change," Bella muttered, as Gabby tried three times to navigate himself on to the bridge.

"Aye, you're right there! And know what I'm thinking? Where on earth did he get the wherewithal to be drunk this early in the day?"

"You still letting him into Dolan's?"

Rachel shook her head.

"Here, talking of that, has yon skinflint pit up yer wages yet?"

"Officially – no."

"Oh, dinnae tell me ye've taken to doctoring the whisky and takin' the money he owes ye oot o the till?"

Rachel just turned away and looked down into the murky waters again.

"Oh, my God. Do ye no ken ye could end up bein' chairged and daein' time for that?"

Rachel's head shot up "Me doctor the whisky? Dinnae be daft. He goes off back to Ireland every month and while he's away I just buy a couple bottles of the real Mackay," Rachel stopped and winked at Bella before adding in a whisper, "Bottles, you know, that fell off the back of a lorry. Then I sell them in the shop for myself. And know something? If you pour it right, you can get nearly thirty nips out of the one bottle."

By now, Gabby had got himself on to the bridge and, as he weaved his way towards them, he pulled a bottle from his pocket and took a long slug from it. He was so bleary-eyed and drunk that he was almost level with Rachel and Bella before he noticed them.

"Weel, weel! If it's nae ye twa. And ken somethin'? Aw ye need is for soddin' Anna to come back frae the deid and the three of ye could play the bloody witches in Macbeth."

"That richt?" said Bella tartly. "And what I'm wondering is, where the hell did ye get the dosh to get so bloody fu?"

"Got a few o my Post-War Credits again. Aye, they come in real handy. Mind ye, at the time they were takin' them aff ma wages I cursed them, so I did. But I'm real grateful noo for the wee lift I get when they pey them back."

"In that case, d'you no think you should be layin' something by for your funeral?" asked Rachel.

"My funeral?" Gabby exclaimed, tottering backwards. "Look, I'm no thinkin' o deein' richt noo. And when I dae dee, ye can bung me in the paupers'."

"No way will you leave my house for the paupers'."

"In that case just gie me to the students to practise on."

"Washed or unwashed?" sniggered Bella impudently.

"An' that's anither thing! When I do d-dee-d-dee ye're no to wash me," said Gabby, wagging his finger in Bella's face.

Bella pulled her head back in distaste. "That richt?" she sneered, "Well, that'll no be ony hardship, cos I'm damned particular aboot whae I wash."

Gabby made to take a lunge towards Bella then seemed to change his mind and began to lurch off. But after only a few steps he turned and sniggered, "An' if they doctors up at the in-fir-mar-ee dinnae want ma pickled liver, then just send me awa in an orange box. An', like yersel', Bella, my darlin', I'm real fussy – so it will hae to be Ootspan or Jaffa."

Bella and Rachel shrugged and looked at each other. "Here, Rachel, talkin' o folk deein'. Do ye ken Rosie's had a bad stroke yesterday?"

"No. But why would that matter to me?"

Bella shook her head disapprovingly. "Look, she does her level best by you and the bairns. She just cannae help it that she's nae match for Ella's green eyes and Johnny's ..." Bella hesitated. "Look, he's no really aw that bad, Rachel. He's just no a coper."

Rachel eyes rolled before she retorted. "Not a coper? He's not anything."

"Maybe so," Bella went on doggedly, "But where Rosie's concerned, ye should mak yer peace wi' her."

Rachel made no attempt to answer at once, which surprised Bella who had expected a mouthful in return. But Rachel was shaken and searching for the right words – words that would say she was sorry about Rosie, yet at the same time blaming her for Johnny having deserted her and the bairns.

She had almost found the right words when Bella called out, "Look, here's yer Sam comin' noo." She paused, looking lovingly towards the young man.

"Aw, God," she murmured with feeling. "Is he no a braw-lookin' laddie noo. An' ye ken something, Rachel? Gabby yased to look just like him."

"No another eejit trying to say my father was once tall, straight and athletic?"

"Weel, he wis! And that's hoo yer Mammy fell for him. But yince the booze and gamblin' took ower, she should hae done a runner."

By now Sam had bounded up to them.

"Did you get a job, son?" asked Rachel tremuously.

"Aye, I start in the office on Monday and I'm going straight into a trade in July. And I'll no need to pay the twa pounds doon at the start."

"You won't?"

"Naw, Mam, and they're gonnae pey ma nicht school fees an aw."

Rachel tried to speak but couldn't. Her beaming face said it all.

"And what trade did they gie ye, Sam?" asked Bella on Rachel's behalf.

"Engineerin'. Same as Will Fraser. I saw him when they took me roond the yaird."

"Him that plays for Restalrig Juniors?" Rachel asked dubiously.

"Aye. His Daddy wouldnae let him sign for the Hearts neither so he works in Robb's aw week and plays fitbaw on Saturdays. And when he's finished his time he's gonnae gae to sea as a ship's engineer."

"Just a minute, Sam, are you trying to say you're thinking of following him to sea an aw?"

"Aye. Soon as I finish my time, I'll be aff to the Merchant Navy."

Rachel looked from Sam to Bella. Not a word could she utter. Her eyes widened in dismay. Was her own precious Sam planning to go out of her life?

"Weel, the sea's in his blood," Bella volunteered helpfully.

"Is it?" A startled Sam looked questioningly from Rachel to Bella.

Again it was Bella who answered. "Aye, son, yer great-grandfaither, Gabby's Daddy, was a maister mariner. An expert on navigation by the stars, they said he was. An' his twa sisters were schuil teachers. Lived in a big hoose in South Queensferry, they did."

Sam said nothing but looked again from Rachel to Bella.

"Surely ye ken aw that?" Bella asked.

Sam shook his head and looked searchingly at his mother, whose face was turning a deep scarlet.

"Look, I never told you where he was from," she said defensively, "cos I didn't want you to know just how far he'd fallen."

"But I ayeways thocht yer Mammy had mairried beneath hersel'?"

"Look Sam, so as far as I'm concerned, if Gabby had been blooming King George himself, she'd still have married beneath herself."

Bella grew uneasy and began to shift from one foot to the other then quickly turned and looked over her shoulder. "Thank you. Thank you," she said, speaking into space. "I'll tell him."

She turned to Sam and said airily, "That was yer Granny speakin' to me there."

"Dinnae be daft! My Granny's alang in Admiralty Street, no standin' oot there on that oily water."

"Naw! Yer ither Granny. Yer Mammy's Mammy that's in heaven. An' she says engineerin' will dae for noo but there's something much better for ye later on." Bella looked over her shoulder again, "Oh, that was her comin' through again, just to remind me to tell ye that, whitever ye dae, ye've no to annoy the Chinese."

"Och, Auntie Bella, it's aw stuff and nonsense this talkin' to the deid. I wish ye wouldnae dae it," Sam shouted as he turned away and raced back along the road.

"Where are you off to, Sam?" Rachel called after him.

"To see my real Granny and tell her aboot my job."

"Hold on a minute, Sam. I've somethin' to tell you – I'll go with you."

Sam halted abruptly and looked at Rachel with a quizzical smile. "You're gonnae chum me to see ma Granny?"

Rachel nodded. "Aye, son, ye see – she's taken a bad turn – and I need to see her too."

Bella nodded.

It was well past tea-time when Rachel jumped into the house

ahead of Sam. "Where have you been, Mammy?" Alice complained with a scowl.

"Getting Sam started into a job and seeing to this and that," said Rachel, glancing warningly at Sam to make sure he'd do as she had asked and not mention Rosie being so very ill – nor that she'd visited her.

When Rachel had arrived in Admiralty Street she'd gone first to the Browns. Willie, now retired, was sitting by the fire smoking his clay pipe as usual. The Browns were such a nice family: decent hard-working folk who had remained very good friends, not only with Rosie all the many years they'd been her neighbours, but also with Rachel.

"If ye've come to see Rosie it's safe to gang in." Willie, who knew why Rachel had come, spoke before she could say a word.

"She's not by herself, surely?"

"Naw, naw. My Mary's wi' her till Johnny and Ella get back," Willie reassured her, taking his pipe from his mouth and spitting into the fire which sizzled and crackled.

Rachel signalled her thanks and tiptoed into Rosie's house where Mary Brown came over immediately and pulled her into a tight, comforting embrace. "Guid to see ye, Rachel. Ye're in time, lass. But only just, if I'm ony judge."

Mary let go of Rachel and went over to the bedside where she gently tapped Sam on the shoulder. "C'mon noo, son," she whispered, "Dinnae greet so sair. Naw, naw! Awa doon the stairs and keep an eye oot for yer Daddy or yer Auntie Ella comin' back. An' if they turn the corner o the street run straight back up here and get yer Mammy intae my hoose till it's safe for ye and her to leave."

Reluctantly, Sam heaved himself up off Rosie's chest but before going he stroked her forehead and put her paralysed hand to his mouth for a kiss. "Bye, Granny," he said sofly as he watched two large tears run down Rosie's face. Mary led him to the door and they both crept into the lobby.

Rachel was still pondering deeply about Rosie and wondering whether she had understood what was said to her when Carrie broke in, shouting, "Mammy, are you listening to me?"

"Aye, Carrie, what is it?"

"Just that at school this afternoon we got taken around all the places that we might find work."

"And?"

"Well, they took us to Smith's Bakery at Hawkhill. And ken that cream that goes in their cream cookies? Well, we all got a lick of it."

"You did?"

"Yeah, we did that – and if you take a job there you can have a lick any time you want. And if they don't sell all their bread by tea-time the workers get it half price."

A deep frown furrowed Rachel's brow before she spoke with undisguised irony. "Right enough, Carrie, that's exactly what I want for you. A place where you can get a lick of sour cream any time you want it and take a stale half loaf home with you every night."

Carrie pursed her lips before exclaiming "Oh, Mam, surely you knew I wasn't going to take *that* job."

"Thank goodness for that."

"No, it's Lottie Glass that's going to stick the jam in their Paris buns."

Rachel sighed. She was feeling guilty for not being with Carrie to help find her a job. But she just had to see Rosie. There were so many things …

Trying desperately to take her mind off her meeting with Rosie, she went on, "And where else did they take you?"

"Crawford's biscuits."

"Aye well, I hope you told them that you had no intention of packing biscuits either."

Carrie ignored that. "And then we went on to Duncan's chocolate factory. I saw Jean Hunt there. She puts the walnuts on top of the Walnut Whips. But I didn't fancy that. I'm really not that keen on walnuts. But I did quite like the hazelnut chocolate they gave us to sample." Carrie rambled on, unaware that Rachel was only half-listening. "Listen to this, Mam. See, in the VAT 69 Bond …"

"VAT 69 Bond? Without my permission they took you into the VAT 69 whisky bond?" fumed Rachel.

"Aye, but we didnae get any samples there because we're too young to drink whisky and when we went round we had to keep our hands in our pockets."

"Why?" Rachel demanded.

"In case she pauchled enough samples to keep Granddad goin' for a week," Sam quipped.

"That right?" Rachel retorted, 'Well, she's your sister, right enough, but she's no that bloody smart."

"And last of all, Mam, they took us to British Ropes."

"Took you to the Roperie?" thundered Rachel. "Are they mad or something?"

"What's wrong with the place?"

"Look, Carrie, you have to be a keelie to work there. Oh aye, that place is so tough that even your common school pals, Lottie and Crystal, would find it hard going."

"But Mam, there are some real nice lassies working there in their office."

"Here! Don't tell me you're thinking of working in the Roperie office?"

"Well, what I would really like to do – that's if I had a choice – is write." Carrie sighed and her eyes misted over.

"You mean, be a clerkess?"

"No, Mam, I don't want to be a clerkess – I want to write for the *Red Letter*."

Rachel sank down heavily on the chair and covered her head with her hands. "Oh no. We're not going down that road again. I've told you already, I couldn't hold my head up around here if folk thought a daughter of mine was responsible for writing the trash that's printed in that apology for a magazine."

"Well, in that case," Carrie challenged, "it might be better for you if I take the job I was offered at British Ropes today."

"What blooming job at British Ropes?" demanded Rachel.

"I told you, Mam. They have an office and they've started to make nylon ropes."

Rachel butted in before Carrie could continue. "Don't be daft, Carrie. Ropes are made from hemp and it's stockings that are made from nylon."

"Mam, I can assure you that the new whaling ropes are made out of nylon."

"That's right, Mam, they *are* made o nylon noo," Sam confirmed.

"You must be joking!"

"Naw," said Sam chortling, "Honestly, Mam, they're made o nylon because nylon is much stronger than hemp. Stronger than ony whale for that maitter."

"Okay, that might be the case, Sam. But you, Carrie, my girl, are going to work in *no* Roperie!"

"But I'll be workin' in the office."

"Look, as I've just said, I'll accept that ropes can be made out of nylon to keep the whaling industry going but there's no way you can persuade me they're made in an office."

"Just listen to me, Mam. The nylon ropes are made in a specially-built factory unit down there and the man in charge is absolutely brilliant but doesn't know how to write out the test papers, the results, the letters, the invoices – or anything like that. So they're looking for someone to be his ..."

"Secretary?" yelled Rachel in disbelief.

"Aye," Carrie nodded. "And the wage – the salary I mean – that they're paying is ten bob a week more than Oxo offered me to be an invoice clerkess."

"But why?" queried Rachel, who was still thinking there had to be a catch somewhere.

"Well – cos I'd have to work with this man and sometimes he shouts and swears when he's dictating a letter and you have to know how to find other words for his swear-words. And as he starts at seven-thirty – so will I."

"But if you don't start at nine the neighbours will all think you're just working in the factory. And I can't have that, Carrie. No. I just won't have it."

"But they'll know I'm staff because I'll be signing in, not clocking on – and I'd have every Saturday off and finish at five every night."

"And why's that so important?"

"Cos I won't get any overalls so I'll have to save up to buy some nice clothes to ..."

"Here, just a minute. There's no way you'll be keeping yourself till you leave this house to get married. And till you do that, you'll hand your wages over to me every pay-day – unopened."

"I know that, Mam, but the wages from my other job."

"What other job?"

"The usherette job I'm taking on at the Palace picture house."

"What?"

"Aye, just three nights a week and every Saturday, Mam."

"And, Mammy, ken something else?" squealed Paul, "she says she'll be able to smuggle Alice and me in for nowt after the big picture has started."

"And do you know something else, Paul?" Rachel retorted, "I think the lot of you have been watching too many bloody pictures."

"Anyway," Carrie went on as if Rachel had made no comment at all, "the money I get for being an usherette will go on tap-dancing lessons for Alice, some nice clothes, a pair of black patent-leather high heels and a bottle of Mischief perfume for myself. And know something else I'm going to buy?"

Rachel shook her head wearily.

"A bottle of that new stuff they've brought out for painting under your oxters. Honestly, Mam, Bernie was telling me, that even if you don't wash for a week you still don't hum if you use it."

"What?" Rachel exploded.

"Aye, Odo-ro-no it's called; and know something else? Even though I'm going to have to work in the Roperie and the Palace, I just know that one day I'll be a famous novelist and be so rich that I'll pay somebody like me to do the typing."

"Oh, my God," Rachel moaned as her head dropped again into her hands.

"And after I'm dead, there'll be a plaque on the outside door stating: 'Carrie Campbell wrote her first novel in this house'."

Rachel looked up at Carrie and then gazed out of the window.

"Nope, Carrie, I just can't see them."

"See what, Mam?"

"Flying pink pigs, Carrie. Flipping flying pink pigs."

CHAPTER 12
LET THERE BE LIGHT

Carrie emerged from the bathroom with a towel wrapped around her head just as Sam shouted from the kitchen, "Hey, Lady Muck, if ye've finished washin' yer hair for the second time this blinkin' week, d'ye think we could hae oor kettle back?"

"Aye," chipped in Paul who always took his cue from Sam. "Some o us would like oor breakfast."

With a well-practised air of indifference, Carrie turned back into the bathroom and lifted the kettle from the floor along with a colander and a jug from the window sill; then picked her way gingerly through a morass of wires, plaster and uprooted floorboards, back into the scullery.

"How much longer are they going to take to put in this flaming electricity?" she moaned, dumping the kettle down on the bunker top.

"Anither twa days."

"Oh, Sam, you don't mean to tell me we have to live in this blooming mess for another two days." Carrie stopped and stared down into the exposed foundations of the house. "Honestly," she continued in doleful tones, "our house looks worse than Clydebank did after the Luftwaffe were finished blitzing it eight years ago."

"And it's Hannah's week-end off and she'll be right upset if we haven't got the place properly redd up."

"Right enough, Alice! She'll be here in no time. And I bet when she sails in she'll already have had a bath at the hospital. In a real bath at that – and with real hot water."

"And she'll hae taken the shampoo off her hair with a real spray – not had to slunge it with a milk jug and colander like you've just done."

"You know, Alice, you're the only one in here that knows

what I'm putting up with."

"Oh, gie it a rest, will ye?" Sam retorted vehemently.

"That's your answer to everything, Sam. Yon electrician said four days and we'd be all shipshape again and here we are at day five and ..."

"I ken. I ken," agreed her twin. "But look, they're gonnae work overtime on it the day so by the morn the lights'll be on and we'll even hae an immersion on the hot water tank. Noo surely that's enough to straighten up yer coupon."

"Are you having me on, Sam? I mean, are you saying we'll really have an immersion heater?" Carrie squealed in disbelief.

"For sure."

"But we had hardly enough money to pay for the lights and plugs to be put in."

"That's richt, but I bunged the heid guy a couple o quid that I'd made frae selling aff the scrap yesterday."

"Oh no! No! No!" Carrie howled, waving her hands dramatically. "I just don't want to know about you selling off Robb's scrap and pocketing the money."

"So ye'll no be haein' a hot soak in the big bath the morn's nicht?"

"Well ..."

Before Carrie could finish capitulating, Hannah opened the door. Carrie, Sam, Alice and Paul all silently waited for her to scream when she surveyed the mess but, to their mutual surprise, she didn't. All she did was to execute a series of precious little pirouettes over the floor until she reached the kitchen.

"Well," she simpered, pretending to be switching on a light, "won't it be just dandy next week when you can just go 'Ping' and the light comes on."

"Aye, but right now what are we going to do?" Carrie expostulated.

"Put the kettle on and have our breakfast," declared Hannah, fishing in her shopping bag and dragging out a large brown paper bag, "And just look," she exalted, "I've brought in some of the Home Bakery's nice hot rolls. One each for us girls and two each for Sam and Paul."

"I'll get the frying pan oot for ye, Carrie. Then we can slap some black pudding and crispy bacon on the rolls," said Sam, starting to whistle merrily.

"I just love Seturdays, so I dae," enthused Paul, getting up to fetch the bacon and black pudding from the cupboard.

"You do?" teased Hannah with a mischievous smile.

Paul, now seated at the table, cupped his chin in his hands and a smug grin lit up his face before he spoke. "Aye, cos on Seturdays ye get bacon rolls for yer breakfast and then Carrie smuggles Alice an' me intae the pictures an' at the interval she sneaks us a drink on a stick."

"And is that all that happens on a Saturday?" asked Hannah, trying to keep her laughter in check.

"Naw. Forbye that," said Paul smugly, "when we get oot o the pictures, Carrie gies us the money to get a bag of chips for oorsels on our wey hame."

"Talking of the pictures, what's on at the Palace today?" Hannah asked Carrie, affectionately ruffling Paul's unruly jet hair.

"*The Third Man*. See yon Orson Wells? He's brilliant. It's been on all week and I'm still not sick of it." Carrie handed Hannah the bread knife so that she could cut open the rolls. "But here, how about me smuggling you in too?"

"Indeed not," Hannah said reprovingly, waggling the knife in Carrie's face. "I have a reputation to keep up, so I'm quite willing to pay my one and threepence. And then ... I'll let you show me to a seat in the two and threes."

"No can do!" said Carrie, mimicking Hannah's tone of voice and gestures. "The two and threes are upstairs and the boss takes the tickets there himself."

"So I'd need to pay two and threepence?"

Carrie nodded.

"That's a bit much for me, Carrie. But I just couldn't possibly sit in the one and threes. After all, somebody might see me."

Carrie, who had taken over frying the black pudding and bacon, sniggered. "Tell you what, snobby, we'll just have to compromise. You buy a one and three ticket and then I'll slip you into the one and nines."

"Aye, and in the meantime," chuckled Sam, "just slip me ower some o the black puddin' that's noo burnt to perfection."

Hannah smiled. Carrie passed the black pudding to Sam. The crisp bacon followed from the frying pan. The kettle boiled. The rolls were all filled. The beano commenced. All were happy.

When Hannah, Paul and Alice came out of the picture house, Carrie was on her tea break and stood waiting for them.

"Look," she said, "the house is such a dreadful mess. And I've got a bob or two in my pocket so how about I treat you to a fish tea in Costa's?"

"You mean a sit-in tea," squealed Alice.

"But there's always a queue out past the door on a Saturday," Hannah argued.

"Aye, but Bernie's working there."

"Bernie's working in Costa's? I thought she worked in the Bonds."

"So she does, Hannah," explained Carrie, "but she's so tired out she needs a holiday. And the only way she can afford one is to work overtime in Costa's chippie three nights a week."

"But surely if she's that tired she shouldn't be –." Hannah didn't bother going on. She knew it was useless trying to explain how illogical it was for Bernie to be working even harder if she was exhausted. Besides they'd now arrived at the chip shop and

Bernie had beckoned for them to come to the top of the queue. She showed them to the only vacant table which had a hand-written card on it plainly indicating it was reserved. It read in fact:

> *Dinnae sit here!*
>
> *Carrie's coming in and she will be in a hurry to eat her chips*

Once Alice and Paul had squeezed themselves at the end of the two benches on either side of the table, their excitement at the thought of a sit-in tea boiled over exuberantly and their gales of laughter echoed around the shop, much to the amusement of the other customers. Hannah and Carrie sat sedately at the outer places facing each other and only then did they look haughtily at Bernie who was standing ready with her pad and pencil.

"Is it just fower fish teas that ye want?" Bernie asked as she spat on the top on her indelible pencil.

Carrie nodded graciously but Paul intervened loudly. "Naw. Naw. I'm haein' a white puddin' supper covered in broon sauce – an' I'll wash it doon wi' Vimto."

"So will I," Alice chimed in.

"So, Alice, ye're gonnae hae a puddin' supper an aw?" Bernie queried spitting once more on her pencil.

"No. I want a fish tea without the tea and – Vimto instead."

Bernie looked from Carrie to Alice and then back to Carrie before laying down the pad and pencil in front of Carrie. "Here, write it oot yersel'. – Fish tea wi' nae tea!" she exclaimed. "Sure, you lot are no the full shillin'."

Silently Carrie wrote out the order and returned the pad back to Bernie who scanned it carefully.

"Did your Alice no say she wanted a fish tea wi' nae tea?"

Carrie nodded.

Bernie stuck the pad under Carrie's nose once again. "But ye've ordered her a single fish and richt enough that comes with nae tea but it also comes with nae chips nor breid and butter."

Carrie sighed and flashed her eyes to the ceiling. "She'll not be able to eat all the chips that come with a fish supper so Hannah and I will give her some off our plates."

"And what's she gonnae drink?"

Carrie pointed to the pad. "Vimto.   See? There's two ordered."

"Aw richt," said Bernie indifferently, though still not convinced that Carrie and company knew what they wanted. "But here," she insisted. "Whit aboot the buttered breid that comes wi' the fish teas?"

"We're all having that as well."

Bernie was about to argue but thought better of it and retired with the order.

"Honestly," said Carrie in disgust. "Here's us getting up in the world, sitting in to have a fish tea, and Bernie tries to take us down a peg by asking if we'll have buttered bread with our chips?"

"I know, Carrie," Hannah pronounced. "But I suppose we just have to make allowances for her. She's not in our class."

Carrie had to go back on duty at the cinema before Bernie had worked out the bill but she left money with Hannah to pay for the feast.

Hannah had just squared up and all three were about to leave when Sam dashed in.

"The cashier at the Palace telt me I'd find ye aw here. Where's Carrie?"

"She's away back to the picture house. You must have passed her," replied Hannah.

"Never saw her. But we'll just hae to leave her for the noo."

"Why?"

"Oh, Hannah, Granny's awfae bad. Dinnae think she's gonnae mak it this time."

"They've been saying that for over two years now," Hannah whispered, putting a protective arm around Alice.

"Aye, but this time they've sent for the priest to gie her the Last Rites – twice. So come on – we must get to her afore …"

"Is Daddy there?"

"Aye, he is, Hannah. Sittin' greetin' in the corner – like the useless constipated wee shite that he is."

It was nine o'clock when Carrie finished at the Palace and it was raining so heavily that when she stepped out into the street she pulled up the collar of her coat and was about to turn into Duke Street when Hannah suddenly emerged out of the shadow of the sweet shop.

"Carrie," sobbed Hannah, clutching Carrie's hand. "You have to go, right now, and see Granny. She's in a real bad way."

"No need. Mary Brown is for ever saying that, but our Granny always pulls through."

"Honestly, Carrie, you have to go right now."

"No!"

"Look, this time I've seen her and I've spoken to the doctor as well."

Taken aback, Carrie changed her tone of voice. "Are the others there?"

"No. Sam took Alice and Paul out of it. You know what Auntie Ella and Daddy are like."

"So it'll be just you and me in the middle of that bunch?"

"Sorry, Carrie, I can only walk you as far as the bus stop."

Carrie's eyes silently pleaded with Hannah.

Hannah shook her head. "I simply have to leave you – I haven't got a late pass. And you know what a bitch the Night

Sister is."

Carrie nodded her agreement – well aware that Hannah wouldn't leave her to go to Granny's all alone if she could help it.

Making their way along Great Junction Street, Carrie found herself slipping her hand through Hannah's arm. "Dear God," she said to herself. "What *will* we do without our darling Granny?"

On reaching Admiralty Street, Carrie hesitated at the entrance to the stair. Mary Brown and Jessie Mack were gossiping in hushed whispers at the foot of the stairs but stopped as soon as they saw Carrie. Seeing her fear plainly, Mary said, "C'mon, hen. I'll gang wi' ye. Ye'll be awricht if ye just haud on to me."

Upstairs, the door of Rosie's house was ajar. They could see people kneeling and praying. A priest was bending over the bed telling Rosie she was dying and that she should make her peace with God. Carrie felt shocked. Shouldn't her Granny be allowed to die in peace without her house being full of nuns and priests. And why were all those candles burning? And that mimosa, whose smell irritated her nostrils: who in the world had brought that stuff in? She knew that for the rest of her life she would always hate mimosa. Burning candles, heavy-scented mimosa and chanting prayers would forever remind her of this night – a night she had never wanted to see.

Carrie's hand was still being held tightly by Mary Brown when Auntie Ella called out, "She's sinking fast. Oh, Mammy, please hear. If I ever hurt ye I'm sorry."

Mary began to drag Carrie over to the bed but Ella was now lying prostrate over Rosie, crying out again and again to be forgiven. Carrie thought Auntie Ella and her father should both ask Rosie to forgive them because when she was last able to speak Rosie had said that she did love them both but that they had broken her heart – Ella because she had been cursed with the green eye and coveted everything she saw. Johnny's unforgivable sin was his desertion of her beloved grandchildren.

As Carrie patted her Granny's hand she became aware that her father, who was carefully avoiding eye contact with herself, was also trying to throw himself over his dying mother. Ella's two boys also felt they should be lying across Rosie but to do so they had to push Carrie aside. Time to leave, she thought.

As she turned away with Mary and left the house, Carrie realised that her father didn't want the new parish priest to know that he was married and that she, Carrie, was his daughter. Or that she was Rosie's blood granddaughter, who was being denied the right to say goodbye to her precious grandmother.

Silently stumbling into the lobby, Mary insisted on taking Carrie into her house where she allowed her to sob. And sob. And sob.

"Weel may ye greet, hen," said Mary, patting Carrie's head compassionately. "But ken somethin'? Ye an' yer brithers and sisters, alang with Davie, were the true loves of her life. The very reason her hard-wrocht life was worth livin'."

When Carrie arrived home in Learig Close the house was in darkness. It was eleven o'clock and she assumed they'd all gone to bed. She had just stepped in the door, however, when Sam called out.

"Let there be licht – and there was licht!" He flicked the switch and the house became illuminated.

"I thought they wouldn't be finished until tomorrow." Carrie muttered.

"Persuaded them to work on, I did. So what do ye think?"

Tears welled up in Carrie's eyes. "Sam …"

"Dinnae greet," pleaded Sam. "Look, I've heated the water for a bath for ye. Ye can hae a soak in the big bath richt noo." Turning his face from her and staring into the louping flames of the fire, he reiterated, "But *please* dinnae greet."

"And Hannah left you a Radox bath cube," Alice blurted out, pressing the cube under Carrie's nose. "Smell it. It's called Ashes of Roses."

Carrie sniffed the bath cube and shook her head as the tears splashed down. "Ashes of Roses, is it?" she said half-hysterically. "Love roses, so I do."

"Noo, look what ye've done, Alice. And I just didnae want her to greet. D'ye no realise – I can staun onythin' but yin of ye greetin'."

Alice went to leave but Carrie grabbed her in a fierce embrace. "Don't worry, Sam. I won't cry any more and we're not going to Granny's funeral either cos ..."

She was about to tell them about what had happened but Sam interrupted her. "Ye're bloody richt we're no," he exploded. "They can go and find some ither puir beggers to insult."

"Yeah, but we'll all go later on in the afternoon and say our goodbyes then to Granny." Carrie paused before going on softly, "You do know she's not going to be buried with Granddad in Seafield? She's going to the Catholic cemetery at Mount Vernon." Carrie turned her gaze away from Sam, Alice and Paul. "Seems funny to me," she remarked, "that Granddad and Granny never let religion separate them in life and now in death others have decided that they should lie miles apart."

Sam, Paul and Alice all stood silent.

Two weeks later Carrie met Sam in Great Junction Street while she was out buying a bag of chips for her tea.

"Pictures busy, Carrie?" asked Sam.

"Aye. Just out for ten minutes. But here, where are you off to?"

"Seeing it's Hogmanay I'm on my wey to see Uncle Davie."

Carrie almost let her chips fall. "He's not there, Sam! Did you not know? Hannah and me went along this morning and Mary

Brown told us he'd given the house up."

"But why?"

Carrie kicked some rubbish lying at her feet and shrugged. "Seems he's now staying with Ella."

"Naw. He couldnae go and bide wi' her. He's a proddie, like us."

"Look, Sam. Don't blame him. The poor soul just couldn't live on his own and our Dad wouldn't go and stay with him."

"An' whar's my wee stool? The yin my Granny yased to save pennies in for me?"

"Forget the stool, Sam. In fact, forget everything that was ever in that house."

"Why?"

"Because our dear loving Auntie Ella – took it all for Mark and Tony."

"Ye saying oor Dad didnae even hae the guts to put up a fight for my wee stool – or for just yin wee reminder of our Gran for us?"

Carrie shook her head.

"What kind of blasted folk are they?"

"Good Christians," answered his sister. "But, Sam, like Hannah said today, these wee keepsakes are only bric-à-brac. The one thing they can't take from us, the most important thing, is that her blood runs through our veins."

CHAPTER 13
GIVING UP THE GHOST

It was a cold February in 1952 and all the children were enjoying Rachel being at home. It suited them to come home to a warm, comforting fire and to find their tea on the table. Carrie, who was now going on eighteen and at five feet five the same height as Hannah, swore that whenever she turned into the street the "Ah! Bisto" aroma of Rachel's mince, tatties and dough-boys would assail her nostrils. Instead of walking she would race along the street to relish the delicacy.

To be truthful, Rachel had also enjoyed the last two weeks. Not only had she managed to have things all redd up for the family coming home every day, but she was able to treat her neighbours to the wholesome smell of bleach and carbolic as she scoured every neuk and cranny in the house. Even the glory-hole, where a store of logs and coal was kept, along with dusters, brushes, indeed anything she wanted kept out of sight, got a right going-over. Her final task had been to whitewash the glory-hole and now poor Sam was having to clean his football boots in the garden before tossing them in there.

Rachel's only problem was that she was now out of a job. It had come as a great shock to her when Paddy Doyle had forced four weeks' wages into her hands a fortnight ago. It turned out he'd heard that Edinburgh Corporation had condemned the pub and the surrounding flats on the Broad Pavement. They were to be demolished and replaced by a multi-storey block – a ten-floor skyscraper in the shape of a banana! When Rachel heard of the proposal she said with incredulity, "A skyscraper in the shape of a banana in Leith? How the hell will the bairns ken exactly whose jam piece it is when it comes winging down from they dizzy heights?"

What she really couldn't understand, however, was why

Paddy should have thrown in the towel so early? After all, the Corporation had condemned Admiralty Street over twenty years ago and here they were in 1952 with some folk still awaiting the bulldozers. The other thing that puzzled Rachel was why Myles Dolan and Paddy, who had been mates for years, couldn't have sorted something out between them? But whatever the problem was she found herself out of a job.

That hadn't bothered Rachel unduly because she assumed she had nothing else to do but find herself another job in a bar. However, smart as she always looked, it seemed that the customers, in all the establishments she applied to, liked their pints served by nubile, blonde twenty-year-olds. There was just no place for an experienced forty-four year old, even if she could make a thirty-five year old look ancient.

Mulling over her problem, Rachel reluctantly concluded that she should try for another week at least to get a decent job. And if nothing came up she would then – and only then – consider Grace's proposal that she should apply to the Eastern General Hospital for a cleaner's job.

Nevertheless, there were more than a few problems with that solution. First, she knew that once she did take a cleaning job there would be no chance of her climbing back up the ladder. Second, it was very easy to hold your head up when you were climbing up the ladder but hellish hard when you were falling off it. Last but not least, Hannah was now about to qualify as a Staff Nurse. She'd done so well in fact that she was the top nurse on her course and would have the pick of the jobs that were available. And as luck would have it, there was a vacancy for a Staff Nurse at the Eastern General and if Hannah took that job Rachel couldn't afford to let her down by being a cleaner in the same place. No. That certainly wouldn't do!

Rachel sighed as she looked out of the window at the thickly falling snow and she conceded that the other problem – the more pressing – was that she had to be earning; and earning more than in the past because Paul needed to be kept for another six years. Why she wondered, had she allowed Hannah, Sam and Carrie to pressure her into letting him go to Leith Academy. All three had promised they'd chip in to give him the chance. Had they hell! Hannah spent her cash on deodorants, nylons and feeding the poor. All Carrie could be relied upon to do was to pay for Alice's dancing lessons and bring home ice cream cones, fish suppers, bottles of red kola – and once a Mars bar that she cut equally into six bits, making sure that she and Alice got the chocolate-coated ends. As for Sam – well, Sam could be relied upon – but at what price? It had never ceased to amaze her that Sam had never once been lifted by the police.

The snow continued to fall heavily. Rachel, deep in thought, was still gazing out of the scullery window when the front door opened and in stomped Alice.

"Oh, Mammy, what a pig-awful day."

Wistfully, Rachel turned to look at her youngest daughter, who was now a willowy sparkling blue-eyed blonde, and tartly remarked, "Aye, so it is. But that doesn't give you the right to forget to wipe your feet on the doormat before coming in here." Rachel gave a backward jerk of her thumb. "So, my lady, if you don't mind, get back out there and get it done."

Alice grumbled loudly and stamped her feet on the mat, took off her Wellington boots and bounced back into the living room – but, since the floor was wet from her first attempt to come into the house, her stocking soles skidded all the way along the highly polished linoleum before catapulting her into the scullery.

"Damn and blast!" she swore, picking herself up and rubbing her bruised backside. "Know something?"

"That you'd better watch your language?"

"No, that life was a lot less dangerous here when we had nowt. That polished lino is a death-trap. Only last week poor old

Granddad tripped over the fireside rug and banged his head on that new-tiled fireplace."

Rachel calmly opened the bread bin and took out a well-fired loaf that she began to saw with a bread knife. "C'mon, Alice hen," she coaxed, "I'll make you some nice toast and tea."

"Oh, great," said Alice, drooling at the thought of the hot crusty toast dripping with fresh butter. Then she seemed to have second thoughts. "But, well, oh, maybe I should give it a bye."

"What for?"

"Well, you know how Carrie got me that job modelling clothes for the Economic Warehouse tick-shop down in Constitution Street?" replied Alice, running her hands proudly over her nubile figure.

"Aye. Both of you are going."

"Well, Carrie says they've chosen the stuff we're going to wear – so we'd better not put on any weight till after the show."

Rachel lifted the slice of bread she had been going to toast for Alice and she looked at it quizzically. "Right enough," she agreed, "this one wee slice would turn you into a right two-ton Tess."

Before Alice was about to say that maybe she could eat just one slice of toast a loud bang on the outside door silenced her.

"You answer that," Rachel said, turning to heat the teapot.

At the door Alice was confronted by a big police sergeant who bellowed, "This the Campbell's' hoose?"

Alice nodded.

"Your Mammy in?"

Gaping, Alice nodded again.

"I'd like a wee word wi' her."

Still dumbfounded, Alice nodded yet again while the sergeant pushed past and strode into the scullery.

"What the hell do *you* want?" Rachel snarled. In reality she was terrified at the thought that Sam, who'd been very lucky never to be caught and charged by the police, had at last landed in trouble.

"Just a wee word wi' ye," said the sergeant soothingly. "Just ye hae a wee seat."

Rachel was about to comply meekly when the door opened again and in bounded Sam and Carrie.

"Mammy! Wud ye believe it that this daftie, oor Carrie, was oot there playing snowbaws with the wee Stoddarts?" bellowed Sam giving his sister a dunt in the chest.

Rachel looked at Carrie, thinking, "Where have I gone wrong with this lassie? Surely at her age she should be behaving with some decorum. But no. Here she is, her coat covered in snow, her good woollen gloves sodden, her hair dripping wet and her high-heeled shoes squelching." But before Rachel could tackle Carrie on why she wasn't wearing Wellingtons, the sergeant went over and slapped Sam on the back.

"That was some gemme ye played on Seturday. Fower goals, eh? Ye should try and get yersel' a job where ye can yaise yer footbaw skills."

A deep sigh escaped Rachel and she rolled her eyes upwards before demanding witheringly. "Are you another idiot that's come here to fill this laddie's head with nonsense – or is there an official reason for you trespassing?"

"Oh, aye," the sergeant nodded. "Thanks for remindin' us."

Rachel braced herself. She'd never quite worked out how she would handle being told that Sam had been found selling nuts and bolts – most of which she was sure had fallen out of his and Carrie's heads. However, when the Sergeant motioned for her to sit down again she knew it was more serious than nuts and bolts.

"Ye are Rachel Campbell, née Forbes?"

Alice, now standing protectively behind her mother, nodded and said, "Aye, she is."

"So ye'd be the next-of-kin," the sergeant said, taking out his notebook and flipping over the pages, "to yin Gabriel Forbes who bides at ..."

Sam muttered under his breath. "The Winter Palace for the Destitute."

The sergeant went on, reading from his notes, "... the Model Lodging Hoose in Parliament Square, Leith?"

"Aye," replied Alice, nodding her agreement.

"Then I'm sorry to report that he's noo ..." the sergeant hesitated and adopted a suitably pious look. "... is noo temporarily detained in Ward One at Leith Hospital."

"Drunk and incapable again?" said Sam warily.

"Naw, son," the sergeant replied. "This time it's mair serious. He's sober and he's raving."

"That's serious. Very serious," said Rachel quietly. "But we'll have something to eat first and then Sam, Carrie and me'll go down and see him."

Rachel took a deep breath as she and the twins strode into the hospital. There was something very comforting and reassuring about the hygienic smell of carbolic and so she made her way almost serenely up the corridor towards the wards. Ward One was at the far end of the corridor on the right-hand side and when Rachel and the children arrived there a nurse barred their way – stating, as she looked at her watch, that the visiting hour wasn't until seven oclock.

"But we're here to see Gabriel Forbes," explained Rachel.

"Maybe so," the nurse said primly, "but as he's on the critical list only his immediate next-of-kin are permitted to see him."

"That's me," Rachel replied, making to push past.

"Really?" said the nurse, but nevertheless directed them to a side ward where Gabby lay propped up on pillows.

Nurse left, quietly closing the door behind her. Carrie, Sam and Rachel all looked at each other in amazement. There was Gabby lying in a bed with the sheets and blankets so tightly tucked around him that he was unable to move. As Carrie well knew, it didn't matter to Sister or Matron if your circulation was cut off and you were in danger of getting gangrene, just as long as the bed looked immaculately tidy.

Gabby lay there as they'd never seen him before – clean-shaven, dressed in a stiff white nightshirt and looking more emaciated than they had ever realised.

They were still trying to come to terms with this when Gabby half-opened his eyes and stretched out a scrawny hand. "Rachel hen. Rachel hen," he gasped. "Thank God ye've come!" Gabby struggled for breath. "Ye've got to get me oot o here."

"Out of here?" exclaimed Rachel. "I'm still trying to figure out how the hell you got yourself in here."

"Collapsed in Dolan's pub, so I did. But listen, Rachel, I *hiv* tae get oot o here," Gabby pleaded, "I just cannae abide that midden o a Sister." Gabby stopped to get his breath. "Which minds me, Carrie hen – ye gae and get the polis and then yer Mammy can hae her chairged." Gabby's breath was now rasping and he waited a full minute before continuing, "wi' theft, arson and ..." he struggled for breath again before uttering ominously, "... *cruelty!*"

"Theft, arson and cruelty!" exclaimed Rachel. "And how in the name of heavens did she manage all that?"

Gabby gasped his answer. "Well, when I got brocht in – first thing – she – had me stripped naked." Lifting his head from the pillow he sought for Carrie's hand and tears welled up in his eyes. "Aye, aff came ma coat, ma jaiket, ma muffler, ma jumpers – aw three o them – ma shirt – ma vest ..."

"They'd need to do that to examine you," Rachel interrupted impatiently. Gabby flung his head back on the pillow and groaned as she went on. "And, as no one'll want them, you'll soon get them back."

These ironic words of comfort only made Gabby more agitated and his breathing become still more erratic.

"That's where ye're bluidy well wrang," he wheezed. "Didn't the auld midden kick them oot the door and then tell the porter to burn the lot. That's right, Carrie hen," cried Gabby, who was now sobbing openly. "The bloody bitch burnt aw my claes. Didnae even leave me wi' a hankie."

"Right," said Rachel complacently, thinking to herself, "Good! That's what I've wanted to do to them for years."

To Gabby, she said, "That takes care of the theft and arson. But, know something? I think you'll have a hard job, a hellish hard job, convincing anybody that it amounted to cruelty?"

Gabby struggled again to speak. "The cruelty bit, Miss Know-all, was wheeling me mither-naked intae the bathroom and then me bein' ..." He was overtaken by a fit of stertorous coughing before he could continue, "... bein' flung in a bath, doused wi' raw carbolic an' then bein' scoured wi' a deck scrubber."

"Oh, that's just awful, Mam," whimpered Carrie. "Can you no do something about it?"

"No, Carrie, I can't. The nurses are only doing their job."

Rachel picked up her bag gingerly and cautiously brought out a bottle. Simultaneously, the door opened and Sister flounced in.

"Mrs Campbell," she announced in the sternest of tones, "that paper bag that you're just about to slip to your, em, father, wouldn't be concealing a bottle of alcohol, would it?"

A deep red glow suffused Rachel's face. "It's just a wee dram, Sister. You see, he's been a heavy drinker all his life."

Sister snorted contemptuously. "That's all too evident. In here, however," and she hesitated before continuing with every 'r' imperiously rolled, "rules are rules and regulations are regulations and the Demon Drink is not permitted on *my* ward."

Gabby struggled to grab hold of Sister, failed and had to be content with a heartfelt imprecation. "Wi' ye, ye frustrated ugly auld coo, there's nae drinkin'. An' nae livin'." He stopped to gather enough breath for the final insult. "See, if ye'd hae been in the murderin' Gestapo ye'd hae been drummed oot for sheer bluidy cruelty."

"Maybe so," the Sister responded coolly, pushing Gabby back on his pillows and pulling the blankets even tighter about him. "And might I remind you to kindly moderate your language while in this hospital?"

"Look, Sister," pleaded Rachel, "surely it's not good for him to be cut off the drink so sudden? I mean it might – er – well – finish him off!"

Sister's only response was to toss her head. Clearly, in her opinion, Gabby's demise would be no great loss.

Three days later, Carrie stood at Robb's Shipyard gate ostensibly waiting for Sam. And when Will Fraser came out he only told Carrie what she already knew – that Sam had taken time off to help Rachel who'd been upset at being asked by the warden of the Model Lodging House to clear out Gabby's locker. The man wasn't really insensitive: it was just that were more homeless people in Leith than there were beds. And everybody recognized that it was highly unlikely that Gabby would ever go back to lodge there – even though he did seem a little better.

Taking time off to help Rachel was natural for Sam. What he could never cope with was Rachel being distressed; so before she could dry her eyes he'd volunteered to go down to the Lodging House and clear out Gabby's belongings. Before he left, however, he asked Rachel if he could borrow a suitcase from the neighbours and she had replied grimly, "You won't need a suitcase, Sam," she said, handing him a brown paper carrier bag. "All his worldly goods that haven't ended up in the furnace will go into this."

Will Fraser again asked Carrie why she didn't know about Sam having taken time off. She blushed slightly and stammered "I – just forgot. You see, I'm so upset about my Granddad. Brought back memories of my Granny who died a couple of years back."

"Can I walk you part of the way?" Will asked sympathetically.

Carrie immediately consented. That had been her objective all along but she wouldn't have had the courage if Sam hadn't told her that Will thought Carrie had the loveliest legs he'd ever seen – even better than Betty Grable's million-dollar ones.

But Sam had angered Carrie by telling Will he was never to look at her legs again – or if he did, he'd end up in bits like the last guy Sam had warned. This was all because Carrie and Alice both had legs like Rachel's – absolutely perfect. Carrie knew they were because Alice and she were always carrying out the "perfect leg test" by taking three half-crowns (that is, if they were lucky enough to have three) and place them between their ankles, knees and thighs. If they stayed in place, that was the all the proof they needed that their legs were indeed perfect.

By the time Carrie had stopped thinking about the perfect leg test, she and Will were walking together along the pavement. They had gone only a few yards when Will felt for Carrie's hand – but not wanting him to think her a fast piece she pulled her hand away and thrust it safely into her coat pocket. Then she wondered whether she'd been a bit hasty in taking her hand out of Will's, because it had felt so nice there – when wallop! She bumped into something hard and solid.

"What idiot put that there?" she cried, rubbing her forehead.

"That lamp post?" asked Will. "It's always been there."

"Has it? I've never seen it before."

"Maybe you should be wearing your glasses." Will

chuckled.

Carrie was furious. Everybody knew that boys, especially those as dishy as Will, didn't make passes at girls who wore glasses. And she had only taken hers off to encourage Will to make a pass at her. Tossing her head, she retorted, "I'm not wearing them cos I only need them for reading."

"Aye, and for seeing lamp posts," chortled Will.

Carrie felt her face burning with embarrassment and she began to stomp off. But before she was out of earshot Will called out, "Hang on a minute, Carrie. I want to ask you something."

She wheeled about to face him again. "Like what?" she yelled.

"Just this – can you dance?"

"You crazy or something?"

Will, who had now caught up with Carrie, shook his head. "No. It's just that I need a pretty girl, with or without glasses, to go with me to the Highland Ball next Friday night."

"You want *me*," Carrie had to gulp before she could go on, "to go with *you* to the Highland Ball on Friday?"

Will vigorously nodded his assent.

Carrie smiled but then bit her lip.

"You do have a ball gown, don't you?" asked Will, worried that Carrie was going to renege.

"One?" Carrie retorted nonchantly. "Don't be silly! I've got two. Which one d'you want me to wear – the pink or the blue?"

Rachel was seated at the table deep in thought. She'd been there for ages, having had yet another row with Paul and Alice. Paul had been cleaning Sam's footballs boots to earn a couple of bob but that morning he'd decided not to clean them in the entry but to do his chore on the floor in the scullery – on the very floor that Rachel had just finished scrubbing. Paul had thought it was far too cold to be cleaning boots outside and was surprised when his mother picked them up and tossed the offending objects into the stairwell. Having got rid of the boots, she turned her attention to Paul. Grabbing him by the scruff of the neck, she indicated by a curt nod that he should follow the boots – and out he stumbled.

Rachel banged the door shut with a sigh of despair, hoping she'd not been too hard. Her Paul was just so thrawn. How often had she told him he was not to have the nerve to take after his father. But that had made no difference. Oh, no. Of all her children it was only Paul who mirrored Johnny – the same jet black hair, slate-grey eyes, olive skin and tall lean figure. The only things Paul had taken from his mother's side of the family were his intelligence and his vaulting ambition.

Rachel was still thinking about Paul when the door was opened – this time by Alice, who waltzed in looking as if she'd stuck her fingers in an electric socket. Her normally straight blonde hair (one of Alice's best assets in Rachel's opinion) was now a mass of reeking corkscrew curls. Her mother could only look on in horror as Alice gazed admiringly in the mirror, preening herself all the while.

"Mam," she said ecstatically. "Now, be honest: What do you think of my new bubble-cut? You know bubble-cuts are all the rage right now."

Rachel could guess pretty accurately who was responsible for Alice now looking like some Rose Street tart. Carrie! Carrie, who seemed to have nothing better to do with her money than indulge Alice's lunatic whims. What Rachel had never been able to understand was why Alice couldn't accept that her hair was not curly – or how lucky she was to have straight blonde hair that was classy, just like Hannah's and Veronica Lake's.

Once Alice realised that Rachel was not going to fall head over heels for her new hair-do, she stormed out of the house to go and see her pal, Florrie. Alone again, Rachel wondered if everybody who had to bring up bairns had the same problems that she seemed to be having. She had just settled down to ponder the question further when a loud knock came to the outside door. It was the police sergeant again.

"Och, don't tell me you're back to talk to Sam about blooming football again?"

The sergeant shook his head and Rachel indicated that he should come in. "Wish I was here aboot yer braw laddie," he said gravely. "But naw, it's aboot yer Dad."

"Has he had a relapse?"

"Naw. Mair than that – he's deid."

Rachel sank down on her chair again. "But yesterday he was on the mend," she protested.

"Aye," the sergeant nodded. "So much so that early this morning he decided to mak a run for it. Only thing was he hadnae realised he'd been moved to an upstairs ward and then when he leapt oot the windae ..." The sergeant grimaced before adding. "Well, it's a fifteen fit drap into the hospital gairdens frae Ward Three."

"Are you saying he broke his neck?"

"Naw. Naw. To tell the truth, he micht hae got ower his faw but when they got him back inside and the Sister insisted on dumping him back in the bath – well – he just gave up the ghost, didn't he?"

CHAPTER 14
BURNING ISSUES

Sam was at the bunker sorting through Gabby's things when he came across an old battered photograph of three well-dressed, cherub-like children standing on a highly polished wooden staircase in a large house.

"Who are they?" he asked Rachel who was busy rolling out scones.

Rachel paused and dusted her hands on her pinny before taking the photograph from Sam. "That's your Granddad and his two brothers at their home in South Queensferry."

"Awa!" exclaimed Sam. "Are ye tellin' me he really did come frae a posh backgroond like that and ended up like this?" Sam pushed Gabby's few belongings along the bunker before picking them up distastefully and throwing the lot into the bucket.

"Aye," his mother answered. "And not only do you have his good looks but he's the one you got your athletic prowess from."

"Whit d'ye mean?"

"Just that in his youth he was a star, Sam."

"A fitbawer?"

"No. But he could run and sprint like a cheetah," Rachel replied wistfully. "Oh aye, he could even have won the Powderhall Sprint."

Sam was looking at his mother as if she were mad. "Ye mean the big race they run every New Year's Day doon at the dug stadium?"

Rachel nodded as she looked longingly down at the photograph again.

"But if he was that guid, whae beat him?"

"Oh, he wasn't beaten, Sam. He took a bribe – sold out."

Sam's jaw dropped. He was speechless but noted that Rachel

ran her hand gently over the photograph before placing it carefully behind the gas meter beside all her other unredeemed pledges.

She began to roll the scones again when the outside door was flung open and Carrie bounced in.

"Oh, Mam," she cried, "I can't get it out of my mind."

"Well, Carrie, these things happen," Rachel murmured.

"Is there nothing we can do about it?"

Rachel looked perplexed. Carrie had some strange notions but imagining they could somehow resurrect Gabby was going just a bit too far, even for her, so all Rachel said was, "Well, to be truthful I'm not sure that I want to."

"So you'd rather see me end up an old maid?" Carrie continued.

"What on earth are you talking about?" Rachel asked, more puzzled than ever, as she got out the girdle to begin baking the scones.

"Will Fraser fancying me, of course."

"Fancyin' ye? But is that no what ye've ayeways wanted?" sniggered Sam. "Efter aw, ye've been daeing five-mile detours just to get him to notice ye."

Carrie's eyes misted over. "And he has, at last, Mam. He's even asked me to go with him to the Highland Ball in Mackies on Princes Street next Friday."

"What's the problem then?"

"Just that he asked me if I had a ball gown and I told him –." Carrie hesitated and carefully distanced herself from her mother, "– that I had two."

"And where the hell are you going to get *one,* let alone two?" fumed Rachel.

Carrie sidled over towards Rachel again. "Well, Mam, if you could lend me a fiver there's a lilac one in the Store sale that would do."

"A fiver for a frock that you'll no be able to wash and wear again?"

Carrie nodded. Sam giggled. Rachel took a deep breath, suddenly realising that Carrie didn't know about Gabby.

"Look, Carrie," she whispered. "Come and sit down. I've something to tell you."

"Like what?"

"Do you know who's dead?"

"Aye! The King ."

"Not just the King, Carrie, but your Granddad too."

Carrie began to sob. "Oh no!"

Before Rachel could comfort her, Sam butted in. "And ken whit? He bocht it tryin' to get yin last dram."

"That's enough, Sam!" Rachel retorted sharply. "'Don't you realise that we're going to have to come up with the wherewithall to bury him?"

Before Sam could speak there came a loud knock at the door. "Right, Sam. Go and see who it is and try to come back with some good news for us."

Sam cautiously opened the door and found Bella, who pushed straight past him and was in the scullery before Rachel knew she was there.

"Whit a beezer o a day!" Bella exclaimed, rubbing her hands together enthusiastically.

Rachel didn't respond. Instead she glared at Sam and hissed, "D'you ever listen to a word I say?"

Sam repressed a giggle with difficulty.

"And hoo are ye, Rachel hen?" Bella went on. "Ye ken, as soon as I heard, I just kent ye would be needin' me. Mind ye, did I no tell ye last week, when I saw that auld craw sittin' on tap o yer roof, that there would be a passin' for sure."

"You did?" said Carrie hysterically.

Ignoring her, Bella carried on. "And, Rachel hen, yer Mammy

came through to me last nicht and asked me to be on haun to comfort ye. An' here was I just comin' alang the street, there the noo, when she came through again just to say ye've nae tae worry as yer Dad's arrived safe and sound."

"That right?" Rachel said with some contempt. "Oh, what wouldn't I have given to be a fly on the wall when my mother got her hands on him again?"

Carrie felt it was time for her to speak but all she could think of was, "Auntie Bella, you don't happen to know anybody that has a ball gown I could borrow?"

Aghast, Bella stared at Carrie. "Oh, hen," she gasped, "ye dinnae wear a ball goon to a funeral. Naw. Naw. A wee black frock is whit ye gang in."

Sam and Carrie had better things to do than cope with Auntie Bella and her ravings so both went out – Sam to meet some mysterious man who wanted to discuss a wee business proposal, and Carrie to cry on Bernie's shoulder about the ball gown. That left Rachel and Bella to do what they were both best at: sitting down with a cup of tea and having a good crack.

Today, however, they were lost for words and Bella, who seemed deep in thought, was idling stirring her tea when she noted that Rachel's tightly clenched fists were constantly rubbing her eyes.

"Ye can greet aw ye want, Rachel, noo the bairns are oot o the road. I ken, as well as ony, that it's a sad day when ye lose yer faither," Bella reassured her, surreptitiously adding a large spoonful of sugar to her tea.

Within seconds Rachel's eyes blazed and she fired back at Bella: "You really think so, do you?"

Bella shifted uneasily in her seat and took yet another spoonful of sugar. "Well, maybe no in your case." And when Rachel made no response other than to offer Bella another warning glower, she continued. "Just to please ye, I went ower to the hospital mortuary and laid him oot. And efter I washed and shrouded him I even pinned a wee bunch of blue violets to his chest."

"That so?" mocked Rachel. "Well, all I've got to say is that they'll be a fine match for his big purple nose."

"Aw, Rachel, dinnae be so sarcastic. The man's deid an' there was some guid in him."

"Like what?"

Bella shrugged. "Like er … Like, just gie me a meenit to think!"

"Oh, Bella, be fair. He died as he lived, a disorganised bloody burden that I've had to take care of."

Bella sniffed and looked away from Rachel, who promptly moved the sugar bowl out of reach.

"And anither thing," said Bella turning back to face Rachel again. "Ye'll hae to tell Johnny."

"Tell Johnny?" cried Rachel so shrilly that her voice reverberated round the scullery. "And why the hell should I tell Johnny that my father's dead? He wouldn't even give a shit if it was me that was dead."

Bella stretched out an arm in attempt to retrieve the sugar bowl. "Ye're wrang there, Rachel. When I telt Johnny aboot Gabby being sae ill that he was likely to dee, he said he'd gae to his funeral. Though – if he was strictly honest – he'd rather gang to yours!"

Rachel shook her head. Why, she wondered, did she put up with Bella? Then she confessed to herself that she knew why. She was truly indebted to this woman who had shared a bed with her when they were just bits of bairns. Indebted to her moreover for her loyalty in always putting out a hand to help, even though she usually ended up making things worse.

"Look, Bella," she said at last, "I've more to worry me the day than Johnny. Don't you realise I don't know what I'm going to do about Gabby?"

"Aw, Rachel, wi' aw that's been goin' on, I forgot to tell ye Sandy's comin' up."

At that very moment a loud knock at the door startled both women but within seconds Bella relaxed and announced: "That'll be him noo. Gonnae tak ower aw the arrangements, he is." And she rose to go to the front door.

"But why?" demanded Rachel.

"Weel, wi' me workin' there and oor Auntie Anna haein' trained him," Bella shouted back, "he's as guid as faimily."

Bella returned followed by Sandy, a tall, gaunt man with sunken cheeks, wearing a long mourning coat and tall lum hat. Rachel knew that Alice would be terrified if he was still in the house when she came in because folks rightly said that Sandy's dead customers looked healthier than he did.

"Sad day, Rachel. Sad day when you lose yer faither," he said mournfully into Rachel's ear as took a seat at the table. Then he added comfortingly, "Well … sometimes death comes as a freend, ye ken."

"Like a wee fly cup, Sandy?" Bella offered on Rachel's behalf.

Sandy's eyes searched around the room. "Ony embalming fluid to gang in it?"

Rachel reached up behind the soap powder and brought out a bottle of whisky which she laid on the table. Bella picked it up instantly and poured a good dram into each of the three cups of tea before lifting one cup to her own mouth and greedily sucking in the warm pungent liquid.

"My, but that's real guid," she said smacking her lips with satisfaction.

"And so it should be! It's the real Mackay," Rachel responded, as she also took a long slug of the medicinal restorative.

Bella set her cup down, lifted up the whisky bottle and

squinted at the label. "Naw, Naw. It's no the real Mackay. See, here it says, Glenfiddich Twelve Year Old." She then turned the bottle around, stared at the back label, and gasped, "Oh, here. Whit's this?"

Rachel bent over and grabbed the bottle out of Bella's hand. "So if it was on its way to Venezuela and got lost in the docks, so what?"

Then she switched her attention to Sandy. "Sandy," she asked plantively, "what am I to do about Gabby?"

"Cremate him. I mean whit else would ye dae wi' him?"

"All I want is to have him put away nice and tidy."

Sandy smiled graciously and patted Rachel's hand. "Nae problem. Ye ken fine I'll dae aw that for ye."

"No problem is it? And will it still no be a problem when you know I cannae afford it?"

Sandy sucked in his lips thoughtfully as he took out a notepad and pencil from his pocket and started to scribble furiously on the pad. Once finished he gave a self-satisfied grin. "Oh, but ye *can* afford it. See!" He pushed the notepad under Rachel's nose. "Wi' a wee bit o faimily discount it's only gonnae set ye back thirty-five quid."

"Thirty-five quid!" squealed Rachel in dismay, sending her chair toppling as she jumped up. "But I've only got eighteen pounds coming from the Pearl."

"Gabby left nae siller?"

Rachel shook her head. "Silver? He didn't even leave any brass." She paused before adding in a voice thick with sarcasm, "Unless, of course, you count his brass neck."

"In that case," said Sandy brusquely, tucking his notebook away in his pocket, "just bung him in the paupers."

Rachel spun round and her head shot up defiantly. "Cannae do that. You know fine he did that to my mother and I've lived with the disgrace of it ever since."

While Rachel and Sandy were arguing, Bella had begun to replenish her cup with tea and whisky. "What a state ye're gettin' yersel' intae ower nothin', Rachel," she said benignly. "Ye're forgettin' aboot the death grant, so ye are. And that alang wi' whit ye've got coming ..."

"Death grant?" Rachel interrupted. "What death grant? Don't you realise he's too auld to qualify."

"Richt enough," Bella reluctantly conceded, before looking up over her shoulder and nodding to some unseen presence. "That was him just comin' through to say he was ayeways too everythin' for onythin'."

Rachel and Sandy both shook their heads and sat in stunned silence. Bella, however, took no notice of their bewilderment and went on to looking over her shoulder. "Oh here, wait a meenit though! Auntie Anna's just come through an aw; an' she says, Rachel, ye've to ask Sandy hoo aboot payin' up the difference at five bob a week."

This unexpected advice from the other world restored Sandy's voice. "B – b – but Anna kens fine I dinnae dae funerals on the never-never." He gulped three times before turning his attention to Rachel and confiding in professional tones, "Ye see, there's nae comeback frae the deid. So it's a waste of time tryin' to sue them."

"That right?" And Rachel gave Sandy a covert wink. "Well, it just might be that my Auntie Anna – who taught you all you know about the funeral business and sorted out all your wee ..." Rachel deliberately hesitated and winked again at Sandy. "your wee problems – that she'll think it'll be in everybody's interest for you to make a small concession in my case."

Sandy swallowed hard, put two of his fingers inside his collar and stretched his scrawny neck. Rachel knew he was wondering how many of the rumours she'd heard about what he and that wee nurse in Casualty had been up to in the mortuary? And if she thought it explained why the beauty spot under the nurse's bairn's right eye was identical to the dirty wee black mole under his.

After much deliberation, Sandy announced, "Aye, aw richt then. But richt noo I've to gae and see about a big bug's funeral, so I'll tell ye what." Sandy drew out his notebook again and licked his lips before writing a brief note. "We'll dae Gabby in Seafield Crematorium, let's say, on Wednesday at fower o'clock."

"Four o'clock? That's just perfect," Rachel almost sang. "Cos that means the bairns will only need two hours off work without pay to go to it." She hesitated before going on, "And we've agreed it'll be eighteen pounds down and the rest at five shillings a week?"

Sandy rolled his eyes, sighed, grimaced and finally nodded in acquiescence.

"And that'll surely include a wee floral tribute? The bairns would like that," Rachel added coaxingly.

Sandy fingered the mole under his eye again. "Aye, I suppose so. Noo I maun be aff. Run aff my feet this week, I am, with everybody wantin' to be upsides with the King and pass away this month." Before leaving though, he drained his cup and asked, "Here! Yin last thing: d'ye want Gabby brocht up here to hae a proper lying-in-state afore the service?"

"Course she does!" Bella interjected. "There'd be nae point in giein' him a decent send-aff if the neebors didnae see it."

Rachel nodded her assent. She and Bella both rose to see Sandy out but by now four cups of whisky-laced tea had taken effect on Bella and she staggered perceptibly before embracing Sandy rather too cordially. Rachel, who had had only two cups of the medicinal tea, was overtaken by a fit of the giggles and spluttered, "Here, Sandy, tell you what! To hell with the expense! Let's give Gabby a right royal send-off, just like the King's getting this week, and send him off in that mahogany coffin with the maroon tassels that you've got on show."

Now it was Sandy's turn to chuckle. "Right enough, lass, so we should. But here – ken somethin'? A funeral like that would set ye back a cool hunner."

"That all?" replied Rachel. "Well then, we'll just take it out the petty cash, won't we, Bella?"

Sandy had only been away for half an hour when Rachel realised that she'd have to put Bella to bed to sleep off the effects of her six cups of tea. Bella had insisted that she was needed down at the funeral parlour to help Sandy. Rachel was of the opinion, however, that Bella was more in need of being laid out than the corpses, so she had hochled her through to Sam's room and planked her down on the bed before throwing her coat over her. She then dashed to the scullery and had just finished getting rid of all the evidence of their impromptu wake when Carrie opened the door and came dolefully into the living room.

"Suppose having a face like the length of Leith Walk means you've told Will you won't be going to the ball."

"Haven't told him yet," Carrie snapped back, flinging herself on a chair.

"And why not? After all, haven't I brought you up to face up to your problems?"

Carrie began to look tearful. "That was the problem. I tried to look him straight in the eye and when I did – oh Mam! His eyes are so blue and they twinkle whenever he says, 'Carrie, darling'."

"Oh, my God. Don't tell me you're wanting to write for that blinking *Red Letter* again?"

"Mam," Carrie whispered pleadingly, "is there no way you could get that ball gown for me?"

Rachel looked out off the window. It was raining again. Like her own life of late, the weather was always storm-tossed. She sighed. "No, hen. You see, I'm having to go into debt because I haven't got all the thirty-five pounds I need for your Granddad's funeral."

"Thirty-five pounds for a funeral for Granddad who wanted to go away in an orange box? Mam, don't you realise my whole life is being ruined just for the want of a five-pound ball gown when you could take out a Mutuality Club loan from the Store?"

Rachel lowered the pulley, methodically took off the towels and sheets, then folded them neatly before replying in a voice that was thick and choked.. "Look, Carrie, there'll be other balls for you and Will; but with a bit of luck we'll only need to cremate your Granddad the once."

Carrie jumped up, grabbed her mother by the arm, and shouted, "But that's where you're wrong! Cos I told Bernie all about it and she says, if I can't go with Will, then *she* will."

Rachel firmly removed Carrie's hand from her arm before demanding, "And what's *she* going to wear?"

"The dress she had as bridesmaid to her sister last year."

Rachel started to smile and she patted Carrie on the cheek. "Then that's your way out. You and Bernie are about the same size, so just you ask her if you can borrow the dress."

Carrie's face fell again and tears ran down her cheeks. "I've already done that but Bernie says that the Bishop says that the Pope has just ordered that Protestants aren't allowed to wear Roman Catholic bridesmaids' dresses!"

On the day of Gabby's funeral, Carrie left work well before lunch-time. She'd been instructed by Rachel to do the shopping for the boiled ham tea because, out of the blue, Rachel had been asked to attend the Queen's Hotel for an interview.

By the time Carrie had gone to McRitchie's in Charlotte Street for the boiled ham, into Lipton's in the Kirkgate for the cheese, to Smith's for the bread and finger rolls, and finally to Rankin's in Great Junction Street for the Canary Islands tomatoes, she was soaked – thanks to the rain and hail that had pelted down relentlessly as she'd trudged from shop to shop. And, by the time she got home with a laden message bag in each hand, she was so ill-humoured that she lifted her foot and furiously booted the door.

She was just about to give another vicious kick when the door opened and there stood Auntie Bella with a feather duster in her hand.

"Oh it's you, Carrie," she said, standing aside to let Carrie enter. "Wi' all that thuddin' I thocht it was the polis."

Ignoring Bella, Carrie went straight into the scullery and dumped everything on the table, muttering, "Hope I got it all." Then she went to the living room.

"Got what?" asked Bella.

Only then did Carrie become aware of the highly-polished coffin lying on its two trestles against the far wall and she uttered a squeak. "Is that my Granddad's coffin? I thought... Well, I never thought it would be so highly polished."

Bella flicked the feather duster over the coffin. "They're always real braw like this when Sandy dis the funerals. Doesnae send onybody awa, he doesae, that isn't completely polished aff. But never mind that, ye were saying ye hoped ye had got it aw. Aw what?"

"All the stuff for Granddad's boiled ham tea. And another thing. Why are we saying that it's Granddad's boiled ham tea and the only one that's not having it – is Granddad?"

"Time for ye to bother is when you get left at the crematorium and the rest of us come back for the boiled ham tea," retorted Bella. "And, by the way, you did get the ham sliced thin? *Very* thin."

"Yes, I did," said Carrie irritably, holding up an imaginary slice. "I told the grocer so often that I wanted a whole pound of it cut very thin that he held up a slice so I could see the light shining through it. Nearly died of embarrassment, I did."

"Talking of deein'. I thocht ye said ye were gonnae hara-kiri yersel' last night?"

Carrie stuck her head arrogantly in the air. "I've had to put off drowning myself until Sunday."

"Oh, so ye've gaun aff gassing yersel'? But then, ye did say ye micht cos ye couldnae really staun the smell."

Bella prattled on about all the other ways Carrie had talked of ending it all. She'd just got to teasing Carrie about how she would have jumped off the Scott Monument if she hadn't been so scared of heights when she realised that Carrie wasn't listening. Instead, she was sitting on the settee sobbing quietly and every so often rubbing her hand under her nose to catch the drips. Bella's deep brown eyes began to sparkle suddenly and she looked over her shoulder, giving several nods of understanding. "Here, Carrie," she said at last. "That was yer Granny Rosie that just came through the noo and she says ye're to stop yer greetin' cos Cinderella ayeways gangs to the ball."

This otherworldly revelation only served to make Carrie cry all the harder and she blurted out, "Oh, Auntie Bella, this isn't the day to remind me about the only person that has ever really loved me."

Before Bella could remonstrate the door opened and both Sam and Paul came in.

"In the name o the wee man!" Sam exclaimed, walking in astonishment around the coffin. "Whit on earth is this?"

At that very moment Rachel dashed in. "What a day! Guid for neither man nor beast," she gasped, shaking her umbrella.

"Aye," agreed Bella. "But happy is the corpse that the rain faws on."

Shaking the water from her hair Rachel was about to reply when her eyes fell on the coffin. "Here, what the devil's this?"

she exclaimed, advancing warily.

"Gabby's coffin," Bella replied nonchantly, flicking the feather duster over the coffin once more.

"Oh no! It cannae be. I told Sandy I just wanted him put away nice and tidy. Surely he realised I was only kidding when I said I wanted the showroom coffin? Quick, Sam, work this out: one hundred pounds, less eighteen, divided by five shillings is how many weeks?"

She'd scarcely finished when Sam answered glibly, "Three hunner and twenty-eight weeks, which is six years, three months and three weeks efter this week that ye'll be – "

"Up to my eyeballs in debt!" howled Rachel. "Oh my God, I should have remembered that Sandy bloody well enjoys makin' a fortune out of other folks' misery."

"Noo be fair, Rachel, ye did say you wanted nae expense spared."

Rachel glowered at Bella and then sprang towards the coffin, tripping as she did so over one of the large floral arrangements lying on the floor. "And they flowers! Where, in the name of heaven, did they come from? Oh no!" she sobbed. "I said a wee floral tribute. I never said I wanted the whole blooming Botanics transplanted."

Bella, Sam, Paul and Carrie all looked blankly at one another, speechless. Not one of them knew what to do or say. So when they finished looking at each other, they all stood and gazed at the three large wreaths. Eventually Bella bent down and picked out a card from the nearest floral arrangement.

"See here, Rachel, and listen tae they nice words." And she began to read reverently from the card: "To dearest Papa who wis oor inspiration an' joy."

"Sarcastic bastard," Rachel replied through gritted teeth. She took another close look at the coffin, checking the lid before yelling, "Quick, Sam, get me a screw driver."

Sam dashed into the scullery while Bella threw herself over the coffin and screeched, "Naw. Naw, Rachel. Ye *cannae* tak him oot o his box."

"No. You can't, Mam," Carrie insisted, wringing her hands. "I mean, what would you put him in?"

By now, Sam was back with the screw driver. Rachel grabbed it from him and smartly ordered, "Get the blanket off the ironing table, Carrie, and we'll wrap him up in that before laying him out on the table itself."

"But, Mam," Carrie protested again, "the blanket is full of burn holes."

"Good," came Rachel's retort. "At least we know it's inflammable."

Before they could do anything, however, footsteps echoing on the outside path paralysed each of them and they looked from one to another again in dismay. Bella dashed to the window and looked out.

"Too late, Rachel," Bella sighed with relief. "It's your Alice and Hannah and they've got the minister in tow."

"Oh, Mam," Carrie cried, "whatever are we going to do?"

"Nothing, hen, except stuff our fists in our mouths when we see a hundred pounds go up in flaming smoke," said her mother despairingly, as the screw driver slipped from her grasp.

At lunch time next day, Bella and Rachel were sitting at the table supping some hot soup when Bella remarked. "Weel, didnae everythin' just go sae awfae weel yesterday. Ye ken, when we arrived in oor limousine and I looked oot and saw aw they respectable folk, I thocht we'd been taen tae the wrang funeral."

Rachel just nodded complacently. She too was thinking about the events of the previous day. Bella was right in saying there was a large turnout of decent folk but then they were mostly

Learig Close neighbours and pals of hers and the bairns. A sly grin crossed Rachel's face as she remembered how everyone had seemed quite gobsmacked when the hearse rolled up. And not only did Gabby's up-market casket come in for envious approval but Rachel lost count of the number of people who commented on the truly tasteful floral tributes. Rachel recalled how she had smiled demurely and maintained her dignified manner even when the minister remarked that Gabriel had been an example to all – an example of what would happen if you succumbed to the twin demons of drink and gambling. She was unable to keep her utter despair in check though when the minister asked all to stand for the committal. He had just reached the words, "ashes to ashes" when a long anguished wail escaped her as she stood and watched a hundred pounds' worth of mahogany being committed to Dante's Inferno.

Rachel's cries were subsequently drowned out by the wails from Carrie and Alice. Evidently the girls were grief-stricken because they could now remember the couple of times that Gabby had had a winner and had bought them in a bag of dolly-mixtures. Carrie herself was also consumed with guilt when she remembered that she never ever did pay back the five pounds she had "borrowed" from him when they were about to be evicted.

At the end of the service, Rachel had stood at the door with Paul and Sam to thank everyone who had come to pay their respects. And when it was the turn of Andra Couper, a drouthie crony of Gabby's, to shake hands with Sam, he remarked that Gabby's coffin was really something; "In fact I've never seen Gabby sae weel dressed afore." Sam responded by asking Andra up to Learig Close for the boiled ham tea and he, along with most of the others that were in attendance at the crematorium, did just that.

Rachel had been mortified. It was true she performed wonders feeding the family out of scraps, but even she would need divine intervention to get a pound of boiled ham, five tomatoes and two loaves of bread to go round forty folk!

Her solution – that none of the family would eat – had angered Carrie. In fact, she had stayed furious all day. First, she was angry that Johnny had turned up at the funeral and had stood at the back. She had seen him there in his kid gloves and Anthony Eden hat and when he realised she was staring at him he had pulled back his overcoat sleeve pretending to look at his gold watch – which was truly gold. She was so angry that she had hung about the front door intending to ask the burning question she had always wanted to put to him. Why, when he'd left them, in the dead of winter, had he taken his Home Guard greatcoat with him when he knew it would leave them with no covers for their bed? But even though she was now fired up enough to confront him she was denied the chance because he had stolen out of the back door like a thief in the night.

Bella was now looking about the kitchen. "That boiled ham on the bunker there?"

"Aye," Rachel answered absent-mindedly, "Bought it this morning."

"This mornin'?" Bella speired, sucking in her cheeks. "Won the pools or somethin'?"

Rachel shook her head as she got up to light the gas under the chip pan. "Just thought, that as Sam and Carrie missed out last night I'd give them a wee treat."

"Spending yer wages afore ye get them again?"

Rachel didn't bother to reply. She knew Bella was referring to her having got a job back at the Queen's Hotel. This time though she was to be the *manageress*, doing the day shift and in charge of purchasing. The only problem with being in charge was that you got paid monthly in arrears and with what had happened this week Rachel was already up to her ears in arrears.

Bella seemed quite unaware that Rachel was deliberately

ignoring her endless stream of chatter, which only stopped when Carrie opened the outside door and slunk into the scullery.

"Look," Rachel said brightly, pointing to the boiled ham she had set out. "McRitchie's, just like last night, and, better still, you and Sam are getting chips and beetroot with yours."

Carrie grimaced before slumping down on a chair. Lifting up her fork and knife she intoned woefully, "Don't tell me you think a slice of boiled ham, twelve chips and two slices of beetroot are going to mend my broken heart?"

"Och, c'mon. Yer Granddad got a richt guid send-aff, so stop worryin' aboot him," Bella coaxed, picking up one of the chips from Carrie's plate and eating it with relish.

"Good send-off?" howled Carrie. "It was a blooming disgrace the carry-on that there was in here last night. Specially from folk that were always going on about my Granddad's drinking."

Rachel gulped. She hadn't meant the funeral tea to turn into a big knees-up and it wouldn't have, if every man that had come hadn't brought one of the bottles of Glenfiddich that somehow had got lost at the docks and needed refuge at 16 Learig Close. "Carrie," said Rachel gently, "you'll get over losing your Granddad."

This statement only made Carrie break down and sob, "Mam, I'm over Granddad. It's the fact that I can't go to the ball tomorrow night that's breaking my heart. Does no one realise I'm in *love* and the only man I will ever love will leave me and go to the ball with Bernie?"

"If he's that thick then aw I can say," commented Bella, as she bent over and pinched not only another of Carrie's chips but half of her boiled ham as well, "is that ye're better aff withoot him."

"Carrie, are you saying you haven't plucked up the courage to tell that bloke you haven't got a dress?" demanded Rachel indignantly, slapping Bella's hand away before she could steal yet another of Carrie's chips.

"I'd rather commit suicide than do that," wept Carrie, taking the last chip on her plate and handing it to Bella.

"Right!" Rachel went on. "You can leave early with me to go back to work."

"Thocht you and me were goin' doon to see Sandy?" Bella reminded Rachel as she swallowed Carrie's last chip and wiped her mouth with the back of her hand.

"We certainly are," Rachel uttered determinedly as she wheeled round on Bella. "And Carrie here can chum us down the road. And while we go in to settle Sandy's hash she can get herself down to the docks."

"Oh God, Rachel," Bella gasped. "Surely ye're no wantin' her to throw hersel' in?"

"Of course not. What I want her to do is tell that Will ..."

Rachel couldn't finish her statement since Sam came rushing in, flung himself on a chair, began to attack his dinner and mumbled, "Sorry I'm late, Ma."

Both Bella and Rachel looked at the clock. Right enough, Sam should have been in fifteen minutes earlier.

"But somethin' big has happened," Sam continued as he grabbed the sauce bottle. "Jist wait till I tell ye."

Rachel held her head. Was she losing it or something? Only last night Hannah had confessed she had something so world-stopping that she simply had to tell Rachel and now here was Sam saying the same thing. Whatever it was Hannah and Sam had to tell her, it would have to wait till she'd straightened Sandy out. So all she replied was, "Tell me all about it the morn, son."

It only took twenty minutes for Rachel to quick march Bella and Carrie to the front door of Sandy's shop. When they arrived, Rachel indicated curtly to Carrie that she should go on her way and tell Will that she couldn't go to the ball with him. Carrie hesitated, hoping her mother might change her mind about taking out a Mutuality Club; but the only response she got from Rachel was a firm shake of the head. This left Carrie no alternative but to leave her mother and aunt and cross the road to where she would have to pass the Leith Provident shop window where the lilac dress was still on display.

Once Carrie reached the window she stopped and stared lovingly at the lilac creation. Why, she wondered with tears in her eyes, was the dress still there? Tempting her. Even mocking her.

Mother and aunt watched her from a distance. "Is there nae wey ye can get her that frock, Rachel?" said Bella sadly. "She fair wrings my hert, so she does."

"*Your* heart, Bella?" Rachel sighed. "Honestly, I would have sold my soul to get her that ball gown. But right now I can't even afford to buy her a pinny."

As soon as the door bell tinkled, Sandy came into the front shop and his customary mourning face lit up when he saw who it was. "Thank heavens ye've come, Bella. Awa ye gang ben the hoose. There's three there needin' washed and shrouded."

Bella was only too grateful to escape from the row that she knew was brewing and needed no second telling to go and get on with the laying-out.

"And noo, Rachel," said Sandy beaming as soon as Bella was safely in the back shop. "Ye'll be weel pleased, awfae pleased, wi' the wey things went yesterday. Best funeral Leith has seen in mony a lang year."

Rachel opened her handbag and fished out the eighteen pounds the Pearl agent had given her that morning. Flinging the three fivers and three pound notes at Sandy she screamed, "You knew I was only joking when I said to send him away in your show-coffin. And I said only *one* floral tribute – not three.

Didn't I, Bella?"

Bella, who had surreptitiously been listening behind the door, made no response except to turn the water tap full on, so that she could hear nothing more than the water as it splashed into the sink.

"Bloody traitor," Rachel hissed to herself as she watched Sandy pick up the money she had just thrown at him.

"Nae need for ye to fash yersel' aboot the flooers, Rachel," said Sandy complacently. Then, adopting his most pious look, he motioned Rachel to a chair. "Noo just ye calm doon till I tell ye aw aboot the big bug's funeral that I did just afore Gabby's."

"What the hell has that got to do with me and the predicament I'm in?"

"If ye'd just haud yer wheesht, I'll tell you. The faimily – real toffs they are – said to put their faither's floral tributes oot in the Garden of Rest and I did just that – but I gied them a wee detour first."

Rachel looked puzzled and wondered if there was some truth in the rumour that Sandy was beginning to lose the plot. Quite unaware of Rachel's concern, Sandy went on. "Sent them up to your hoose, so I did, so aw yer snobby neebors could get an eyeful."

Rachel relaxed somewhat lower into the chair. "So I've only got that bloody Chippendale casket to cough up for?"

Sandy looked carefully all around the room. Then a sly smirk crossed his face. "D-d-dinnae ken h-hoo to tell ye this, Rachel," he stammered, hardly able to keep his laughter in check. "But ye see, yer faither wasnae in the Chippendale."

"Wasn't in that coffin?" Rachel howled, catapulting herself out of the chair and covering her face. "So he's no dead after all," she muttered, collapsing on to her chair again.

"Oh, but he is! *Very deid*" Sandy chuckled.

"So he's no been cremated then?" Rachel asked, becoming

suddenly aware that Gabby's posh coffin was now back on show.

Sandy shook his head. "Oh aye, that's been done an aw. Ye see when I got hame efter seein' you, I had a wee word with your Auntie Anna."

Rachel's eyes bulged and all she could do was shake her head pityingly. Here was yet further proof that Sandy was indeed losing it. Not only was he talking to his past customers, who were all dead, but they were now answering him back.

"And," Sandy continued, quite unaware that Rachel was panicking, "she said that I should grant Gabby his last wish – and send him awa in an orange box."

"An orange box!" Rachel exclaimed, leaping out of the chair once again. "You put my Father away in an orange box?"

"Well, er, no quite," said Sandy, weighing his words. "Ye see Outspan an' Jaffa are baith oot o season, so I had to knock up something close to it frae some balsa wuid."

Rachel's jaw dropped but Sandy seemed oblivious and carried on serenely. "So when I had him safely boxed in that, I had the boys take him ower to the crematorium early yesterday – and then I sent oor show-piece," Sandy now gestured at the mahogany coffin, "up to your hoose."

Rachel didn't know whether to laugh or cry but she did manage to articulate the right question. "So I only owe you seventeen pounds because I gave you eighteen the now."

Sandy shook his head. Rachel grimaced, thinking, "I should have known it was all too good to be true." She then braced herself for Sandy's answer but all he did was to take two fivers from the money she had flung at him and hand them back to her.

"What's this?" she asked with a puzzled frown.

"Just a wee somethin' to help keep yer feet clear while yer waitin' for yer first pey – sorry – salary."

"You mean it only cost me eight pounds to see the back of Gabby?"

Sandy shook his head again. "Naw. Three pounds twa shillings and fourpence but wi' double faimily discount I'll settle for three quid."

Rachel was speechless. She wanted to thank Sandy effusively but the words stuck in her throat.

"An' here," Sandy added. "I want ye to tak this ither fiver and go ower to the Provi and buy yourself a new winter coat. That pony-skin ye're wearing is that auld they widnae even tak it in at the knacker's yaird."

"Buy a new coat? But why?" asked Rachel in utter perplexity.

"Cos yer Auntie Anna and me think that Gabby should dae what he never did in life –pit a warm coat on yer back."

"Cannae do that, Sandy," Rachel sobbed, jumping up and kissing him lavishly on each cheek. Then she turned and raced out of the shop.

"Where the hell is she awa to in sic a hurry?" Sandy asked Bella, who by now had sneaked back into the front shop.

"Och," Bella sobbed, rubbing her nose vigorously with the back of her hand. "Rachel's just awa to tell Cinderella she can gae to the ball."

CHAPTER 15
DOUBLE BOUNCE

The day after Rachel heard the good news from Sandy about the cost of Gabby's funeral, she had started work at the Queen's Hotel on Princes Street, taking over from the woman she was to replace. At the interview she had insisted on the stock-takers doing their job in the presence of herself and the outgoing holder of the job, Dorothy Clyde.

Rachel had worked under Dorothy before and knew that every time there was a stock-taking due Dorothy would bring in bottles of spirits that she'd bought from an off-licence to bolster the stock. As the years rolled by, more and more bottles had to be brought in and over the last few years Dorothy had even been forced to enter into a sale-or-return arrangement with a licensed grocer in South Queensferry Street in order to keep the stock-takers and hotel management fooled.

When the senior manager at the Queen's sent for Rachel to offer her Dorothy's job, on her own terms, she had suspected things were now so far out of control that Dorothy would probably do a runner. Instinctively she knew Dorothy must have been quite desperate to have gone the length of giving in her notice – because leaving the Queen's would be a sore miss for her. Dorothy revelled in the affluent standard of living that the Queen's had provided and was very grateful that, through her highly creative bartending, she had also been able to send her two children to prestigious fee-paying schools.

As soon as the stock-takers had finished their work, Rachel became quite upset, since without any warning they promptly called in the police and a distraught Dorothy was now in custody. That left Rachel having to convince herself that there was no way she could have taken over, other than by insisting on a full stocktaking. If she hadn't, Dorothy would have walked away scot-free while Rachel, who also had two children to educate, would be left to explain the discrepancies. Unless the senior management duly understood that it was all Dorothy's mess, she herself might end up doing time. And that was certainly not an option for Rachel who would never contemplate jeopardising her children's well-being. She sighed, reluctantly conceding that her children's welfare had been the only reason she had never carried out her frequent threats to murder both Gabby and Johnny.

Because of all the carfuffle at the Queen's, it was past four oclock in the afternoon by the time she got home. A deep feeling of relief suffused her when she entered the house. This place was her home where she always felt safe. Yet even those stout walls couldn't entirely alleviate the guilt she felt about Dorothy. Lifting the poker to stir up the fire she argued to herself over and over that there was never any question that her children and their needs would have to come first. And, okay, she might occasionally, like Dorothy, do things to boost her income that weren't strictly honest; but she always had the wit to balance the books somehow or another and so satisfy the management.

Having poked up the fire, Rachel set about redding up everything for the children coming home. Once satisfied, she sat down at the table with a cup of strong tea and began to mull over the events of last week. Thinking of Gabby and his funeral brought a smile to her face and when she thought how wonderful Carrie was going to look in her lilac ball gown that night she almost shouted with glee. Indeed she only just managed to stifle her cry of excitement when the door opened and in waltzed Hannah.

As usual, Hannah was dressed in her navy blue staff nurse's Burberry coat with her nurse's hat neatly secured to her long fair hair by four hair grips – and looking at her daughter Rachel fairly bristled with pride. Hannah had more than met Rachel's dreams for her. Yes, she thought rather smugly to herself, all the sacrifice of putting her Hannah through the nursing had been so worthwhile. And she just knew that one day Hannah would be Matron at the Royal Infirmary in Edinburgh where she'd been trained and was now the proud recipient of the Pelican badge. Rachel didn't even have to close her eyes to imagine what the future held. All she had to do was to look at Hannah as she was today.

"Mam," said Hannah with a smile that lit up her whole face, "I've something to tell you."

"You've been offered a Staff Nurse's job at the Royal?"

Hannah shook her head. "I never applied to the Royal."

"You didn't. And why not?"

Hannah took a deep breath. "Because I'm going to live on Benbecula."

"Benbecula? Where the hell is Benbecula?"

"It's a remote wee island in the Outer Hebrides."

"The Outer Hebrides!" Rachel exclaimed. "But what on earth for?"

"Mam, I've met a man. A fisherman."

Rachel's mouth fell open and all she could do was gape at her daughter.

"We're to be married and then we'll go and live on his croft."

"Just a minute, Hannah! Are you saying I sacrificed all of the others, so you could be trained as a nurse, and now you're going to throw it all up to marry a fisherman?"

"Yes, because I love him, Mam."

"Love? For heaven's sake, Hannah, whatever would a bible-punching Wee Free know about love?"

"He's not a Wee Free."

"That doesn't matter up there. All the Protestants there are Holy Willies that insist that *they* are the head of the household and that their wives must submit to their every demand."

Hannah sat like a marble statue as Rachel raved on. "And you just wait till you've spent the Sabbath among them," she mocked. "No working, no laughing, no nothing but reading the Bible all day and going to the church not once but six times."

Rachel finally stopped ranting and fired Hannah a warning glare before demanding, "Is that really what you want?"

Hannah sighed in exasperation. "But, Mam, I won't have to put up with all that because he's not Protestant. He's *Catholic* – and so am I now!"

Rachel half rose and her hand flew to her mouth, "You've changed your religion without asking me about it?"

"Yes. Jamie and I are going to be married in St Ninian's Chapel at Marionville a week on Saturday."

Rachel felt as if she was being beaten senseless. Could she be hearing right? Was it a dream? A horrible nightmare? Hannah had always been so special to her. She had always put her eldest daughter's interest first – and here was the girl throwing away her career to marry a man who would take her hundreds of miles away. *And* he was a Roman Catholic and so was she now!

"Hannah," she pleaded, "don't do this. Don't you realise that you'll spend all of your life being pregnant. Catholics don't practise … er … restraint."

Hannah let out an excited giggle. "Mam, didn't you hear me? I love him so I wouldn't want him to … you know … what you said."

By now Rachel could take no more. She leapt up and before realising what she was doing she struck Hannah hard across the face.

Taken completely by surprise, Hannah could only run a hand over her stinging cheek before she backed towards the front door. Still facing Rachel, she whispered, "Oh, Mam, it was you who taught me to think for myself. Now I'm doing it, why are you objecting?"

"Objecting? Of course I'm bloody objecting to you throwing yourself away. And if you think I'll come and watch you do it, then think again!" said Rachel venomously before turning her back on Hannah.

"Somehow I knew that this would be how you'd take it." Hannah sighed wearily before adding quietly, "Thank goodness I bumped into Dad today and he's offered to give me away."

"Give you away!" Rachel croaked as tears sprang to her eyes, "That sod gave you away years ago, Hannah."

Hannah was silent.

"Oh, I see," hissed Rachel. "You seem to have forgotten that. Just as you've also forgotten it was me, and only me, that stood between you and a bloody orphanage."

Hannah shrugged but still said nothing.

"Shrug all you like, my girl," Rachel persisted, "but it won't change the fact that is was *me* – who put the clothes on your back. *Me* – who put the food in your belly. *Me* – who begged, borrowed and stole to educate you so you could think for yourself."

Advancing towards the outside door, Rachel flung it wide open and with a dismissive nod ordered Hannah out. Before Hannah could make her escape, however, she had to stand back to let Carrie enter.

"Oh, Hannah, are you not going to wait and see me get all dressed up for the ball?" urged Carrie excitedly.

"No, she's in too much of a hurry to collect her thirty pieces of silver," retorted Rachel, banging the door shut on Hannah.

Carrie had wrapped her hair in a scarf so that she wouldn't disturb it when she took her bath. The hairdresser down at Restalrig Brae had set it. She had complimented Carrie on her natural kink – and now that it was professionally set, the golden highlights that streaked her soft brown hair shone like dazzling crystals. When the girl told Carrie that she had a natural kink she'd been taken aback because Sam was always telling her that. So when she realised that the hairdresser was talking about her hair and not her nature she'd laughed out aloud. Funny, thought Carrie, as the warm suds relaxed her, how she'd always cursed having curly hair. Now that it lay in long deep waves, complementing her oval face, she was glad of those curls.

She would have loved to linger in the comforting bath with her reminiscences but, conscious that her darling Will would soon be coming for her, she got out, dried herself and went into the bedroom, only to discover Alice sitting on the bed.

"Nice frock, Carrie," chirped Alice, running her fingers over the lilac net before picking up one of Carrie's silver shoes admiringly.

Carrie stopped pulling on her stockings and looked quizzically at her sister. "I get the feeling that there's something bugging you."

Alice shook her head vigorously. "It's nothing really. It's just ... Oh, Carrie, I've been picked to play the lead in the school play."

"You have?"

Alice nodded and a broad smile lit up her face. "Yes, I'm to play chief handmaiden to the Greek god, Dionysus. You know – him that inspires poetry and music."

"He does?" was all Carrie could say.

"Well, that's what Miss Leishman says he does," Alice pouted.

"Oh then, that part will be just great for you," Carrie enthused with genuine feeling as she went over and hugged Alice. "And you'll do it so well because you have all the experience of our back-green concerts behind you."

Alice looked askance at that. Back-green concerts were hardly what she'd call good experience for a Greek drama. As far as she was concerned, Carrie had only organised these so she could charge the other children in the street twopence to get in – and anyway the profit always went on ice-cream pokes smothered in raspberry sauce when Tony Boni arrived on his ice-cream tricycle.

"Have you told Mam?" Carrie asked, unaware that Alice was thinking of ice-cream days – days when they were all just bairns and when a penny to buy an ice-cream cone was all they longed for.

"Tried to," answered Alice dreamily, "but she said she didn't want to hear another word from any of us tonight."

Carrie grimaced. "Well, she'll have got over Hannah by the morn and you can tell her then."

Alice nodded but Carrie could see she was disappointed that Rachel hadn't shown any interest in her news, so she rubbed Alice's nose comfortingly before saying, "Never mind. Now, come and help me on with my dress."

When at last Carrie made her triumphant entry into the living-room she was startled to find that Will, splendidly attired in his Highland outfit, was already waiting for her. To pass the time he had sat on the settee chatting to Sam but as soon as he saw Carrie he jumped to his feet and a long wolf-whistle escaped his lips.

This alerted Rachel, who was in the scullery, and she quickly ran into the living room where she was confronted with a vision of Carrie as she'd never seen her before. She tried to speak but the tears she'd been shedding ever since Hannah left started to surface again.

"Well?" asked Carrie, giving a twirl that made the tulle skirts of her dress billow out invitingly.

"Fine," Rachel nodded. "Aye, fine feathers make fine birds," she muttered thickly –acknowledging that Carrie had indeed been transformed into a swan.

"They certainly do!" Will said, taking Carrie's coat and placing it on her shoulders.

Once Carrie and Will had left, Sam asked, "Ony tea left, Mam?"

"Aye, I'll just heat it up."

"Richt, and while ye're daeing that I've somethin' to tell ye. Here, Alice – awa ye gang to the chippie and get me a bottle o Vimto." And he flipped Alice a half-crown so that she could go for his favourite brew – and be out of the way.

Rachel said nothing as Alice went out but she did remember Sam wanting to tell her something earth-shattering yesterday. Well, she thought, I could do with some good news after the bombshell Hannah has just delivered.

"Pit my notice in, I hae," said Sam casually.

The fish-slice that Rachel was using to turn the fried potatoes slipped from her hand. "You've what?" she gasped, turning to face her son squarely.

"Pit my notice in."

"But why? You've got three years in and in another two you'll be a fully qualified marine engineer."

"Aye, but the polis …"

Rachel's hand flew to her mouth. She had always wondered why the stupid police hadn't caught up with Sam before – but why now of all times? Och, she argued to herself, why couldn't his luck have held out till he'd finished his time – before he had to do time of a different kind?

"Mam, are ye aw richt?" asked Sam, coming over to turn off the gas under the frying pan that by now was sending billows of blue smoke about the scullery.

"All right, you ask?" she demanded. "You're about to do time and you think I should be all right?"

Sam began to chuckle, "Dinnae be daft. I'm no gonnae dae time."

"Just probation?" Rachel squealed as relief flooded over her.

"Weel, I'll hae to dae twa years' probation richt enough, but

I'll no be startin' that till I come back."

Rachel shook her head and gesticulated wildly. "Sam, you talk in bloody riddles, you do. Now can we please go back to the beginning?"

Sam nodded "Richt-oh, Mam."

"You've put your notice in because the police have caught up with you? Is that right?"

"They've no exactly caught up with me. I kent ever since last week that they were efter me."

"Then why the hell did you no stop doing what they were after you for?"

"Because I like playing fitba', Ma."

Rachel shook her fist in exasperation and when Paul and Alice, who had just returned, came into the scullery, they thought Rachel was about to explode. And she did, grabbing Sam by the front of his jumper. "Are you saying you were lifted by the polis for playing bloody football?"

Sam struggled free of his mother. "No lifted, Mam. I've been offered a job wi' them and I ..."

"What!" Rachel, Sam and Alice all yelled in unison.

"Aye."

"But – you're a bandit, Sam! You're the robber no the cop," giggled Alice setting Sam's bottle of Vimto on the table.

Sam was not amused. "Okay, so it was the reference frae the sergeant, that runs the force's fitba' team, that got me the interview. But an Inspector also had a wee word wi' me efter I came tap in the entrance exam. Oh aye," Sam cocked his head jauntily. "He telt me that they'd been lookin' for somebody like me for a lang time."

"That right?" said Rachel, still perplexed. "But don't you realise, Sam, that you'll have to do your National Service now you've given up your apprenticeship?"

Sam explained patiently: "That's anither thing I've to tell ye.

I'm joining the Royal Scots next week."

Rachel's face became drained of all colour as she remembered the day on the bridge when Sam had got the job at Robb's and Bella had warned that Sam should never annoy the Chinese. "No, Sam," she groaned, hitting her chin with her clenched fist, "the Royal Scots are being sent out to Korea and there's a war going on out there. Shooting and firing at each other, they are."

"That's right," Paul joined in, growing fearful for Sam as well. "And they're daein' it wi' real guns and bullets that can kill ye stone deid."

It was after one o'clock in the morning when Rachel heard the taxi draw up. She'd been sitting by the fire with the light out since Sam, Paul and Alice had gone to bed. In her mind she had gone over and over the events of the day. How could life yet again be so cruel to her? Hannah's betrayal – as she saw it – had been the hardest to bear. Sam's departure from sanity had been easier for her to cope with because she could see that he would probably make a great career in the police. After all he'd always be one jump ahead of the thieves he was chasing. She smiled to herself, picturing Sam in the CID chasing Chalky who was finding it hard to fathom if Sam was running away *with* him or *after* him. Suddenly she realised that Carrie had still not come in. She tiptoed over to the door and listened before softly opening it. Carrie and Will, who were leaning against it, nearly fell on top of her.

"What's going on here?" Rachel demanded, becoming aware that Carrie's coat was open and that Will's hands were inside.

Carrie's face fired. "It's just that Will's hands are cold, Mam."

"That right?" Rachel snorted, hauling Carrie towards her. "Then you just tell him to buy a pair of gloves."

"Mam," said Carrie plaintively, "Will and I have an

understanding."

"That's right," echoed Will, "We have an understanding."

"You have an understanding, do you?" Rachel cried in maternal rage, "Well, let me tell you that *my* understanding is that *your* understanding thinks that you can molest *my* daughter. So I want *you* to understand that, even if you do have an understanding, you are *never ever* to put your hands inside my daughter's coat again until you have more than an understanding. And now do you understand my understanding?"

"Oh, Mam," wailed Carrie. "All Will and I are trying to say is, that he's going away to sea and when he comes back we're going to get engaged and then get married."

Rachel exhaled loudly as she hauled Carrie further into the house, before banging the door firmly on Will.

"Why did you do that, Mam?" bleated Carrie, as she tried to push or pull Rachel away from the door. When she finally realised her mother was immovable, she retaliated: "Are you frightened I'd end up like you?"

"What do you mean?" shouted Rachel, as a deep fear rose within her.

"Well, I managed to work it out. You got married in October and Hannah arrived the following April. So you see, you were expecting her long before Dad and you got married!"

Rachel swallowed hard but stayed mute, biting on her lip.

"And I think that's the reason you've always loved Hannah more than me."

Rachel still said nothing but her thoughts raced. How, she wondered, could she possibly explain to Carrie that she loved her every bit as much as Hannah? That she had only been trying to make it up to Hannah for the fact that she had tarnished her – that she had somehow conceived her in sin.

"And it wasn't like how you think, Mam," Carrie sobbed, breaking into Rachel's thoughts. "He only had his hands inside my coat."

"Inside your coat the night, Carrie," Rachel, who still had her back to the door, whispered more to herself, "but by tomorrow you'd find his hands ..." She didn't finish what she was about to say for she didn't need to. Carrie had stomped off into the bedroom to take off the ball gown. As it tumbled to her feet, she felt the warm magic of the night drift away to meet the cold reality of dawn.

By the following Friday night the row between Rachel and Carrie had been long forgotten and Carrie was sitting at the table in the scullery reading her beloved *Red Letter*. She had been there ever since Rachel, Paul and Alice had gone to bed two hours ago and had just about reached the climax of the story when the front door opened and in came Sam. He and the boys he worked with had been out for his farewell do.

"Whit are *ye* daein' up?" Sam asked Carrie as he struck a match and lit the gas under the kettle.

"Thought you might be stottin' fu' and you'd need me to put you to bed," she giggled, relieved in truth to find him quite sober.

"Me drunk? Nah! Whenever I'm tempted, the sicht o Gabby staggering aboot wi' his big blue neb ..." Sam made a circle with his finger and thumb and ringed them around his nose, then wobbled his middle finger. " ... has put me aff drinking for the rest of my life, so it has."

"Well, I know the pong coming off you is a fish supper in that pocket," said Carrie with a smile, pointing to the bulge in Sam's right-hand overcoat pocket. "But what in the name of heavens is that bulge in your other pocket?"

"The king of drinks," Sam sang, digging in his left pocket and bringing out a bottle of Vimto. Then, reaching into the other pocket, he brought out the newspaper-wrapped delicacy. "C'mon noo," he coaxed, winking at Carrie, "let's sit doon and hae a guid tuck-in."

Carrie took the fish supper from Sam's hands, unwrapped the newspaper and spread it out on the table. Sam opened the Vimto and they had both just lifted the first chips to their mouths when they found themselves faced with pyjama-clad Paul and Alice coming into the scullery. "Aw, God!" exclaimed Sam, "Noo I'll hae to share it amang the fower o us."

Alice confirmed that by going over to get four cups from the cupboard. She had just sat down again when Paul pranced over to the cupboard, lifted out a bottle of tomato ketchup and was about to splash a large dollop of it on to the chips when Sam grabbed him by the arm.

"See you, Paul?" Sam teased playfully. "Ye've aw the big bricht ideas aboot being a lawyer and ye dinnae even ken that it's muck sauce that goes on fish and chips when they're being washed down with Vimto   nae tomati."

Undaunted, Paul pulled himself free, went back to the cupboard and took out a plate. And, as they all silently watched, he picked up a handful of chips along with half the tail of the fish and put them on the plate before picking up the bottle and liberally dunting some tomato sauce on to them. To their amazement, he then lifted his cup and toasted them boldly, bragging, "And I *will* be a lawyer. Oh aye, I'll mak a fortune out of defending aw them crooks that you're gonnae nick, Sam."

All four looked from one to the other for a second, then their laughter rang gaily round the room.

"Aye, ye just micht," Sam chortled, before his voice changed as it became choked with emotion, "Ye see, Paul, things werenae too bad for you and Alice. Ye grew up in the palmy days. Ye're getting' to bide on at schuil and Alice is gettin' tap-dancin' lessons – no robbed like Carrie and me – an' maybe puir Hannah even mair so."

"Robbed? Robbed of what, Sam?" Carrie queried in amazement.

"Oor childhood! Never allowed just to be bairns and just to play." Sam sniffed before he continued. "Oh aye, cos we were deserted and betrayed by oor ain kith an' kin, we were foisted wi' responsibilities awa beyond oor years."

"Be fair now, Sam," said Carrie, who was desperate to get Sam's mood to lighten. "By the time Paul was ready to go to Leith Academy we could afford the blazer for him."

"A second-hand yin, if ye don't mind," Paul chimed in.

"Aye, but yer scarf and tie were new. Brand-new. I ken that cos I went wi'oot to buy them for ye," Sam reminded him.

"That's quite enough, Sam!" Carrie fulminated.

"Aye, ye're richt enough."

Realising he was upsetting everyone, Sam got up and ruffled Paul's jet black hair in a gesture of reconciliation. "A lawyer ye want to be, son? Me? I just wanted to be an ace fitba'er." He paused and then added wryly, "But I stopped believin' in fairy tales when I was eight years auld."

"Did you really, Sam?" laughed Carrie. "I've never stopped believing in them. Oh no! I remember dreaming that one day I'd have a half-loaf all to my self and a whole tin of condensed milk to spread on it – and I got it. And then I dreamt about a whole Mars Bar for myself …" She stopped and giggled as she grabbed hold of Sam by the arm. "And now that I can afford one, I'm sick if I take more than one wee slice. And know something else?" Carrie's eyes became dreamy. "I know that some day Will and me will have one of those semi-detached houses with the rose gardens over on the posh side of Learig Close."

Now it was Sam's turn to laugh, "Semi-detached hoose, Carrie? Ye were ayeways semi-detached."

Desperate to get in on the game, Alice heaved a sigh and blurted out: "I remember how we used to dream about having electricity and enough hot water to fill the bath in the bathroom. And now we have hot baths and wash our hair, not in that old fashioned Dreen, but in posh Amami shampoo every week."

Before Sam could snub Alice, Carrie lifted her hand to warn him that it would be cruel to remind her how she and Paul had had life easy compared to the older ones. Sam heeded the unspoken advice and joined in the game. Picking up a chip that he had dragged through the muck sauce, he teased, "D'ye remember, Carrie, hoo I'd dip my chips in yer egg yolk? An' cos we were the mankiest, we'd be the last to be dumped into the wash tub and scrubbed clean by Mammy."

Sam's eyes moistened and his face grew more serious. "An' I hinna forgotten yer ornaments, Carrie. Oh aye! Some day I'll get yer Dresden shepherd and shepherdess back for ye." Sam stopped, and then his eyes twinkled as he nudged Carrie. "Mind ye, I dinnae ken hoo lang it's gonnae tak but I do ken that some day – I just will."

Carrie smiled and, stroking Sam's cheek, whispered, "I don't think these ornaments were so important. What was important was that Mammy kept us all together and that we got there in the end."

Sam nodded. "Aye, we never sterved. Never got chucked out by the cooncil. Never got lifted by the polis. And Mammy never …"

Alice interrupted Sam. "Know what you mean. And know something? If this house could speak it'd tell better stories than you're going to write one day, Carrie."

Carrie nodded. "Wish Hannah was here right now. Mammy's still real upset about her."

"Nae need to fret aboot Hannah and Mammy," said Sam reassuringly. "They're special tae each other, an' afore ye ken it, Hannah will hae a bairn an' aw the sea atween Oban and Lochboisdale will never be ower rough or ower deep enough to keep them apairt."

Carrie's eyes began to sparkle and she looked upwards over her shoulder. She nodded again and again and again. And she kept repeating "Thank you! Thank you! Thank You!"

"Och, dinnae tell me ye're anither yin that's gonnae be speaking to the deid," teased Sam, rolling the newspaper into a ball before flinging it lightly at Carrie.

"Just being like you and Auntie Bella – foretelling the future."

"And what *is* our future to be?" Alice gasped, desperate to know if one day she would really go to Hollywood and take over from Alice Faye.

"Ah well," said Carrie, in mock imitation of Bella, "that was our very own Granny Rosie that came through there just now. She says we all have a long, long, road to travel and ..."

Sam broke in: "We'll hae oor ups and doons and oor successes and failures, cos that's hoo life is. But when ye've had a Leith education ye can bounce back frae onythin'."

Carrie nodded. "Aye, and ..."

Sam interrupted again, "Cos we were lucky enough to be brocht up by oor Mammy – we hae the backbone, no only to dae a double bounce, but to dae it wi' class!"